The 49th Day

The 49ᵗʰ Day

Helen Noble

Winchester, UK
Washington, USA

First published by Soul Rocks Books, 2014
Soul Rocks Books is an imprint of John Hunt Publishing Ltd., Laurel House, Station Approach,
Alresford, Hants, SO24 9JH, UK
office1@jhpbooks.net
www.johnhuntpublishing.com
www.soulrocks-books.com

For distributor details and how to order please visit the 'Ordering' section on our website.

Text copyright: Helen Noble 2013

ISBN: 978 1 78279 593 3

A CIP catalogue record for this book is available from the British Library.

Design: Lee Nash

Printed in the USA by Edwards Brothers Malloy

We operate a distinctive and ethical publishing philosophy in all
areas of our business, from our global network of authors to
production and worldwide distribution.

CONTENTS

Acknowledgements

Gratitude, love and respect to:

Imelda for holding the space;
Gerry for his kind hospitality and entertainment;
Margaret for sharing the mythological secrets of the hills;
Mary for her other-worldly insight and practical advice;
Jordan for her art;
John for his reading and reflections;
Emma for being;
Gareth, for his enduring support and encouragement.

Prologue

The icy prickles on the back of Celia's neck pre-empted the shriek that pierced the dark silence. Within seconds she was out of her room and at the bedside of her daughter. "Katherine! Wake up, you're dreaming again." Celia gently shook the fragile shoulders of the young girl, whose body lay tangled in the sheets.

Disoriented, the girl sat up in bed, sobbing, "He was here again, the man..."

"It's only a dream," Celia whispered, wiping away her child's tears.

During the seven months since the death of her father, Katherine had woken at night terrified by the presence of an intruder in her room; she insisted that the menacing figure was not just a figment of her imagination.

"He came to the side of the bed and he put his hand around my throat," Katherine gasped, relaying the recurring scenario. Celia knew what was coming next. "I tried to call out but I couldn't hear my own voice, and then he squeezed until I could no longer breathe." The young girl gulped, the words catching in her throat. She broke into a choking cough.

"I could hear you." Her mother reassuringly rubbed her thin arm. "I am here. I'm always here. You have nothing to fear. He's not real, it's just a dream." She looked directly into the sunken, grey eyes of her only child, stroked her soft, chestnut hair and hugged her tightly.

The presence of this man was casting a despondent gloom over their world, one already fraught with grief following the death of Lieutenant Commander Walsh.

Katherine's father had passed away early one morning, at home, following a premature heart attack. The tragedy had been witnessed by the unfortunate girl and her mother. Katherine had stood in a surreal stupor watching, yet not hearing Celia screaming down the telephone receiver. She played the role of a silent witness to the ensuing frenzy of the emergency services. Stepping back into the shadows of the house, the child had largely gone unnoticed by the paramedics in their frantic efforts to revive the dying man; she had looked on lifelessly as his limp body was finally stretchered away. Celia crumpled; her spirit fragmented and her body slumped to the ground. Mother and daughter had never since spoken of the event.

In the wake of their loss, Celia had a desperate urge to leave the family home. With the late lieutenant's service pension as their only source of income, they were plunged into the unfamiliarity of a new house, on the edge a large estate, and forced to face the challenges of a tough inner-city school.

The only child of a naval officer, Celia had spent her youth moving from one military base to another. When Katherine came along she had decided that it would be more beneficial for the family to remain in one place. However, as her friends, the wives of other servicemen, continued to move on and the lower orders closed ranks, she had become an increasingly isolated figure. She had failed in her attempt to provide the support network she was hoping to build for her own child. Lonely and in unfamiliar surroundings, Celia's grief and depression deepened and she became increasingly reluctant to leave the house.

Nine-year-old Katherine found herself running errands and performing household chores in addition to her schooling. On the surface, she appeared to be coping rather well. She was putting on a brave face and her school report indicated that she had settled in and was making steady progress. However, her night terrors were indicative that all was not well in her world. Celia was forced to acknowledge that her daughter was in need of extra help, and without any extended family to reach out to, professional help was the only answer. She booked an appointment with the family doctor.

Listening to her claims that her sleep was broken almost every night by screams from her daughter's bedroom, Dr de Courcy prescribed sedatives for Celia.

"Of course, in the circumstances, this sort of thing is to be expected," he advised, trying to dismiss his patient's concerns.

"But it's just the same dream, over and over," Celia explained. "She falls asleep but cries out until I wake her up. She tells me there is a man in her room; always the same man. I reassure her that no one is there, but she insists he is real."

"If it's a lack of sleep that's the problem, maybe I can prescribe something for the child? Just for use on a temporary basis, you understand?" Once again the doctor reached for his prescription pad. Celia gratefully accepted a signed script in her daughter's name. Folding it up and slipping it into her coat pocket, she rose to leave the room. Katherine remained seated, looking straight at Dr de Courcy who stood to usher her out.

"Take the medication," he ordered, patting her on the shoulder as if to soften the blow of his bluntness. Then turning to Celia, he added, "If there is no improvement over the next couple of weeks, bring her back to see me."

Katherine had refused to take the medication. When her mother handed it to her, she had turned away and slipped it into her pocket, waiting for an opportunity to flush it down the toilet. The awful man who came to her room at night was real. Maybe her mother could not see or hear him but *she* could see, hear, and feel him there in the room, at her bedside. He was as real as any of the other people around her; she could hear his heartbeat and feel his breath on her, just as she could feel the nudge to her shoulder of the strangers sitting next to her on the bus, or passing her in the street.

The dark circles refused to fade from under Katherine's eyes and Celia arranged another visit to Dr de Courcy. This time the staid old man had tried a different approach. Endeavouring to engage the child in conversation he had asked, "Are you worried about anything, my dear?"

Katherine was worried about everything. Her mother hardly left the house, she complained constantly about not having enough money and she shut herself away for hours on end, without explanation. When she stood outside her mother's bedroom door asking after her, the only response was the sound of Celia's sobs. The young girl had not yet made any friends at her new school and was afraid to ask if she could invite anyone around at the weekend, as her mother always seemed so sad and tired. And each night she feared closing her eyes because the man would appear at her bedside. But when old Dr de Courcy questioned her, she remained tight-lipped. She knew he would not believe her.

"Katherine, we want to help you but you must talk to us," he had implored her in a whisper. "Tell me what's troubling you." The girl looked towards her mother and then at the floor, her lank brown hair hanging over her face. She simply refused to speak. Why should he believe her, when her own mother had refused?

Realizing that he was not going to make any progress with her, the doctor had asked her to wait outside while he had a word with her mother. She was glad to leave and quickly let herself out of the room. Inside, he broached the subject of counselling with her mother. Having her nine-year-old daughter on medication was one thing, whereas being directed to take her child to see a therapist came as a shock to Celia. In naval circles, wittering on about one's 'abnormal' feelings was simply not the done thing.

"Is there something wrong with her mind?" she had asked.

"No, no, no, I'm not suggesting that," the doctor said.

"Well then, what purpose would it serve?" Celia had no idea. "It's just that she has lost her father and perhaps she would benefit from speaking to a professional, someone trained to help in these sorts of situations," he suggested with a shrug.

"Surely it won't do any good to stir it all up again?' Celia couldn't stomach the thought.

"Bereavement therapy has become a very popular form of treatment amongst adults," he replied. "And now its use is being applied to children. It's still early days in this country, but I understand that the approach is very popular in the United States. I know of one lady who seems to be very good with children."

With the popular American TV image of a shiny leather sofa in a plush psychiatrist's office, a reluctant Celia questioned the doctor as to the cost of such a service. Dr de Courcy reassured her that in this instance she would not be required to pay.

Maggie Brown's consulting room was anything but luxurious. The functional office in the children's department of the city's Social Services building appeared hostile to Celia, a far cry from the private medical consulting rooms that she, as the wife of a naval officer, had encountered. Even now, the notion of accepting help from the civilian state was alien to her. She was uncomfortable sitting in public waiting rooms amongst people with widely different backgrounds from her own. She shuffled uncomfortably in her seat, avoiding eye contact with staff members and clients alike, often holding up a handkerchief to her mouth to stifle her nervous cough; whilst a silent Katherine slumped, motionless on the scuffed, plastic chair beside her.

A plump, middle-aged mother of three, Maggie was an experienced clinical psychologist specializing in childhood behavioural issues. Private referrals from general practitioners were not commonplace and so she had been surprised to receive a letter from Dr de Courcy explaining the unfortunate family circumstances. It was obvious that the medic had a long history of treating the family, and Maggie agreed to take on the matter out of curiosity, despite groaning under an ever-increasing caseload. Known for her sharp insight and soft demeanour, Maggie was inspired by the resilience of children and therefore happy to afford a little of her time to see if she could help in any way.

Celia, reluctant to engage emotionally with the therapist, sat in silence at the back of the room, hiding behind the defeated expression on her face. During these sessions she simply faded away into her imaginary world, where she could gain some momentary respite from the harsh realities of life without the guidance and protection of her husband. She surfaced only occasionally to confirm or correct a point raised by Maggie; who in turn focused more attention on Katherine, whom she found to be a very bright, but troubled child. The small girl sat stiffly in the office armchair, and Maggie noted the serious expression of someone with experience beyond her years. Although she appeared happy to participate in an assessment of her own IQ and to answer questions about her day-to-day existence, it took Maggie a little time to win Katherine's trust and learn all about her nocturnal terrors.

It was the third session before the child began to open up and felt able to speak freely, without fear of being disbelieved, or having her explanations shut down.

"Can you tell me how his face looks?" Maggie used simple words to question the delicate child.

Katherine's small pale face looked up her with interest from underneath a heavy tousle of hair. Although her test scores placed her in the 'highly intelligent' bracket of the general population, Maggie was still amazed at the succinct detail with which the child recounted her recurrent nightmare. Looking straight ahead as if the subject was standing directly in front of her at that very moment she described him, "There are four deep lines in the middle of his forehead as he frowns at me, and when he leans in closer I can see my own face reflected in the black of his eyes. He has long, dirty hair and only a few teeth. When I can smell his hot, sour breath on my face, I close my eyes. I hear him groan and I feel his scratchy nails on my neck. Then he presses his cold, hard fingers around my throat, squeezing the breath out of me and I try to scream. But all I can hear is his deep laughter."

Maggie always acknowledged the girl's words. Never challenging nor validating what was being said she simply confirmed to Katherine that she was being heard. In return, Katherine warmed to her, finding that each time she spoke of the images from her dream, she felt a little less afraid. Maggie noted the startling consistency in her description of the recurring dream. Despite being asked a number of times and in a variety of ways about the experience, the details never varied. Struck by the accuracy of the child's memory, she knew in her heart that this was no ordinary dream.

"What is the man's name?" she ventured to ask during the fourth session.

Katherine remained silent and thoughtful for a few minutes before replying, "William, his name is William."

Maggie knew this was not the name of her recently deceased father. Through skilled questioning, she had determined the estranged nature of the relationship between Katherine and Lieutenant Commander Walsh. It appeared that the officer had spent little time at home during her early childhood as Katherine had spoken of often being alone with her mother on the naval base. Her factual, emotionless account of the death of her father sounded to Maggie as if there was little love spared between them. This would undoubtedly have repercussions for the girl's future relationships, but Maggie's remit was to address the immediate problem.

"Who is William?" The therapist pushed a little further.

Despite her desire to please the kind woman, Katherine

struggled hard to answer this question. Maggie realized that for some unknown reason, the girl was simply unable to articulate how, or why, he figured in her dreams.

Maggie mused, *sometimes imaginary figures are the unconscious internalization of an abusive figure in the life of a child*. She made enquiries as to the men who could have played a part in her early years. However, further investigations on the subject proved fruitless, and the therapist found herself at a loss to make any connection between the unconscious creation and any possible previous contacts. This was the first time, in a case such as this, that she had drawn a complete blank. Maggie knew that she would have to switch tack if she was to make any further progress. There had been few occasions when she had found herself working with such an articulate child and, although at first she had found her manner cool and her intellect disconcerting, she also felt that there was a sadness beneath the child's exterior, someplace which she would dearly love to reach. Intuitively, it felt to the therapist as if there was an emotional aspect of the little girl which had always remained inaccessible to those around her; a cold spot in her heart. She firmly believed it was in this chamber that the nightmarish figure reigned with terror.

With a warm, Scotch blanket around her shoulders and her hands wrapped around a mug of hot milk, Maggie spent a sleepless night of her own, sitting in an empty, silent lounge at home, whilst her own children slept soundly upstairs. Mulling over her intuitive insight, she found herself hoping, for the child's sake, that Katherine was not experiencing some form of precognition, a vision of the future. Then there was the notion of the collective consciousness to consider. Perhaps the child had accessed another level of memory where the imagery was not necessarily representative of her own personal experience? Of course, there was the possibility that this phenomenon was an early symptom of schizotypy, or some other form of psychiatric illness or psychological disorder. If that was the case, then she would undoubtedly be brought to the attention of the medical establishment at some point in the future. Maggie would be sure to keep full and accurate records of their work together so as to be of some use, should that happen. But for now, despite the lack of scientific evidence for the efficacy of the treatment, there was only one technique she could think of to try to help this child so devastated by her own dreams.

One bright, autumnal morning, Maggie opened the office window to let in the cool breeze and the sound of birdsong. She told Katherine that she understood all about the dreams and how they made her feel. She also explained that there would be no more questions.

Just this simple act on Maggie's part lifted the mood of the young child who felt as if a magic carpet had appeared beneath her to carry her to a safe place. For the first time, she felt lighter and hopeful that things might be different for her.

"I would like you to try one thing, Katherine," Maggie simply instructed her. "When you reach the point of the dream where you feel scared, I want you to just tell yourself the words: '*This is only a dream and I can wake up as soon as I wish*'. This will enable you to stop the dream before you get to the scary part. It is as simple as that. I believe this may work for you." For the first time in two months, she witnessed a light flicker in the grey eyes of the little girl and watched a smile spread across her sad, little face. The spark of hope warmed Maggie's heart; her job was done.

That night as the ominous shadow closed in on the fragile girl, she faced her fear and spoke in defiance of the steel grip. Focusing her intention beyond the dead eyes of her assailant as his malevolent fingers reached out towards her, she uttered the words, "You do not scare me anymore. I will no longer let you haunt my nights. This is only a dream, you have no power over me in the real world and I can wake up as soon as I wish." The grip loosened from around her throat, she braved a breath and opened her eyes. He was still there; yet his presence felt weaker. She had disempowered him. He dropped his hands and stumbled away from her. No longer could he reach out and hurt her. Despite his cruel sneer he would not torment her; she could not hear the vile words that spewed out of his mouth.

The silent dreams lessened and William faded from Katherine's dreams. On the few occasions that she recognized his face through the nocturnal hours, it now held no power over her. He surfaced only momentarily before merging into the fabric of her dreams. Katherine's mother noticed how her mood lifted and her expression brightened and no longer herself being awakened by the anguished cries, Celia believed her daughter was finally cured. She was happy to consign the experience to the young girl's medical records, never again mentioning the unfortunate interlude in their life.

Week One

Amant de Passage

"Yes!" Katherine gasped in satisfaction, whilst holding firmly onto Henry's shoulders to maintain her balance. She flamed fiery red, the heat rushing through her body before she melted, momentarily merging with the man lying beneath her. Opening her eyes, she saw a bead of sweat trickling between the well-formed pectoral muscles of Henry's chest. Katherine gently traced its trail and then massaged his left nipple with her moist fingertips. His chest expanded suddenly as he took a deep breath, shuddered, and let out a low groan of abandonment. In that moment she understood why some called it *le petit mal*.

Time stilled and energy dissipated, creating a uniquely calm state of existence; their racing heartbeats slowing to a subtle hum, their minds curiously devoid of any angst or struggle.

Gently lifting her hips and rolling over to lie beside Henry, she nestled her cheek onto his shoulder and watched him as he snoozed. A few years had passed since the last time they had made love. There were more grey hairs on his chest and a few more lines around his deep, brown eyes. Yet the instant familiarity and tenderness between them confirmed the true nature of their relationship. Henry would always love Katherine. After all, he truly loved himself, and anyone else who happened to feature in his world, at any given time. It was she who had grown restless in the relationship, wanting to leave the comfort of campus life with an older man, to experience a fuller life, with the hope of a family and career in mind.

As Henry slipped into a deep sleep, Katherine's thoughts dwelled on their time together before she left to work in publishing. He had been her first-year university tutor and the also the first person who had expressed any adult interest in her. She was in awe of his knowledge of the Classical world, even attending the unpopular early morning lectures to hear his passionate speeches. However, she soon relaxed in the comfort of their individual tutorial sessions. Knowing that she was not the first student to be charmed into his bed, she realized that she would not be the last. Every autumn semester there was a steady stream of new and impressionable young women ready to adore him.

Henry was both a very handsome and approachable man; a combination which ensured that many of his students quickly warmed to him. He had offered Katherine a sense of security and shelter when the world had seemed a large and unfriendly place to her. Comfortable with his role in life as a popular and respected academic, his lecture slides depicted his extensive travels in search of new perspectives on the Classical world and now, in his early fifties, apart from occasional speaking engagements further afield, he was largely content with his life in academia. Celia disapproved of the relationship and refused to visit the couple. Katherine's contact with her mother became less frequent, as seemingly appreciated by both of the women. However, a few years after graduation, Celia contracted pneumonia and her mournful spirit finally left its defeated body. Katherine felt both a sense of relief and guilt at her mother's passing. It also provoked a deeper, unconscious response in her psyche and she started to focus more intently on her future. Tired of the repetitive nature of university life with Henry, and the threat posed by each new intake of adoring and impressionable female students, she started to think how different her life could be and to wonder at what her future would hold if she stayed.

Suspicious over his prolonged absences and distant manner, she had one day opened his mail to find an appointment for a vasectomy. Feeling that was the final straw in a tired and tenuous seven-year relationship, she decided to strike out on her own. Henry had offered little resistance when she announced her intention. "Of course I don't *want* you to leave, but I can't, I *won't* stop you if it's truly what you want." He sighed. He had recently sensed a shift in the tension between them. He also believed that she would come back to him.

Leaving her research post at the university, she pitched herself at a career in publishing. Katherine had experienced tentative success with her own academic papers, and she left for the opportunities of the city. There were many lonely nights when she ruminated over her choice, pondering the wisdom of leaving the familiar comfort of the campus for the cold isolation of a single life. However, memories of Henry had gradually faded when, within the year, she met Darrel, a city financier from a privileged family. He had been celebrating his birthday with friends and champagne in a local wine bar. Foolishly, she had given him her number, and he had pursued her relentlessly, until she agreed to have dinner with him.

For Katherine, stepping into Darrel Hewett's life had been like walking through a magical doorway into a kaleidoscope of dreams. He wasted no time wooing her with expensive trinkets, against the romantic backdrops of the world. It was during a moonlit walk on a secluded beach in the Indian Ocean that he offered her a teardrop diamond engagement ring. Katherine was dazzled.

Six months later at the age of 28, she found herself returning from their first New Year celebration together in New York, as his wife. His mother had organized the whole event, including the wedding dress. Katherine stifled her feelings of cold isolation out of a misguided sense of guilt. How ungrateful she would seem to show the slightest dislike of any of the meticulously planned event. She would no doubt, in time, get to know the unfamiliar guests at her own wedding breakfast. In the future she would point out the people in the photographs to her children, who would recognize them as old family friends.

"Darrel told me that you have no close family, my darling. That is why I was so happy to arrange everything for you," Mrs Hewett senior had whispered, yet within earshot of the friends she had invited to the event. "I know how busy you both are. I was just so happy to be able to help."

Katherine felt powerless, a pawn in a secret game of stealth and strategy. She was aware of the conversation passing between strangers, commenting on every aspect of her appearance and personality. Smiles to her face were swiftly followed by snide comments behind duplicitous fingers as her close-fitting bodice pinched a little tighter. Looking across the bloom-bedecked lobby of the Manhattan hotel, her laughing husband appeared to occupy a different dimension; paradoxically a stranger in a curiously familiar form. She knew that she had made a terrible mistake.

Katherine realized that she was just one of Darrel's many missions which, once accomplished, became subject to instant abandonment. The thrill was purely in the chase for the driven and talented financier, who spent many hours poring over the details of his hedge funds but failed to notice when his wife cut her long brown hair and coloured it red.

Weary from enduring a year of long absences and cold disinterest, she protested about his many nights away from home. He called her ungrateful and suggested that she obtain a prescription for anti-depressants. On reflection, her role had been simply to complement his life. Their friends were long-time acquaintances of his, and they regarded her as just the latest in a long line of 'Darrel's girls.' She suffered their company only for as long as was socially necessary in the circle, and was grateful that none of them showed any interest in her as a person in her own right. She occasionally joined the crowd from her office for after-work drinks to celebrate birthdays and promotions, but many of them were recent graduates, younger than her, and too outspoken to mix with Darrel's city set. Any attempt to further develop these potential friendships was further hindered by Darrel's controlling behaviour and demands on her time. He often used her to unburden himself of his work-related frustrations and annoyance with his work colleagues, but he offered her no emotional support in return. He was simply not interested in hearing about the challenges of her day.

On the last occasion that he returned home in the early hours, drunk and dishevelled, he was greeted by an empty bed. Katherine had decided that her life was no longer going to be spent waiting around for him. When he found her in the guest room of their home, a fight ensued and her act of open defiance cost her a black eye and a bruised neck. She vowed that although this was the first time he had resorted to violence against her, it would also be the last. It stirred something inside her; some sense of herself which she felt had lain buried for quite some time.

Over breakfast the following morning, he expressed great remorse and begged for forgiveness. However, Katherine could not conceal her feelings of contempt for him. On leaving the house he headed straight for a consultation with his lawyer. He had no cause to worry over the marital finances as Katherine was only interested in her freedom, not his money, and had signed a pre-nuptial agreement to that effect. He was concerned only that a divorce with allegations of mistreatment would take up his valuable business time and adversely affect his reputation. However, she knew that the marriage had been a mistake. Once the initial enchantment had worn off, it was clear that as individuals they held widely differing values. Katherine wondered how and why they had ever crossed paths. They lived in separate worlds.

Against the backdrop of the global recession, Katherine had found working in the publishing industry a highly pressured and thankless task. She was feeling alone and adrift in unfamiliar waters. Her haunting childhood nightmares of the strangling man had returned, and were persisting, despite her attempts at waking herself from the dream-state. She desperately needed to find something meaningful and rewarding in her life.

On handing in her resignation, she had been told to leave her desk immediately. She was now officially on garden leave and had decided to head as far away from London as she could afford. Having lived on the south coast of England all her life, Katherine intuited to head west in the hope she would again find herself and develop some sense of belonging. An only child, she had lost her father at the tender age of nine. Her mother had passed away following a lingering illness, some three years previously, shortly after her marriage to Darrel. She had not seen Darrel's US-based parents since the day of her marriage to their only son. There was simply no one and nothing to keep her in London.

Henry was the only person she had thought to contact. He was more than happy to meet up, once he had cancelled his previous arrangement with this year's finals student. After all, she would be out of his life at the end of the semester. He had been delighted to hear Katherine's voice as she explained she would be passing his door en route to a little-known Welsh island retreat. The place had caught her attention during an Internet search. She explained how a colleague had been talking about her research for a book on Reiki and the subject had captured her imagination. The retreat centre offered a variety of alternative therapies which she was hoping to experience. The stunning coastal setting had seduced her sensitivities and Katherine had been keen to soak up the expanse of the sky and breathe in the fresh, sea air.

Not expecting to stay the night at Henry's place, she came unprepared. As the evening had progressed and they had finished a bottle of calvados, Henry's favourite apple brandy, he told her that he was not romantically involved with anyone else and she told herself that there would be no harm in sleeping over, just this once. Talk of happy memories led to shared laughter and their mutual desire to relive their intimacy soon became apparent. Now lying awake, alone with her thoughts, and feeling that all traces of the energy of her estranged husband had been erased from her body, she set her mind on the future. Today she would be pioneering westwards in search of a new destiny, whilst Darrel would be opening a copy of her divorce petition posted to him from the court.

Last Rites

"Tell her I'm s-sorry."

Darrel slurred the message on the voicemail of a sleeping colleague. "It's wrong, it's all gone wrong. It wasn't meant to be like this." He ended the call and clicked on the 'contacts' icon on his smart phone, diligently deleting every entry in the folder except for one. Next, he turned his attention to the list of texts and emails, consigning each to anonymity in the memory of the device. Draining the last drops from his glass, Darrel stood up and placed his glass and the empty bottle of vodka at the back of the drinks cabinet. With one last look around the lounge, he decided that everything was just as he wanted to leave it, picked up his car keys from the hall table, and staggered out to the garage. He would take the Barchetta. It was his first and favourite Ferrari. He still prided himself on its glossy, black exterior and loved the firm feel of its interior, particularly the Nero racing seats. He never failed to feel the thrill of the powerful engine through the seats, and he remembered how Katherine had loved riding with the wind in her hair.

Darrel's research was thorough, his plans meticulous in detail. Even his failures were delivered in a grand and impressive manner. He had a specific route in mind. He would drive one lap around the city, in acknowledgement of all of the places and people who had played a part in his life, before heading out towards the Kent coastline. When the city lights were behind him, he turned up the volume of the music playing in the car. He had recorded some favourite tracks, in a specific order, on his iPod, having worked out the exact duration of the drive from London to Godington Gap. There, the beachfront was only 150 metres in width and he would have to bear well to the right to avoid the beach huts and café located there. He was confident that there were likely to be few, if any, holidaymakers resident in the small caravan park midweek, following the May Day bank holiday weekend. The lyrics of the songs were reinforcing the self-destructive loop of thoughts going around in his head now as he improvised with his own twisted notions.

Finally, the roads closed in and Darrel found himself on the narrow, unmade track leading to the empty field at the top of the cliff. With his heart beating a new rhythm, he turned down the volume of the music and listened to the purr of the engine as the car idled some 50 metres from the cliff edge. To the end, his master plan was executed with spectacular precision. The words, *'who wants to live forever?'* lingered in the darkness as the car disappeared over the edge of the cliff, broken only by a quadruple flash of flames from the paired V12 exhausts as they pirouetted towards the beckoning crest of the midnight sea.

The following afternoon, Katherine stood on the harbour quay with a rucksack on her back, being lashed by the Welsh seaside wind and rain. There were others waiting for the boat across to the island, but it seemed as if no one was in the mood to make polite conversation. Due to the wild sea conditions, the waiting passengers had been informed that if the sailing was cancelled, they would have to wait until the following day to cross over to the island. Unsure if the boat would be able to make the journey, Katherine was trying to formulate Plan B: searching the Internet on her phone for details of local hotels on the mainland. She knew it was too far to head back to Henry's place.

At first, she had felt uptight about this hiccup in her schedule. She had not expected such inclement weather in May. However, on reflection, she realized that there was nothing to rush for and the whole idea of this break was to just 'let things be.' *Perhaps this is the first lesson?* Eventually the captain made his decision and the word was passed along the line. This would be the last sailing for the day, conditions were rough and set to get worse but they should be able to safely make this crossing. The six passengers climbed aboard the old fishing boat and sat around the edge on wooden benches. There was no shelter from the driving rain. The captain advised them all to remain seated for the journey as the vessel rocked violently. Still anchored in the harbour, Katherine momentarily considered getting off the boat. However, she was calmed by the smile and kind words of a fellow passenger.

"It'll be fine, Cariad," said a wise-looking, elderly lady sitting huddled next to her. "We'll get there safely. We've been through far worse conditions than this!" A knowing smile spread across her round, friendly face. The familiar rhythm of her emphatic speech assured Katherine. She pressed her back into the bench and gripped the rail running around the boat. This was only a short crossing; she was sure that she could stomach the nausea and battle the wind for some twenty minutes. However, she let out a loud scream when the salty spray crashed over the front of the boat, drenching her from behind. The angry face of Darrel flashed into her mind. Katherine quickly buried the unwelcome image in the sea-chest of her imagination, cut the rope and watched it sink to the deepest trench of her memory. As she sat squashed between wet strangers, looking intently at each new face from beneath the hats and waterproof anorak hoods, Katherine wondered about the life stories of her new companions; how many, like her, were running away from miserable lives? She asked herself if they could all find the peace and solitude they were seeking.

The Island

With wobbling sea legs, the six bedraggled travellers were met on the shore of the island by the course director, and made their way on foot to the retreat house. On reaching the reception desk of the main house, the old lady from the boat removed her hood to reveal long, silver hair pulled back neatly from her face and fixed firmly in a homely bun. Hanging up her sensible waterproof coat, she put on a housekeeper's apron. "You're always welcome in my kitchen, Cariad," she said, tapping Katherine lightly on the shoulder before heading off to prepare the afternoon tea.

Where have I seen her before? For a split second, Katherine thought she recognized the well-rounded lady. Her manner was odd, yet familiar. The remaining four retreaters revealed themselves as they peeled off their saturated outer garments. Katherine saw shy and friendly faces emerging from beneath their assorted apparel. She understood that some were here in the hope of gaining some respite from relentless work or family pressures; she would respect their privacy. However, one smile caught her eye as it was flashed around the room. It belonged to a tall, slim man with short fair hair, congenially shaking hands with everyone. His clear blue eyes held Katherine momentarily transfixed. With a shy smile, she smoothed her windblown hair and turned away. Turning back just a few seconds later, she saw that his gaze was still fixed on her and she blushed. Reminding herself of the reasons she was here, on retreat, she focused on finding out the details of her accommodation.

Having booked in for a long stay, Katherine had been allocated one of the modest cottages on the estate. She was given a key and directions to the lighthouse keeper's cottage, which would be her home for the next six weeks. However, the receptionist advised her to stay at the main house for afternoon tea and a chance to dry off before heading back out to brave the wind and rain. Katherine thought this would at least give her the chance to learn more about her surroundings and the retreat amenities. She was led along with the others down a short corridor from reception which led to a large L-shaped room with two sets of bow-shaped bay windows, revealing sweeping views of the beach below and the sound beyond. The room contained one long dining table, laid out in a formal manner, and a lounge area with comfortable sofas and tables with lamps; all arranged around an open fireplace, itself housed within a wall of shelves, containing a rich selection of old and new books. The paintwork on the wood had yellowed with age and the décor looked a little faded, yet despite the frayed corners and the faint mustiness she could see herself sitting comfortably here, reading under the evening lamplight.

Whilst Katherine browsed through the bookshelves, the director of retreat events introduced herself to the group. She was a thin, freckled, red-haired lady with a quiet and gentle manner who addressed them as they relaxed in the lounge. Outlining the events scheduled, she also acknowledged that some people were here for the solitude and explained that whilst participation was always welcome it was by no means an expectation. The multi-faith centre had amongst its staff a resident counsellor, a hypnotherapist and a Reiki practitioner. The Reiki healing appealed to Katherine who figured it would be, in essence, an opportunity for some deep relaxation. She believed that what she needed most was to feel free to breathe again, to walk on the deserted beaches in the spring sunshine, or in the wind and rain if the current weather front persisted. She wanted to loosen off the shackles of her personal and professional lives and quieten her mind, so she could hear clearly what it was that she really wanted from life. If Reiki or any other alternative therapy could enhance her sense of wellbeing, she was quite open to exploring it. Being here on the island would, hopefully, allow her the time, space and freedom to do so, at her own pace and on her own terms. She could eat at the main house and join in with the activities if she felt the need for human company, or she could simply take shelter in the solitude of her cottage if she so chose.

She knew that there would have to be solicitors' letters and maybe court hearings if the divorce from Darrel became contentious, as she suspected it would. And at some point she would have to find herself a new job. Until then, she was treating herself to a hiatus from the hustle and bustle of her hectic life in the 21st century. Hopefully the break would help her re-evaluate her genuine responsibilities and simplify her life.

She was tired of the struggle with all the 'shoulds' and 'musts' that had been thrust upon her over the years by her mother, teachers, boyfriends, and employers. She had reached the stage where she was no longer sure what exactly she was doing, or why she was doing it. One thing she did know: she certainly had not been doing it for herself. Feeling that she had lost sight of her inner self and seeming to be losing her grip on her outer life, she knew that the time had come to stop and rewind the many strands of herself that had been pulled out in various directions. She told herself that the time for flailing about in the lives and roles that other people wanted her to lead was over.

Feeling refreshed, Katherine collected all the information about the island that she could find and, having confirmed the time for the welcome dinner at the house, she headed out whilst there was a break in the rain to find the cottage which was to be her home for the next six weeks. There was a Norman chapel situated on the island which welcomed visiting pilgrims, which she would get around to sightseeing at some point; now she was far more interested in locating the deserted lighthouse on the island. As relatively late additions to the island, the lighthouse and the keeper's cottage had been built in the 1820s. Katherine had viewed photographs of their interiors on the Internet and was struck by the beauty of their simplicity and magnificence of the sea-bound outlook.

At low tide she could reach the cottage by way of a short beach walk but as the tide was on the turn she took the course director's advice to take the cliff path around the headland. With her rucksack on her back, she enjoyed the wind in her hair and the freshness of the coastal air as she walked, filling her lungs with deep breaths of freedom. She shook out her shoulder-length red curls and let her arms swing freely by her sides as she strode along the narrow path, happy to wear the natural windswept look for a while.

Turning the key and lifting the latch of the old wooden door of the whitewashed cottage, she felt she was entering a unique space. This was somewhere of her very own. There was no one to judge or criticize her choice; there was nothing she needed to do to please anyone else. Standing in the centre of the small and sparsely decorated single-storey abode, she closed her eyes and offered up her gratitude. Unpacking her rucksack, she switched off her mobile phone and placed it in the side-zipped pocket. Next, she lit the two church pillar candles displayed on the sill of the tiny bathroom window and filled the old-fashioned tub with hot water. Soaking in the local lavender oil, a bottle of which had been placed most thoughtfully on the small wicker stand just inside the room, she smiled serenely, enjoying the luxury. This was it! This was how life was to be, for the next six weeks or so. She was going to immerse herself in a world of wellbeing, indulge herself with peace and inner calm. She would celebrate this new beginning alone, with an early night. Settling between the clean cotton sheets on the creaky wooden bed, Katherine welcomed the silence she created by lying perfectly still. This was a blissful contrast to the luxury of sleeping in a king-size bed with silken sheets, trying to recharge after the exertions of an adrenalin-fuelled to-do list of the day. The pleasure now lay in the knowledge that she was no longer anxiously waiting for anyone to return home and would not be rudely woken by an early morning alarm.

The Dream

Katherine was standing at the water's edge. She was mesmerized by the shimmering reflection of the moon as it danced on the waves. Her eyes followed the rippling light as it played hide-and-seek with the night sea. Her trance was broken by a flash of lightning which lit up the sky and on hearing the distant rumble of thunder she became aware that she was on the beach in the dark, wearing only the thin, silk shift she had worn to bed. Cradling herself with her bare arms in an attempt to keep warm, she knew that she had to find her way back to the cottage. As the rain started to fall, she found herself clambering over the wet rocks in bare feet. With the rising tide close on her heels, her heart pounded in her chest as she climbed the treacherous steps to the cliff top.

When the storm clouds hid the moonlight she was forced to feel her way along the cliff path, scraping her toes on the stones, and crying out at the scratching of the hedgerow briars on her bare skin. She reasoned with herself that any time soon she would be reassured by the intermittent flash from the lighthouse that she was on the right track. However, on approaching the clearing where she hoped to find the cottage, she became confused and disoriented. She was sure this was the exact spot where she had soaked in the bath and slept in the cottage bed. However, she found only a small clearing with a ring of stones circling a burned-out fire, and the sound of her mobile phone, alerting her to a call.

'Run!' Something or someone was telling her that she needed to leave this place.

Katherine raced, barefoot over uneven ground, feeling the sting of sharp stones on the soles of her feet. As her legs tired and the ground beneath her took on the form of ascending, circular, stone steps, she struggled to climb to safety. There was someone behind her now and she knew he intended her harm. As her breathing became more laboured and her pace slowed, she could feel the hot breath of an angry man on the back of her neck. If she turned around to see his face, she knew it would be the last one she saw. Katherine struggled on until the stairwell opened out into the battlements of a ruined castle, perched high on a windy promontory. Although the black night prevented her from seeing the ocean spread out in front of her, the sound of the crashing waves and the spray of saltwater on her skin told her she was at the edge of the land. The only way to escape with her life would be to plunge into the waters below.

'*Jump!*' a voice urged. '*You will be safe, I will catch you.*'

In the dream, Katherine took the chance to freefall. She felt the initial euphoria of weightlessness until she was gripped by the gravitational pull. The wind whooshed past her face and through her hair, her speed increasing until her landing was cushioned by the sail of a large ship. In the dim light of oil lanterns, she could make out stout figures stumbling about on the listing wooden deck. Her fear gave way to overwhelming nausea and she searched for a way to get to the bottom of the ship. If she could just find a cabin and hide away, Katherine felt certain that she would be safe. She scrambled down into the hold and from the small porthole of a storeroom in the bowels of the ship, her small, pale face peered out at the rough sea surrounding her. She knew all she had to do was to lie low until they reached land, when she could breathe freely again. She found respite in snatched moments of sleep, until she became aware of a large shadow falling across her hiding place. She felt a menacing presence; a rough hand grabbed her shoulders, pulling her away from the porthole. From behind, she felt the tightening of a ligature around her throat. Grappling to loosen the noose, the flesh on her fingertips and knuckles was sliced to the bone by the spiked wire. The taste of her own blood splashing across her face during the struggle for her life was the last thing of which she was aware, before blacking out.

Faces, Old and New

Katherine awoke with a start on her cold bed at the cottage. The blankets and quilt lay on the floor, thrown off as she struggled in her sleep. Her throat felt bruised and every muscle in her body ached. At first she was disoriented, unsure of where she was or what had happened to her. No stranger to frequent nightmares and dreaming in graphic detail, she soon came to her senses; she remembered that she was in the cottage on the island and relaxed. On realizing that she was safe from the horror of the dream, she took a deep breath and reached over to pull up the covers, stretching out in the bed. She allowed herself to sink back into the soft mattress, consciously relaxing every tense muscle in her body. The air in the bedroom was cool and fresh, with a faint hint of lavender from the sprig placed in the small glass vase on the white bedside table. She breathed slowly, savouring the unusual silence and enjoying the sense of deep relaxation, lying awake, eyes closed, sensing the peace surrounding her, before finally dropping back to sleep.

She was awoken a short while later by a gentle tapping sound on the bedroom window. No longer hearing the distant hum of the city traffic or the sounds of the neighbours closing their car doors and pulling off from their gravel driveways, it was the sounds of the country which now acted as her morning alarm call. Resisting her daily habit of rushing out of bed and careering headlong into an endless series of tasks, she turned her back to the window in the hope of relaxing further. However, as the sound persisted she reluctantly threw back the covers, rose from the warm bed, and pulled aside the curtain. A bold, red-breasted robin perched proudly on the outside sill of the bedroom window. He tapped his beak once more on the pane as if to acknowledge her, then he shifted nimbly on his tiny feet before flying off. Katherine opened the window to hear the sound of the waves breaking into the cove below and she started to recall the scenes from her dream. With a feeling of uncertainty in the pit of her stomach, she gently rubbed her neck, half expecting to feel the ligature wounds. Checking in the bathroom mirror for marks, she was relieved to see only her pale, smooth skin. Next, she searched for her phone in the zipped pocket of her bag. It was still as she had left it, switched off. She sighed in relief and, resisting the temptation to check for new messages and missed calls, she replaced it inside the bag.

Over breakfast at the retreat house, she was surprised to hear the topic of conversation turn to dreams and found herself talking with the others about her own experience. In her absence, the company of guests had gelled over the previous night's dinner and so the morning's conversation was freely flowing. Happy to join in, she explained her confusion at her inability to find the cottage. However, she held back the fearful ending to the dream as it was still looming uncomfortably large in her memory. Her companions were keen to suggest various interpretations of the beach scene in her dream; one of the guests intimating that it was symbolic of the nature of the retreat, and that she was here to gain respite from the rising tide of her emotions. Katherine warmed to the hazel-eyed, middle-aged lady whose suggestion was delivered in a good-natured manner. She was reminded of Maggie Brown, her childhood therapist. However, it was something the smiling, blue-eyed man said that caught her attention.

"Perhaps you were here before the lighthouse," he suggested in a gentle Irish lilt, as he reached for another piece of toast.

"What do you mean?" Katherine asked.

"The lighthouse was built around 1830," he explained. "Perhaps the time of your dream predated that era on the island." Katherine looked straight into his eyes and saw both kindness and mischief in his expression.

"Fintan Byrne, call me Fin, full of all sorts of useless information!" He offered his hand for her to shake. Katherine smiled in acknowledgement and reciprocated.

"Katherine Hewett, soon to be Walsh," she said, taking a sip from her cup of strong coffee.

"That's a good Irish name you're getting there," he remarked.

"Oh no," explained Katherine, "it's my family name. I'm going back to my maiden name and they are all English, from the south coast."

"That may be so," Fin continued, "but the name is Irish." His comment unsettled her even though it was said in a friendly manner, and she did not understand the reasons for her discomfort. Perhaps she was feeling more sensitive than she realized? After all, this was new territory for her. She was all alone for the first time in years, with no one dictating what the future was to hold for her. She was not open to considering such personal comments from a stranger, however handsome or charming he seemed. She was grateful for the timely appearance at the table of the familiar-faced cook, offering a tray of freshly baked crompogau. Katherine chose one of her buttermilk pancakes and reached for the blackberry jam on offer. The old lady had been listening to the conversation and on turning back to Katherine and Fin she said, "The Welsh and the Irish have an ancient connection, you know. Since olden times, our two Celtic nations have been intertwined. It all started with the marriage of our king's sister, Branwen, to the Irish King Matholwch. Of course, it all ended in disaster."

"How do you mean?" Katherine asked.

"Well, the jealous brother of the Welsh King Bran of Harlech was enraged that their sister's betrothal had been arranged without his consent and he set about slaughtering the Irish king's horses." Katherine recoiled at the image of such needless cruelty. "King Bran made good by offering up a magic cauldron to his insulted counterpart, one which was said to restore life to the dead," the cook continued.

"And they all lived happily ever after?" Katherine asked tongue-in-cheek.

"Branwen was mistreated by her husband and sent a message for help from her family over the Irish Sea, by way of a starling," the cook replied.

"So was she saved?" asked Katherine, now becoming amused by the impromptu breakfast entertainment.

"Alas," replied the elderly lady, casting her gaze at Fin, "after much bloodshed, only seven Welshmen survived and on her return to the Welsh shores Branwen died of a broken heart."

Katherine was intrigued by the seriousness of the old lady's delivery.

"I love folklore," she said in an attempt to lighten the moment, "although I'm more familiar with Ancient Greek mythology. That's full of tragedy too!"

"It pays to know our history; our collective history. We can learn much from our ancestors and, perhaps most of all, we can learn that wherever we come from, we are all the same."

The old lady nodded at Katherine as she spoke her words, before leaving the table to return the empty pancake plate to the kitchen. For the duration of the meal, Katherine enquired further from the group members as to the nature and benefits of Reiki, casting only furtive glances across the table at Fin.

Reiki

Later that afternoon, Katherine lay on the soft table in the fragrant treatment room at the top of the retreat house in a deep state of relaxation. Although at first feeling slightly uncomfortable with the warm palms of the Reiki master hovering over her eyes and face, she found herself feeling progressively more at peace as the concentration of energy moved down through her body. She found it easy to place her trust in the hands of the mature woman who had explained a little about the modality, and that the term master was bestowed on both male and female therapists achieving the most advanced level of practice. She let her thoughts wander through varying levels of consciousness, elicited by the therapy, as the session progressed.

She was experiencing all shades of the colour blue, and the cleansing feel of strong emotions washing over her with every deep breath she released. It felt good to let go of all of her circular thoughts and pent-up feelings which had kept her wired over the past few months, even if she was unsure of what was to follow. Deep relaxation was a new habit that she was developing with pleasure.

As the master's hands reached above Katherine's lower abdomen and hips, both of them felt a surge of heat and momentarily an image of Henry's face appeared in Katherine's mind. The master's hands tingled with a curious, new energy and she hovered a little longer, as if trying to solve a puzzle, before moving on to Katherine's thighs. It was at this point that Katherine sensed there was someone else in the room with them. As she felt the urge to open her eyes to see who it was, a strong shade of aqua emerged from her mind's eye and she felt the smooth flow of satin against her cheek. It felt comforting somehow, as if to reassure her that she was safe. Katherine felt herself sink into a deeper level of peace and relaxation.

She was unsure how much time passed before she became aware that she was no longer in the treatment room. Instead, she was in a much older building with a high ceiling, lying in a large, four-poster, oak bed placed in the centre of the room. There was a set of arched windows to her left, through which she could see woodlands in the foreground, and the sea in the distance. She watched as an old lady wearing a white, cloth bonnet and a long, heavy, woollen tunic came into the room carrying a bowl and a cloth. Placing the objects on a narrow trestle table positioned alongside the window, the woman then bowed her head in her direction before leaving the room.

Katherine came round in response to the Reiki master's voice, telling her to remain in the reclined position for a few minutes and asking her if she would like a glass of water. She was back in the treatment room.

"How are you feeling?" the Reiki master asked, when Katherine managed to sit up and take a sip.

She replied that she felt very calm and was keen to tell the master about her experience. "I must have fallen asleep at some point," she explained. "I dreamed that I was in an old building with a high ceiling and arched windows." Katherine traced the outline of a gothic-style curve in the air with her finger as she spoke. The master listened in silence, smiling to herself. As she recalled the four-poster bed and the encounter with the woman in the tightly-fitted bonnet, Katherine's hands fell to her abdomen where she absentmindedly rubbed herself.

"It was me, but in a different place and a different time...oh, how intriguing...if it was a dream, it was very different to the usual sort that I experience." She was surprised at her own realization.

There followed a thoughtful pause before the Reiki master said, "You seem very sensitive. Have you had many experiences of such 'seeing' or 'feeling' in situations such as this?" Katherine explained that this was her first experience of Reiki, although she had always experienced vivid dreams.

"Your description was very detailed," commented the master. "Have you ever tried past life regression therapy?" she tentatively asked. "It's like hypnosis, but it's for healing."

Katherine replied that she knew nothing about the subject, but she was becoming interested in exploring these new avenues opening up in her life.

Blood

That evening, Katherine stood with her face under the warm flow of the shower in the cottage. Eyes closed, she let the water massage the frown from her forehead and smooth out the laughter lines from her cheeks. She was imagining herself standing naked under a rock-sheltered, tropical waterfall. With her skin a shade of sun-kissed gold stretched over her lithe limbs, the image softly framed with vines of deep red bougainvillea and pale pink Plumeria blooms. She breathed in the exotic scent and heard the splash of the sparkling beads of fresh mountain water, as it fell over and around her into a clear aqua pool. Just one week into her remote island retreat and Katherine was feeling refreshed and ready for whatever the world was going to bring this day to the door of her cottage.

She stepped out from the shower and onto a soft, white towel. Wrapping another around her glowing body, she noticed some brown specks falling between her feet. She frowned, not expecting her period for another week or so. Reaching for a tissue and wiping gently between her legs, she saw that she was losing some pinkish-brown blood. However, she was not experiencing the usual cramping pains or monthly lower backache. Shrugging it off as a bodily reaction to the changes in her routine and environment, she chose to see it as another sign of the end of her old life and the start of the new. However, as she paused in reflection images of Henry whispering into the ears of other women flashed into her mind. She heard his lascivious laughter and she shrank in her mind's eye, standing small: the loneliest girl in the world. Her thoughts shifted to a later time in her life and feeling choked, she tried desperately to swallow her emotions. However, her throat was firmly in Darrel's grip. She shivered, and his face smiled as he tightened the steely grasp around her neck. Her cheeks were awash with tears. The end of her cycle usually brought Katherine's emotions closer to the surface, however this month she was not shedding tears of sadness: these were tears of relief. She was overwhelmed by a sense of release. Closing her eyes, she stood with both arms outstretched and allowed the towel to fall at her feet. Then, standing naked and free, she lifted her chin and said out loud, "I now release all of my regrets and forgive myself for each and every one of my past mistakes."

Retiring to bed that night in a deep state of relaxation, she drifted off easily into a long and comforting sleep. In her dreams, Katherine found herself between the old, stone walls of a kitchen on a cold winter's morning. Warming her hands over the open fire, she was comforted by the warm smell of freshly baked bread. Looking around her, she could see pieces of holly and mistletoe wedged into the gaps between the old grey stones of the walls, and she had the sweet taste of toffee on her lips. Then she heard the voice of the retreat house cook say, "Come along now, Cariad, it's time for Plygain."

"I don't want to go to the church," she heard herself protesting in a small, quiet voice. "It's cold and dark out there. Why can't we stay here and listen to the harp a while longer? It's my turn to drop the taffy into the water and see the initials of my future husband."

"Come now, child, it is Christmas morning and the church will be warm and brightly lit with candles. You know that after the singing you can return home to feast in front of the fire in the Great Hall, with all of your family. Today all of your favourites will be on the table, as well as roasted goose." The cook sought to persuade her with a warm and encouraging manner. "There's much more to look forward to. Soon it will be time for the Calennig."

"Will I be allowed to carry it this season?" Katherine asked, feeling a surge of excitement at the thought of making the traditional gifts to donate to the neighbouring tenant farmers.

"I'm sure your brothers will be pleased to escort you around the estate," the cook replied.

"When will I be allowed out of the castle grounds?" the young girl asked.

"When your mother returns, then she will decide where you are to go." The cook's voice had developed a serious tone. "We can't have you getting bloodied by the St Stephen's holly whilst she's away, can we?"

"When will Mammy come home?" Katherine heard herself ask in a small voice. "Will she be here for the New Year?"

"Soon, Cariad, soon," the cook said, trying to soothe the young girl. Katherine felt a pain in her chest when she heard the cook's response.

"It's no matter if she's not," the cook quickly asserted. "You can stay here with me in the kitchen, away from the Mari Llwyd, if that's what you're worried about." An image of a horse's skull bedecked with ribbons and a bedsheet flashed into Katherine's young mind. The curious creation was a common caller at the servants' quarters of the castle at New Year. Unfortunately, in the hands of the local farmhands, what was intended as an intellectual challenge – a battle of wits with an animal spirit – degenerated into a drunken puppet show. The young girl recoiled at the memory of the clicking of the dead animal's jaws and the slurred, jeering words of the puppeteers.

In her bed at the cottage, Katherine shivered in her sleep.

Week Two

Sylvan Spring

Katherine had been enjoying the simple, home-cooked meals offered at the retreat house. Her tastes were changing and she was enjoying experimenting with new flavours. She had found herself appreciating the pure taste of simply prepared vegetables, free of the sugar and fat of processed food, flavoured only with fresh herbs and spices, and she wondered if the new flavours so relished by her taste buds were to be a permanent change. Perhaps it was a result of the detoxification effect of the diet that she found herself overly sensitive to the scent of oranges placed in a bowl at the centre of the breakfast table? She also found herself avoiding the coffee pot and opting for peppermint tea in its place. She was sleeping more soundly too, and often missed breakfast at the house; hence following her daily morning walkabout on the island, she had a voracious appetite for lunch.

The temperate weather of late spring on the island made it a very pleasant place to explore. Observing the changes taking place in the natural surroundings, she developed a fascination for the variety of plants and trees she witnessed in bloom and she found herself researching the different species and documenting them in a journal. She was amazed at the details of life that had passed her by, unnoticed, when she had lived and worked in the city. Now, she felt grateful for having the opportunity to witness the minute miracles of nature unfolding in front of her very eyes. She smiled at the irony when she learned that the alternative name for the daffodil, Darrel's favourite flower, was narcissus. *How fitting!* she thought to herself and watched the few remaining proud yellow plants fading, seemingly giving up their space to allow the bluebells to carpet the woodland at the centre of the island; followed closely by the first appearance of wild red poppies springing up in their singular fashion atop the traditional Welsh hedgerows.

Before her time on the island, deadlines had replaced days, weeks and the seasons; meetings, not birthdays or holidays, had been marked up in red on her calendar, and at the slightest hint of downtime some additional commitment had been hastily scheduled by Darrel in their domestic life to make valuable use of the time. This usually meant dinner with some boring man and the latest adoring young woman on his arm; an engagement with the sole purpose of building Darrel's portfolio and furthering his career. Now the rhythm of her life was allowing for greater exploration of her own personal needs and desires. She was becoming increasingly aware that she alone was in control of her habits and she was beginning to shake off any guilt inculcated by repetitious demands and enjoy the freedom from having to account to others for her actions.

As the tourist season was starting to spread to the island, the farm shop was filling up its shelves with products made by local farmers, using ingredients from the kitchen garden at the church. Katherine had sampled some of the perfumed products such as the lavender bath essence and soaps. Now she found herself gazing at the selection of locally produced confectionery on display in the fully stocked shop. She had stopped eating chocolate when her mother had convinced her that no man could ever love a fat girl. This notion had been reinforced in later life when Darrel had kept a close eye and a controlling grip on her diet, concerned that she might lose her slim figure. Was it a sudden craving, or an act of rebellion that prompted her to buy a large box of Farmhouse Shortbread biscuits and a variety of chocolate bars? At any rate, she delighted in the realization that she could buy and eat as much of these as she chose. She found the milk-chocolate honeycomb crunch the most delicious, its sweetness a welcome replacement for the curious chemical taste she often experienced in her mouth. She managed to eat two bars whilst walking to the house for lunch, and decided to store the remaining bars and shortbread in the cottage.

Arriving at the retreat house before lunch was due to be served she wandered into the kitchen to chat with the friendly cook. Looking up when she heard Katherine enter, the old lady smiled and welcomed her, using a curious mixture of English and Welsh.

"Croeso, Cariad, come on in!"

"Good morning," replied Katherine. "I'm just wondering what's on the menu for today's lunch. Something delicious, I'm sure."

"Well now, I have some cawl cennin on the hob and some bara lawr keeping warm in the oven," the cook replied. Then reaching out to the bake stone, she lifted off some small, round Welsh cakes, placing them on a side plate. Handing them to Katherine, she announced, "And here are some of your old favourites, teisen maen! Here, take them."

Katherine had never eaten one of these cakes. She was amused that the old lady had referred to them as 'your old favourites.' Politely, she took the plate and tasted one. They were flavoured with currants and were very sweet and moist, but not at all familiar to her.

Puzzled, she simply thanked the cook and returned the plate. The old lady winked at her and turned her attention to stir the pot of stew on the hob.

"Of course, there will also be salad and quiche and fresh fruit on the table," she commented, "for those amongst us who have forgotten their liking for the traditional recipes!"

Who are you? Katherine found herself thinking.

"Have we met? I mean, at some other time or place?" she asked. Continuing to stir the pot on the hob, the old lady simply smiled to herself. "This might sound really weird," Katherine started to explain, "but it's just that I had a dream. I was a child in another kitchen, with you. It was a much older place than this and it seemed like a different time..." Her voice trailed off.

"Cariad, this is a place of healing," the cook said as she sprinkled some freshly chopped herbs into the pan, "and sometimes strange things happen here, strange but usually good things."

"Yes, it felt as if you were helping me through a difficult time," Katherine ventured.

"Cariad, I am here to feed your body, only you can nourish the cravings of your soul," replied the wise old woman.

An agreeable mealtime relationship was developing between the retreaters, who were always enthusiastic to hear about each other's discoveries and experiences. Katherine was enjoying a strong appetite for both the food and the company at the house. She had discovered that the good-natured, hazel-eyed lady was named Shirley and that she had recently retired from a career in teaching to take up counselling.

"It was how I spent most of my working day," she had explained. "Taking kids outside the room and helping them to calm down so the rest of the class could get on with their work. I thought I might as well get qualified for the job. Then I decided I might as well become a full-time counsellor. The funny thing is, now I'm in private practice getting referrals from GPs, I now have the parents of those kids coming to see me, suffering from anxiety and depression, telling me they can't cope with their own children! The system is all wrong. These people need interventions at an early stage, before the behaviour of the kids gets out of control and the teachers and the rest of society are left to pick up the pieces," Shirley vented.

Katherine was firmly reminded about her own childhood experience of counselling, the first time an adult had actually listened to her speaking about her disturbing dreams without telling her that her fear was imaginary. Maggie Brown had provided a safe haven for her as a frightened young girl, where she could speak freely without fear of being judged. She was certain that she had Maggie to thank for her managing to cope with life in the wake of her father's death. As she had grown up, Katherine had learned that the images in her mind were simply not visible to other people and that others around her became uncomfortable when she spoke about them. Accordingly, she had learned to keep her nebulous experiences to herself. With Maggie's help she had once become empowered to take charge of her own internal world and she silently thanked the woman once again for allowing her the space and the time to figure out her own coping strategy. All she needed now was to reclaim that power.

Katherine could see how both the children and the parents would warm to Shirley, with her no-nonsense, down-to-earth approach.

"Once you step out of the city rhythm, you have to move out," she had explained to Katherine, who noticed that her usual buoyant look had given way to tired eyes and a weary expression. "When you get to my age, you just can't be doing with all the bullshit, all the red tape that these larger inner-city schools get themselves caught up in. It's no good fighting it when it's time to move on." She explained how she had left the city and was looking to set up a practice in a rural area, where there would be fewer people and more time to spend working with each client. Her words resonated strongly with Katherine who smiled warmly at the woman.

Fintan Byrne was also listening closely to the conversation. Intrigued by the attractive redhead's distracted expression, he was curious to know what was going on in her mind and determined to engage her in a conversation which would last a little longer than the few minutes of polite exchange of pleasantries around the table. It was a feat he had yet to achieve. However, it was the course director who spoke up and caught Katherine's attention.

"I can highly recommend it," she was saying, "and I don't advertise anyone's services unless I have personal knowledge or experience of them. I'm talking about my third regression session with Peter; it was simply amazing." The group was entranced by her expressive green eyes and enthralled by her experiences as she recounted the discoveries she had made about her past lives under the influence of hypnosis. The group director spoke calmly about how she had suffered with pain in her lower back since she was a child.

"The doctors could find nothing wrong with my bones or muscles and had informed my parents that I was suffering from growing pains!" she exclaimed. "The pain continued into adulthood and worsened when I became pregnant with my daughter. During the third session with Peter, I discovered that I had been a child who had been sent to the workhouse in Victorian times, by my widowed mother who could not afford to feed me. I realized the root cause of my back pain came from my situation in that era. My job had been to blacken the great fireplaces in the grand rooms of the owners of the monstrous house, all alone. If they were displeased with my work they would instruct the kitchen not to feed me any supper that night. I would have to try to sleep despite the hunger, and never knowing if I would be given another chance to please those who decided my fate. When I released the feelings of fear of abandonment and scarcity back into the time to which they belonged, the pain resolved itself. I stopped taking handfuls of analgesic and anti-inflammatory medication and started sleeping properly for the first time in decades."

There was a ripple of response to her words from around the

table. Many were keen to find out more about her experience. With all the talk of hunger, Katherine found herself choosing a large slice of spinach quiche for her plate. Fin tossed the blue cheese and fresh walnut salad in its bowl before offering it to her. She smiled as she took the wooden utensils from his hands and he caught a sparkle in her eyes as she hungrily filled her plate.

"There really is nothing to fear," the course director continued. "It's a very gentle process and Peter is highly experienced. He guides you through the relaxation and asks you some simple questions. He also makes a recording of the session so that you can listen to it, if you wish. He's back on the island this Thursday, so if anyone wants to book a session with him just let me know."

The course director then turned her attention to the bowl of steaming cawl set before her. As Katherine reached to break off a piece of the freshly baked loaf placed at the centre of the table, she had to concede that even if it was all just sales talk it had a compelling pitch. It seemed to have had a profound effect on the woman and it had set off everyone else around the table talking about the subject. With the suggestion of the Reiki master also echoing in her mind, she was keen to try out the experience. Swallowing a mouthful of homemade fruity coleslaw, she enthusiastically booked herself in for an evening session the following Thursday.

The Abduction

In response to Katherine's matter-of-fact statement that she knew very little of her family history, Peter Wheeler explained that past life regression was wholly different to genealogy. He asked her if there was anything of a physical or psychological nature troubling her, which they might explore in the session. He emphasized the healing intention of this type of hypnosis and Katherine, although evasive about her broken marriage, was clear in her mind that throughout her life she had experienced feelings of powerlessness which had led her to make what she believed to be the wrong decisions. Peter asked her if there were such things as *wrong* decisions and sat in silence whilst she thought it through for a few minutes.

"So you believe in predestination?" she asked him. Peter explained that he believed essentially in the power of the mind, that it contains all the information people will ever need to navigate their way through life and that hypnosis was one way to tap into this knowledge.

"Ultimately, we have power over the decisions and choices we make," he asserted. "We may not always be aware of the underlying reasons or subconscious knowledge influencing our actions. Hypnosis is just one way of accessing that information. Some people even use self-hypnosis simply as a way to achieve a greater state of relaxation."

As he spoke, Katherine studied Peter's earnest face. From the faded hue of his sandy hair and deepening expression lines on his forehead, she surmised that he was probably in his mid-fifties. Although in his manner he appeared at first a little detached, she felt it was out of a sense of politeness. The issue of trust momentarily raised its head for her and looking closely into his eyes she saw only compassion. Having enjoyed the experience of Reiki healing, she felt open to experimentation if it consisted of another opportunity for deep relaxation. Tired of looking outside of herself for guidance and approval, she felt good about investing in the contents of her own mind, even the unconscious parts if necessary. Katherine was genuinely curious to find out what might come to light and so she gave her consent for the session to be recorded and lay back into the soft reclining chair in the drawing room at the retreat house. Checking that she was in a comfortable position, Peter asked her to close her eyes and gently guided her to consciously relax each muscle in her body. Katherine engaged fully with the relaxation, focused on her breathing, and soon felt her heart beating more slowly and evenly.

She was asked to see herself walking slowly down some steps and when she reached the bottom Peter instructed her to walk through the doorway she found there and into a walled garden.

As Peter's voice faded in and out of her mind, Katherine became aware of the scent of the roses and the gentle brush of the breeze on the back of her neck. She heard a flutter of wings and watched a ring-necked dove settle on an apple blossom branch. She felt calm and relaxed as she walked between the ancient oak trees through the garden, pausing to watch some swifts splashing in the limestone bowls of a sparkling fountain. Katherine knew this beautiful garden was a creation of her imagination and yet its beauty somehow spoke to her of truth. Although she knew it did not exist in her world of today, she was strangely comforted by its familiarity. It was as if she had returned to a place of fond memories, where the beds of purple, pink and white primulas she could see so clearly had bloomed here forever.

She caught the sound of children's laughter being carried on the breeze and she turned to see what was happening around her. Her eyes fell on an unfamiliar wooden bridge straddling the stream at the bottom of the gentle slope. She struggled to see where it led, but the view of the bank on the far side of the bridge was obscured by a curious mist. Compelled to walk towards the bridge, she could just make out a hooded figure emerging from the mist. Hesitating, she heard Peter's voice assuring her that this person was here to help her and that it was safe for her to meet them on the bridge. As she approached, the rounded figure appeared taller than her, and the walk across the bridge was taking longer than she had anticipated from the top of the garden. She had to lift her arm to reach the wooden hand rail and as she got closer to the figure she heard the woman's voice scolding her, as if she was a young child.

"There you are! Come along now, Cariad, we've been looking for you."

Katherine looked up at the faintly familiar face of the young woman. Something stirred in her memory at the sound of the strong Welsh accent. She looked like a younger version of the cook at the retreat house. The woman turned to go, clearly expecting her to follow. However, feeling a deep sense of foreboding, the girl lingered a while on the bridge, looking into the slow-moving stream below. The clear spring water darkened as the mist enshrouded the bridge and Katherine was startled by the loud cawing of a raven as it landed next to her on the handrail of the bridge. She shuddered, backing away from the piercing eyes and large hooked beak of the shiny black bird, knowing she had no choice but to continue her journey across the bridge.

Peter sensed that Katherine was experiencing something intense and he intervened, telling her that she was safe and encouraging her to look about her once more.

"Where are you? Can you tell me what you can see?" he asked in a slow, calm tone of voice.

"It's cold and dark," she responded, shivering. "I'm by the water's edge, outside the castle, and I'm scared."

Peter picked up on her small, quiet voice. "How old are you?" he asked gently.

"I'm six years old," she replied. Peter then asked Katherine for her name.

There was a long silence before she whispered with a Welsh lilt, "My name is Angharad Fitz-Gerald."

"What is the year? Can you tell me, Angharad?" he continued.

"It is the year of our Lord, eleven and nine," she replied.

"Who are you with?" he asked. "Is there anyone else here?"

Then it was his turn to shiver as the little girl's voice replied that she was alone. It wasn't very often that he had found himself interrupting his client's memories to prevent any harm coming to them, but he feared this situation was potentially damaging for Katherine. He would have to listen carefully and handle this regression with the greatest of care. Peter took a deep breath before asking, "Angharad, what are you doing alone outside the castle in the dark?"

"I'm looking for my mother," replied the quiet, childlike voice. "She was taken by the men who set fire to the castle. My father and the soldiers have given chase on horseback and I have been left alone here on the river bank. I think they have forgotten about me." As she started to weep, Peter knew that he would have to take her out of this situation and guide her to a different time in her life.

"You are safe," he reassured her. "What happened back then, when you were a small child, is not happening to you any longer. You are just watching an old memory replaying in your mind. You no longer carry the sadness and the fear that you felt at that time. You can see that it belongs back in that time. We are going somewhere else now, forwards to a different time in your life. Listen to me. I want you to take a long, deep breath. I am going to count to five and when you open your eyes you will be in a different situation, at a later stage in your life."

Anxious to get Katherine out of that situation, Peter deliberately counted in a sure and steady tone of voice, watching carefully for any abreaction from his client. When her face was wearing a more peaceful expression he again spoke directly to her. "Open your eyes and tell me what you can see."

Katherine's eyes remained firmly closed, however she appeared calm as she described herself lying in a large wooden bed in her room, at the castle.

"Are you alone, Angharad Fitz-Gerald?" Peter asked.

"I am Angharad de Barry," was the response in a mature voice, "and the nursemaid is here with me. She is bathing the baby."

"What year is it?" Peter continued with his gentle questioning.

"It's 1146," she replied.

Peter sat up in his chair and took a deep breath before asking,

"How are you feeling, Angharad?"

"Tired, I am so tired after many hours on the birthing stool," she explained. "We have a fourth son now and I am going to make sure this one is not going to war," she announced in a resolute manner. The therapist was intrigued.

"Which war, Angharad?" he questioned.

"The war in Ireland," she explained. "Not content with their land and fortunes here, my husband, my brothers, and my eldest sons are travelling over the Irish sea to take the land and fortunes of others. I am tired of the warring and the bloodshed."

"What do you want for your fourth son, Angharad?" Peter asked.

"I want him to live a peaceful life, perhaps to become a man of the cloth. I couldn't bear to lose all my children in war. If my cruel husband has his way, he will sacrifice all his sons for glory."

"Who is your husband?" Peter enquired.

"He is a proud man who has become consumed with wealth and power. His name is William de Barry," Katherine replied. "He once built this beautiful castle for his family, and now he is hardly ever here. He is only interested in sailing over the water to conquer new lands and he will leave me behind, without my beloved sons."

Peter noticed how colourless and drawn her face had become and how her breathing had slowed. She looked as if the life force was draining out of her body. When her speaking ceased and her breathing became barely audible, he knew that it was time to bring her back to the present. In a firm voice he advised her that he would leave her to sleep as she was feeling very tired but she would soon be waking up and feeling refreshed. Peter counted her back into waking consciousness.

Fireside Tales

In the evening quiet of the drawing room, Katherine was thinking over the revelations from her past life regression therapy. She had replayed the recording three times and noted the names and facts in her notebook. However, there were still many questions in her mind. Was she that frightened young Welsh girl in a past life? What had happened to her? She was curious to find out who she had married and to learn of the fate of her four sons. Was it all just her vivid imagination at work? Growing up on the south coast of England, she knew nothing of medieval Welsh history. Her higher education had focused on Ancient Greece and the Classical world. She also felt strangely removed from the events she had witnessed herself recounting. It had seemed as if she was listening to a familiar voice, retelling a well-known tale. Katherine could not say that she felt emotionally moved by the story. However, it had aroused a great deal of curiosity in her. Mulling and musing as to what was real or not, she had missed dinner. Thinking that at this late hour the dining room would be empty of guests, she decided to browse the shelves to see if there were any books on local history which might offer a few insights. She found the room empty, although the open log fire was still alight and a book lay open on the arm of a chair. She was browsing the shelves, not really knowing what she was looking for, when she heard a voice from behind.

"Good evening, Katherine." It was Fin. Why did she always feel on edge when he was around?

"Sorry! Were you sitting here?" She cast a glance at the chair and the open book. "I didn't mean to disturb your peace," she apologized.

"Oh, that's not a problem. There's plenty of room in here and it's good to have some company." Fin beamed at her and walked over towards her, holding his hands out to feel the warmth of the fire.

"The evenings are surprisingly chilly considering it is May, don't you think?" he asked. Katherine smiled, not really knowing how to reply and turned back towards the bookshelves.

"Are you looking for something specific?" Fin continued.

"They're arranged in alphabetical order but within date order too, so it can be a bit confusing."

Katherine wanted to respond but could only manage to bite her bottom lip. There was something about his presence that unnerved her. However, at the same time she felt a jolt of excitement at being here alone with him. "I'm looking for some local history from the 12th century," she eventually explained. Then with a dismissive wave in the direction of the books, she said, "but I'm not expecting to find what I'm looking for here. I guess I'll have to get a boat to the mainland and find a café with a wireless network so I can consult the great Google!"

Fin walked over to the left side of the fireplace and scanned the top shelves. "I'm sure I saw something along those lines around here the other day. Ah! Yes, here it is," he announced triumphantly, pulling a large volume off the shelf. "*Annals and Antiquities of Pembrokeshire Families*; written in the 19th century, chronicling as far back as...let me see...1066. I think this must be a reprint, not the original work," he said, handing her the heavy text. Katherine was taken aback with the finding.

"Do you have a background in academia, history, or something related?" she could not help but ask, as she reached out to take the book.

"My only qualification in historical tradition arises from the fact that I'm from Ireland, where everyone's business is subject to public discussion; even a hundred or so years after they've passed away," he laughed. "I've some school days' Irish history; mainly the mythological stuff from way back when, but nothing more extensive than that!" Katherine warmed to his lightly self-deprecating humour. She was done with good-looking men who took themselves too seriously. Some sparks of interest in Fin had been ignited in her imagination. She wanted to know more about him.

"How about you?' he asked. "Are you an historian?"

"I studied Humanities and Classics at university," she

explained. "But I worked in publishing until very recently," she added, her voice trailing off quietly towards the end of the sentence.

"I'm looking at a career change at this point too," Fin announced, pleased to have found some common ground with this attractive, intriguing woman.

Katherine sat on the sofa and started to flick through the entries in the book. They appeared to be in the format of notations from the Calendar of Pembrokeshire Public Records and the commentary to the 11th- and 12th-century Episcopal Acts pertaining to Pembrokeshire, in addition to extracts from the writings of prominent medieval Welsh historians, such as Gerald Cambrensis, and such works as the *Chronicles of the Kings*. She was instantly drawn into the detail, looking for names and dates which might match and validate her past-life memories. Reaching for a notepad and pencil on the desk next to the sofa, she scribbled down the following: '*1066 – Norman Conquest of England: Agreement reached between William I and Rees ap Tudor for the said Welsh king to retain sovereignty in his own kingdom. 1087 – Death of William I, succeeded to the throne by William Rufus. 1093 – Rees ap Tudor killed near Brecon by the Norman Marcher Lords who established the Marcher Lordship of Pembrokeshire. 1100 – Death of William Rufus, ascension of Henry 1 to throne of England. 1102 – The king holds Pembroke Castle under the custodianship of Gerald de Windsor. 1109 – Owen ap Cadogan abducts Nesta, wife of Gerald de Windsor.*'

Katherine was stopped in her tracks by the reference to the abduction of a woman in 1109. She double-checked the notes she had made from the hypnosis recording, but she was sure that she had spoken about a similar incident in the very same year. Intrigued, she wondered how common an occurrence of abduction was in medieval times, and thought it likely that the historical recording of such an event would only be noteworthy if it involved a member of the ruling classes. She was inspired to find out more about Angharad and her family history.

Fin had his focus fixed firmly on the present and he wanted to find out more about Katherine. "There's always the local Registry of Births, Deaths, and Marriages which may be useful if it's your own heritage that you're researching," he suggested, hoping she would volunteer some more information.

"I'm not sure if it's my own heritage," she replied. "Something came to light in a past life regression session and I'm just curious to see if it was a real occurrence or just my imagination at work. I'm not sure how I would feel if it was for real; there was talk of war and abduction!"

"Oh, how interesting!" Fin's bright, blue eyes sparkled at the revelation. "My own experience was just so vague and boring, guess I must have been a simple farmhand throughout the ages."

Katherine smiled again. She was finding Fin's company very warm and reassuring; he was easy to be around. "So what career change are you looking for?" she now felt comfortable enough to ask. "Are you heading for the bright city lights?"

Fin took a deep breath and answered, "No, I'm done with the city in this life. I've spent too many hours in the darkness of the London Underground. I'm heading for some fresh air and open spaces with lots of trees and a big sky, and not quite so many people."

Katherine could relate to those sentiments. "Yes, I guess I have the same ideal in mind, hence the time-out here," she laughed. "Although I'll probably end up back in the rat race at some point," she added dismissively.

Fin beamed as he explained that his time in corporate management was well and truly over. "No more late-night strategy meetings under the harsh strip lighting of city office blocks for me," he stated confidently. "I recently inherited some old family land over in Ireland and I'm going back to manage it."

"Oh, which part of Ireland?" asked Katherine, not really knowing the reason for the question, as she knew nothing about the country.

"On the east coast, in the Wicklow Mountains," Fin explained. "Were you ever there?" he asked.

Something in Katherine wished she could have said yes. Wistfully, she replied, "No, I've never been to Ireland."

Her words brought a wide smile to Fin's face. "You'll have to come," he said. "It's too beautiful to miss."

Katherine was struck by the link between her past history and the present; there had been talk of the sons of Angharad going off to fight in Ireland. She felt a flash of realization course along her spine, lighting up her imagination. She was keen to find out more about her past life and if there was a link to Ireland.

"Do you think they'll mind if I borrow some of these books?" she asked.

"I can't see why they would mind," replied Fin. "Although I don't think they would want them to leave the island."

"I was only thinking about taking them back to the cottage for a few days," Katherine explained. "I would like to research the local history in greater depth."

Mammy, Dearest

'As the daughter of Welsh Prince Rees ap Tudor, Nesta was the Princess of Deheubarth, South Pembrokeshire, in the 12th century. Also known as Helen of Wales and Mother of the Irish Invasion, in 1095 she was married to Gerald de Windsor, a close friend and ally of King Henry I of England. With the Manor of Carew featuring as a part of Nesta's dowry, Gerald established a Norman castle on the site of the existing Celtic fort at Carew, a limestone bluff overlooking the inlet.

However, whilst Gerald was engaged in the king's military business in Wales, his wife's beauty was said to have excited wonder and lust throughout the principality. During the 1108 Christmas feast, when the Welsh chieftains were gathered at St Davids, Owen ap Cadogan heard for the first time of her exquisite charm. He plotted to lay siege to Carew castle and steal her away from her English husband.

Making his way from the north of the county, he and his men set fire to the castle and attempted to break down the door of Nesta's bedroom. Awakened by all of the commotion, Nesta helped Gerald escape from the castle by climbing down a rope and out through the castle drain. However, she and two of her children were captured by Owen and carried out of the county, whilst the castle was left to burn. The abduction led to a war between the Welsh and the Norman Marcher lords, which resulted in the return of the Nesta to her husband, and with Owen fleeing to Ireland. When Gerald died in 1135, he left Nesta alone with their three sons, Maurice, William, David, and a daughter named Angharad.'

Katherine stopped her note taking to sip her peppermint tea. She had been feeling a little queasy and wondered if an early lunch might settle her stomach.

Sitting at the kitchen table in the cottage all morning, enthusiastically interrogating the pile of old books on the kitchen table, she was pleased to have established that a young girl called Angharad had indeed existed in the 12th century. She was enjoying the mystery that these old texts were conjuring up in her mind. She tried to imagine a time before the proliferation of the Internet when such limited information would be locally resourced and available only to privileged, educated people. This served to reaffirm in her mind the notion that knowledge is indeed a firm requisite for power. She reflected on how much of her educational research had been enriched and indeed only made possible, in some circumstance, by the extensive use of computerized information. Now she was greatly enjoying this new experience of delving into ancient books and having to read between the lines.

The clouds had now cleared, revealing a clear blue sky over the island and a shaft of spring sunlight appeared on the page open in front of her. Katherine felt a yearning to be out in the warm sunshine, but she was also very interested to learn more about the fate of Nesta and the four children following the death of their father. She was certain that the abduction she had recalled was that of the princess and she was keen to learn more about her past-life mother. She felt as if she had been presented with an intricate and magical jigsaw, her own spiritual map, where each piece she discovered could help complete a path through the forest of her past lives and perhaps unearth a deeply hidden secret. She took another sip of tea as her stomach did a little flip. *Secrets can be wonderful,* she thought, gently biting her lip as she remembered that sometimes secrets can also be very dark...

'*It was rumoured that Nesta was also mother of two of the English king's illegitimate sons, Robert of Gloucester and Meyler Fitz-Henry, who were born before her marriage to Gerald de Windsor. The Welsh beauty was also said to have conceived a child with Owen, her abductor, and to have given birth to a son she named Robert Fitz-Stephen during her subsequent marriage to Stephen, Castellan of Cardigan.*'

Katherine stopped to take a deep breath. This was some woman! Her mind was spinning at the thought of negotiating so many men and marriages. She was aware of the average medieval lifespan and how both facts and fiction were often blended to form a more entertaining historical account. The odds of surviving multiple childbirths were heavily stacked against women, so having produced eight children in the 12th century was no mean feat.

She found herself feeling strangely empowered before her thoughts turned to her own mother. Paralyzed by self-doubt and fear, her mother had limited her own aspirations and, maybe unwittingly, those of her daughter. Until she had left home for university, Katherine had little idea of the extent of her personal strengths and abilities. Although at first she had been daunted by the prospect of making her own way in the world, she had actually found it quite easy to make friends and successfully manage her own needs. Her way into the world of adulthood was a gentle awakening, and by her second year at university she had developed an attractive, if quiet, sense of self-confidence.

Her mind shifted to Angharad. She wondered about the influence of a strong mother such as Nesta on the character of her only daughter and she spent the next couple of hours searching zealously though the volumes for the smallest snippets of information about Angharad, as a Fitz-Gerald and a de Barry, in an attempt to piece together a picture of the woman and her life in the 12th century.

Her trance was broken by a gentle tapping on the window. She smiled to herself, thinking it was the robin who was becoming a regular visitor to the cottage. His presence always lifted her mood. However, as she looked up it was Fin's smiling face she saw at the kitchen window. As she stood with the intention of walking over to open the cottage door to him, Katherine felt weak and light-headed and she tried to grip the back of the wooden chair to stop herself from falling.

Fin saw from the window that she had lost her balance and hurriedly let himself into the cottage. "Katherine, what's wrong? Are you okay? Sit yourself back down for a moment." He pulled out the chair and helped her to take a seat. "Put your head between your legs for a few minutes, I'll get you a glass of water."

Picnic on the Beach

"Yes, I'm fine!" Katherine insisted with mild irritation. Fin had suggested a walk in the fresh air and perhaps a little time to unwind and take in the scenery. They had ambled towards the cove and Fin had laid out the blanket on the sand.

"I had been sitting at that table with my head in those books for hours. I just tried to stand up again too quickly, that's all. It's no big deal! And I hadn't eaten anything, just drank a few cups of peppermint tea. The fresh air and exercise has made me feel much better. Now, shall we eat?"

Fin had noted her absence from lunch at the retreat house and packed up a picnic basket to take over to her at the cottage. He had no idea whether or not she would be pleased to see him but he was willing to take the chance.

Secretly, she had felt very glad that he had turned up at that moment, a bit unnerved at the thought of what might have happened to her if she had fallen and perhaps injured herself.

The afternoon weather was fine, the beach was a little breezy and Katherine enjoyed sitting outdoors in the sunshine. Fin had brought some bread and soft cheese flavoured with garlic and herbs. She helped herself to a large, crusty baguette, spread generously with a layer of the strong cheese. He had also managed to source some red grapes, a few slices of iced carrot cake and a bottle of elderflower wine. The two ate and chatted as the afternoon passed them by. It was with ease that they came to understand one another's sense of humour and engaged in a discussion of the island and the retreat. Some of his observations made her laugh out loud and he was encouraged by her smiles.

"I'm sure that cook has it in for me," he joked. "I think she blames me for the ancient feud between the mythological Welsh and Irish kings! I'm sure never to be the first one to taste one of her breakfast pancakes!" he laughed.

As she reclined on the sands, listening and laughing, Katherine was feeling relaxed and carefree. Her mind was occupied with the sole pleasure of breathing freely. In a moment of silence, where the conversation came to a natural close, she sipped on her glass of wine and looked wistfully out to sea, wondering what the future held for her. Fin watched as the breeze blew her red curls back from her pale face and found himself entranced by her gentle smile. Sensing that she was being watched, she turned to fix her grey eyes in his direction. Just for a moment it felt as if the wind and the waves stilled and a shaft of sunlight landed on Fin's face illuminating his shining, blue eyes. She took a deep breath and smiled from the deepest part of her soul. It felt as if a dark chamber from the depths of her heart had been opened and its dank interior flooded with fresh air and light. If she had been asked to describe the feeling, her answer would have been that for the first time in her life she had experienced '*a sense of belonging*'.

A wave of nervous energy simultaneously ran through Fin's body and he rather unexpectedly jumped to his feet. "We should be getting you back to the cottage," he insisted. "The tide is on the turn and it comes in quickly. We don't want to be cut off from the path and have to scramble over the rocks!"

Fin

In the kitchen, Katherine offered Fin her thanks for the lunch and explained that she would not be at the retreat house for dinner that evening. She was feeling tired; perhaps she was coming down with a cold. However, she offered him a cup of tea before he left and Fin gratefully accepted.

They sat at the table, continuing their conversation. Fin told her that he was the younger of two sons and that his brother had emigrated from Ireland to the States. They had not met up in over seven years.

"Our parents died within one year of each other and I haven't seen Cillian since their funerals," he said with a hint of sadness in his voice. He described how he had since spent every holiday working on the family property.

"The hillside farmhouse and its outbuildings had fallen into disrepair and the fields had become so overgrown that it had been impossible to see where the farmland ended and the forest began," he laughed. "I had to organize the large-scale clearance of the property and the field before focusing on the painstaking restoration work of the house and the farm buildings. The project had been the main focus of my life for the previous seven summers and it was only a few weeks ago that I made the final break with life in England. After finally negotiating the sale of my apartment, I resigned from my position and froze my pension contributions and so now there's no looking back! I'll be heading over the Irish Sea when I leave the island."

Katherine's heart sank a little when he told her he had booked into the retreat for only three weeks.

He explained that he just needed to stick around until the sale of his flat had been completed and as the buyer had requested the opportunity to decorate the property in the interim he had to find somewhere else to stay for a few weeks. "I chose the island retreat as I'm interested in some of the traditional farming methods used here," he said eagerly and his face lit up as he explained. "And it will be useful to learn more about the types of trees which grow in this climate, as it is very similar to that of the Wicklow Mountains."

Suddenly she realized how much she liked having him around. She wanted to know more about him. Would he be going back to Ireland alone? Was there anyone in his life? "Perhaps there is a childhood sweetheart waiting for you in the homeland?" she asked.

Fin smiled self-effacingly. "There was someone, but it's been over for a while now." Katherine sensed it would not be wise to push for any further information on the topic. To even out the conversation she volunteered some information about her own life.

"I was the only child. My father died when I was very young, aged nine, and my mother never really got over it. I hardly knew him. He seemed to be away from home much of the time. He worked for the military. We lived on a naval base until he died and then we had to move and find a new home. Such long periods of time passed between his visits that on his return I never felt sure he was the same man. I can't remember any family outings or get-togethers. If I had any aunties, uncles or cousins, I never got to meet them. I guess the navy was our family. Then, when he died, it was just my mother and me. Looking back, I think she must have really suffered when he died and there just didn't seem like there was anyone else around to help. When I passed my A-level exams and got a place in university she wanted me to live at home and travel in for lectures. But I needed to make the break from home. I don't think she ever really forgave me for not staying with her. She refused to come and visit me when I lived on campus." Then it was Katherine's turn to smile, however hers was an attempt to conceal her sadness. "She passed away over three years ago so now there is only me. I didn't inherit any family estate," she confessed with a shrug.

Fin paused, trying to harness his thoughts before speaking. He did not like to see the sadness beneath her smile. He wanted to comfort her. "And now you're free?" he suggested in a soft tone. It worked. Katherine was both comforted by his gentle smile and excited by the sparkle in his eyes twinkling under inquisitive, arched eyebrows. Yes, he was right. She was free! Free from any family or relationship constraints, from any career expectations and also from anyone's disapproval. She was finally free to do exactly what she pleased, with whomever she chose. Her heart skipped a beat at the sudden, empowering realization.

1146

Despite having felt so tired earlier in the day, Katherine was unable to settle down to sleep that night. The events of the last two weeks were all competing in her mind for attention and in spite of the realization that she was indeed free, she was still thinking in ever-decreasing circles. She was still looking for answers to the questions created by her trip into the unconscious realms of her mind.

After two hours of tossing and turning, she finally switched on the bedside lamp and reached for a book. What became of Angharad and the four sons she had talked about during her hypnotherapy session? Katherine checked the date she had also mentioned under hypnosis and searched through the index for any significant entries noted in that year. She read:

'1146 – Birth of Giraldus Cambrensis, or Gerald of Wales: the son of

William de Barry and Angharad, at Manorbier Castle. He was the youngest of four brothers, three of whom took part in the Anglo-Norman conquest of Ireland. Whilst Gerald's brothers became loyal Norman knights, the young priest seems to have concentrated on his Welsh ancestry. He studied the history of the Church in Wales and saw that it was suffering under Norman rule. Known as "the Little Bishop", he studied under the guidance of his uncle, David Fitz-Gerald, Bishop of St David's, before travelling to study at St Peter's Abbey in Gloucester.

Later, he travelled to study law in Paris. He was a cleric, a distinguished scholar, and a social historical commentator who wrote many books including "A Journey through Wales" and "Conquest of Ireland", charting the expeditions of his uncles and brothers in Ireland.'

Katherine lay back against the pillows in an attempt to let the information quietly settle in her mind. So Angharad had her wish? Her fourth son did not become a soldier, but a man of the church and a writer and historian to boot! She rationalized that there were probably only two options available to the sons of the ruling classes in medieval times. Wondering how much influence Angharad had exerted on the choices of her youngest son, she read on:

'In his endeavours to be declared Bishop of St David's, Gerald visited the Pope in Rome on three occasions between 1199 and 1203; however he died aged 77, without being ordained due to resistance from the English Crown. It is believed he was buried in the grounds of his beloved cathedral at St David's.'

At least she had been spared the agony of a violent death for one of her children, Katherine mused. Now she was eager to find out what had happened to Angharad. She scoured the indices and footnotes of the historical texts until the early hours of the morning, and yet could find no further historical information on Angharad de Barry. Katherine wondered if she had followed her husband and sons to Ireland. That could be one explanation for the lack of any further mention of her in the old Welsh texts.

However, she remembered quite clearly the tone of Angharad's voice when she described her husband as a cruel man and the fact that he was often away from home. She considered the age of Angharad in 1146. If she had been born circa 1103, as Katherine recalled reading, she would have been aged 43 when she gave birth to her fourth son, Gerald. She wondered about the average lifespan of women in medieval Wales. *Perhaps she had never physically recovered from the birth and died in her bed?* Katherine switched off the bedside lamp and lay down to sleep. Drifting in and out of consciousness, with her imagination full of knights and castles, she saw an image of Darrel as a tall, proud man wielding a sword. She felt a shiver of fear as his leering face loomed large in her mind's eye. Then his face changed and she recognized the cruel features of William de Barry.

In her dream, Katherine spoke bravely, "No, William, this youngest son of ours is not going to be a soldier. You are not going to sacrifice all our children in your bloodthirsty quest for land and power." However, her tone changed when she saw the steely glint through his narrowed eyes and felt his ice cold fingers close around her throat. "Please don't hurt me," she begged.

"Silence, woman! Who are you to challenge me? We are all leaving and you will stay here, with your English-loving mother, Henry's favourite concubine. We, the de Barry family, will seek our fortune overseas. We do not need the patronage of the King of England and we have no need for you, a half-breed whore." Katherine felt the constriction around her throat and saw the whites of William's eyes. Then she saw herself, as Angharad: a pale, ghostly figure in dishevelled nightclothes, lying motionless in the bed. Katherine finally realized her past-life fate.

3

Week Three

The Castle

Katherine stood at the edge of the slipway in the early morning, fearing that this was going to be a big mistake. She had woken feeling nauseous and was about to board the boat to leave the island. Looking at the choppy waves, she prayed that the crossing would be swift and that she would be able to contain her sickness. Fin sensed her discomfort and placed an arm around her shoulder. She closed her eyes and breathed in the salty sea spray, enjoying its refreshing sensation on her clammy face.

As they stepped off the boat jetty and onto the mainland, Fin asked if she would like to stop for a cup of tea or a bite to eat before they caught the local bus to the castle. Katherine gratefully accepted the offer. The colour had drained from her cheeks and she felt weak and shaky on her feet. Still feeling somewhat repelled by the smell of strong coffee, she sipped on a weak cup of Earl Grey whilst Fin picked out an information leaflet and studied the map. "It's only a short walk to the castle from the village bus stop," he informed her. "There's a café and gift shop in the castle grounds and, from this photograph, the beach below is only a short walk. There's also a medieval church in the vicinity," he explained. Katherine's heart sunk a little. She had been hoping that the castle would not be full of tourists. However, on arrival she was not disappointed. She was struck by a familiarity with this place that she had never previously visited. Despite the Norman castle now lying partly in ruins, she was swept up in its enchantment as they walked over the wooden bridge across the moat and into the inner bailey. They walked across the courtyard, through the walled gardens and climbed the steep stone steps to enter into the Great Hall. It was here that Katherine felt a surge of energy which made her feel light-headed and giddy on her feet. As she held onto the moss-stained, curved stone wall surrounding the open fireplace, she closed her eyes and heard the roar of the wind in the great chimney. She could smell its fresh wood smoke and sensed the bustle of people moving around her in the vaulted room. However, the place was empty except for her and Fin.

"I've been here before," she informed her friend with such conviction that he did not doubt her. "It was a happy time," she added. "I have a feeling there were many celebrations in this hall, in the early days, when it was safe."

Looking around, Katherine imagined the room filled with heavy oak furniture and woollen tapestries adorning the walls. She visualized a long, wooden table covered with a coarsely woven cloth and earthenware crockery. She could hear the hum of muffled voices and the distant sound of a low-key string instrument. Venturing over to one of the window seats, she smiled in excitement at the view over the bracken, marshland, and the beach beyond.

"Of course, a forest and a vineyard were here at that time," she explained. "Can we get upstairs from here?" she asked Fin. "From there, we will have an even better view of the deer park."

The two were pleased to find a spiral staircase leading to the chamber directly above the Great Hall. Once in the room, Katherine walked about as if she was retracing her steps. Stopping, she explained to Fin that she had found the location of the bed she had lain in during her past life regression session, and the birthplace of Angharad's fourth son, Gerald. As she spoke, she could feel shivers of realization. She suddenly felt very cold and fell silent. Fin noticed the change in her demeanour; she had become very pale and listless, with a sad expression on her face. He commented on the drop in temperature and suggested they go outside where the afternoon sun was shining.

"Shall we explore the ramparts?" he asked.

"Yes, let's get to the top of this place," she agreed with renewed vigour. Together they climbed the castle battlements and looked over the parapet and out to sea. Katherine quickly spotted a curious round building just below the castle on the slope leading down to the beach.

"What's that?" she asked, and then answered herself out loud. "Oh yes! That's the dovecote, beside the pond in the meadow. I seem to remember picking blackberries from the bramble hedge around there."

Fin could see only a heap of grey stones lying in a circular arrangement in an otherwise empty field.

"Is this the Irish Sea?" she asked, gesturing towards the shoreline lying to the west of the castle. Fin replied that it was the Severn, the channel of sea between the south coast and France. To look across the Irish Sea, they would have to travel to the north or south west of the county.

"I wonder how long it would have taken to sail to Ireland in the 12th century," she pondered aloud.

"Well, from the dock at Pembroke, here in the south, it takes some three or four hours by car ferry these days," Fin explained, "and if the high-speed catamaran from the port of Fishguard in the north is in service, it makes the crossing in about half that time. Then it takes an hour or so to drive into the Wicklow Hills."

Katherine wondered in which part of Ireland Angharad's family had settled, following the Cambro-Norman invasions. She resolved to do some further research when she was back on the island.

During a gentle stroll around the walled garden, the bright marigolds caught her eye and she asked Fin if they could just sit for a while amongst the shrubbery, soaking up the afternoon sun. She liked that they could sit in silence together for a while, without any feelings of discomfort. Fin headed over to the gift shop, returning with a glossy, illustrated history of the castle, remarking that the past owners of the castle had included Irish families from County Meath. With the warm, spring sunshine on her face, Katherine closed her eyes and allowed her thoughts to wander. She wanted to know more about the way of life in the castle in the 1100s. In the Great Hall, and here in the garden, she felt a great sense of security and comfort. However, in the solar chamber above the hall she had felt very cold and lonely. She wondered especially if her feelings were linked in any way to the life of Angharad centuries ago. Perhaps the only way to find out any more about Angharad and her life here in the castle would be through another past life regression session. Her flow of thoughts was interrupted when Fin gently pointed out that they needed to catch the next bus to ensure they were back at the harbour in time for the last boat back to the island.

As they headed for the gatehouse, Katherine felt another wave of sickness wash over her. This time it pooled low in her abdomen and refused to shift. She felt as if her life force was draining away and as the darkening sky closed in around her, she collapsed onto the stone steps.

The Book of Leinster

When she regained consciousness, Katherine was being attended to by Fin and the assistant from the shop. As she opened her eyes, she saw Fin's shocked expression relaxing into caring concern and she sat up on the steps, insisting that she was fine.

"I just don't know what happened," she said. "One minute we were crossing into the gatehouse and then everything went dark."

The shop assistant asked if she would like a glass of water and offered her a seat in the café. "We're due to close to the public shortly," she explained, "but if you need to sit down for a while…should I call a doctor?"

Katherine politely shook her head.

"Do you want to arrange a medical appointment?" a concerned Fin asked Katherine when they were alone in the castle café. "It's the second time you've fainted in as many days."

Katherine frowned.

"I'm sure it's nothing," she said dismissively.

"Is this a common occurrence for you?" Fin enquired.

She bit her lip before replying, "No, it's never happened to me before."

The two sat in silence.

"I feel fine!" she insisted after a few minutes. "If it happens again, I'll go to see a doctor. But I'm sure there's nothing wrong; I just have seasickness or something of the sort."

Fin consulted the local bus timetable and concluded that if they wanted to make the last boat crossing to the island, they would have to get a taxi. He asked the shop assistant, who had turned the sign on the café door to 'closed' and had started to cash up the day's takings in the till, if she had the contact details for a cab. Shaking her head, the young woman explained that such services were rare this far off the beaten track, but if they were not going far she could offer them a lift as she would be leaving soon. When Fin explained where he and Katherine were staying, she checked her watch and explained that they were unlikely to catch the last commercial boat to the island which sailed earlier on Sundays. She stated that unless they had access to a private boat they would be well-advised to seek alternative accommodation on the mainland, for the night. Fin was about to ask her advice about the nearest B & B when she picked up the telephone and he heard her ask someone if any rooms were available for the night. Replacing the handset, the young woman advised him that the pub where she sometimes worked in the evenings had a room spare, and that Fin and Katherine were welcome to get a lift with her, should they wish to stay there.

"The Mill on the Pond is a nice place," she explained. "It was once the castle watermill; the food is good and it has a great view over the tidal estuary."

Fin ordered a steak and a pint of Felinfoel ale. Katherine opted for the fresh local salmon in a hollandaise sauce. The two felt as if they were on a forbidden venture.

"So, Katherine Walsh, where do you see yourself in six months' time?" Fin teased.

She was comfortable in the cosy restaurant, sipping on a glass of sparkling white wine and feeling able to freely speak her mind. "I'm hoping to find a position in academia somewhere. I still have contacts at my old university, but I'm open to the idea of trying elsewhere. I'm just open to any ideas at the moment," she explained enthusiastically, "and I'm not really in any hurry to make decisions right now!" Fin listened attentively, offering only encouraging nods and smiles.

"At the moment, I'm more intrigued with the past," she continued. "Do you believe in reincarnation?"

He looked up from his plate and straight into Katherine's eyes. "Who really knows? Lots of ancient cultures and religions were based on the notion; take Buddhism, for example. The Buddhists' beliefs have remained largely unchanged for centuries and are only now gaining popularity here in the Western world."

"How about Irish culture and beliefs?" asked Katherine.

"Have you heard about the legend of Fintan Bochra?" Katherine shook her head and Fin smiled before launching himself enthusiastically into his explanation.

"Fintan Bochra was married to Cesair, one of the many grand-daughters of the biblical figure, Noah. You've heard of him, right?" Now it was Katherine's turn to grin. Fin's demeanour changed when he was in the middle of a tale. He became far more animated and entertaining, his hand gestures competing with his words for her attention. He continued, "Fintan was the only person believed to have survived the great flood. Legend has it that he turned himself into a salmon. He rode the waves for 40 days before turning into an eagle and then a hawk before finally returning to human form many generations later as Fintan the Wise, a teller of lore and advisor to the many invaders of Ireland. It's all in the *Book of Leinster*, an ancient Irish text dating back to the 12th century, which I believe is currently kept at Trinity University. There are a number of ancient texts, such as the *Book of Glendalough* and of course the famous *Book of Kells*. However, it is also written that he survived by taking refuge in a cave at Tul Tinde in Tipperary overlooking the River Shannon."

Katherine looked apologetically at the salmon on her plate and Fin laughed out loud.

"I suppose the point is that the idea of reincarnation has played a part in human civilizations throughout recorded history. It seems an integral part of our collective psyche."

At that point, a waitress arrived asking for a dessert order. Katherine said that she could not eat anything else and Fin ordered two Irish coffees for them to drink in the pub lounge. Despite her doubt, she enjoyed the taste of the sweet, creamy drink and thanked Fin for introducing her to something new. When he excused himself to visit the bathroom, she walked up to the large bay window in the room and took in the view. Following the flow of the river upstream she could see the outline of the ruins of the large Norman castle around which they had wandered earlier that day, now eerily lit from behind by the setting sun. In a flash, Katherine was transported back to the night as Angharad when, as a child of six years of age, she had searched the riverbank for her missing mother. She could hear the fast rush of the water at her feet and as she turned to look back at the castle, the deep red rays of the disappearing sun became the burning embers of the fire, glowing through the apertures in the silhouette of the building. Then she became aware of Fin standing at her side.

Placing his arm around her shoulder, he asked, "Are you ready for bed?"

The room was clean and comfortable, with a double bed positioned to take in the view of the millwheel over the river. On the left-hand wall there was a cast-iron fireplace filled with dried flowers, with a soft armchair and a small side table standing alongside, facing the door to the bathroom. Katherine rooted around in the wardrobe and took out some spare blankets, handing them to Fin. He looked around the room and reluctantly placed them on the chair.

"I'll take the chair?" he said, in the hope he was mistaken about her intention to sleep alone in the bed. She passed a pillow from the bed to him. Then feeling a little guilty at taking the whole of the bed to herself, she lifted the throw from the bottom of the bed, wrapped it around herself and sat up against the padded headboard of the bed.

"Sleep well," she said quietly, switching off the bedside lamp. The room fell into darkness and Katherine could soon hear the sound of Fin's slow, deep breathing. Her mind was far too busy for sleep. She reflected on the fact that it was just three weeks since she had issued divorce proceedings against her husband and here she was alone with a virtual stranger in a rented room. However, this was her reality; it was the life and loves of the last seven years that now seemed to her to be a work of fiction. She felt safe in his company and yet there was also an edge of excitement when they were alone together. Conversation with Fin always flowed easily and Katherine often found herself enchanted with his vision. He had a way of drawing her out of her own corner of the world and enveloping her in his world. She reminded herself firmly of the dangers of allowing herself to be swallowed up into someone else's existence once again.

She was feeling grateful that Fin had not objected to sleeping on the chair this evening. Although, as she watched his motionless shadow, she could not deny the part of her that wished that he had. She revisited parts of their conversation, searching for clues that would indicate that he wanted more than a casual liaison with her. She believed he found her attractive, but unless he actually said or did something to confirm this she was not willing to make any moves towards becoming more intimate with him. She was all too aware of her own strong physical attraction to him and with every warm smile and self-deprecating laugh she could feel herself drawing closer to him. However, their mutual touch, excepting polite offers of steadying hands, remained frustratingly elusive.

Her thoughts looped repeatedly in this way, until in the early hours when she fell into a restless sleep, wracked with vivid, disturbing dreams. She witnessed a dismembered body burning atop a funeral pyre and through the flames she saw the fierce faces of human-like creatures, glaring out from beneath skull-adorned headdresses. Waking at dawn, she saw two dark-rimmed eyes looking back at her from the bathroom mirror and gently rubbed them in the hope the dark rims would fade before Fin awoke.

Sunrise Over the Estuary

Quietly, Katherine lifted the latch on the bedroom door and let herself out into the hallway hoping she would be able to get out of the pub without having to disturb anyone. She was in luck. The cleaner was just starting her early morning shift.

"Don't worry," Katherine assured the old lady as she unlocked the front door to let her out. "I'm not leaving without paying! I'll be back in time for breakfast. I just need to get some fresh air."

The old lady nodded and told her that she would leave the door unlocked for her return. "There's no one else likely to be around at this time of the day," she explained, somewhat grumpily. Outside, Katherine breathed in the cool, misty air of the morning and tried to work out which direction was east. She was hoping to watch the sunrise. Figuring that her best bet was to cross the bridge and walk along the riverbank towards the castle, she started to walk on but then she hesitated. Then she reasoned that spirits and memories could only hurt you if you allowed them to. Whatever had previously come to pass on this path was now only a faded imprint of energy. It would only become emboldened if she gave it her attention. Hers was the strongest energy at this point in time and all she needed was to be brave. She would simply walk and breathe. As she moved away from the mill and towards the castle, Katherine's resolve strengthened with every step; each inhaled breath helped to refresh her mind and every exhaled breath cleared and calmed her thoughts. Picking up her pace, she could feel the blood pumping around her body, warming her hands and feet and recharging her sense of enthusiasm for the challenge ahead. As she crossed the bridge, the temperature around her seemed to drop and she had to walk faster to keep warm. Looking back, she could see the mist lifting from the surface of the still water and she hoped she would now be able to watch the sunrise. As she continued, she started to feel her energy draining from her. She realized that she was fast approaching the spot where she had stood in the dark as an abandoned child, some 800 years ago. Her heart started to race and her body slowly became numb. However, she was determined not to disappear into the black hole of fear that was beckoning her soul. She would stand her ground, just as she had done in a previous lifetime. She knew that all she had to do was to stop and acknowledge the memory. In doing so, she would disempower it. Through closed eyes, she saw herself once more standing lost and scared. She allowed the fear to ricochet through her body, searching for a place to hide. This time there were no dark places for it to fester. Katherine reminded herself that she had survived this incident, and that her 12th-century mother had eventually returned home to be with her at the castle. In her mind's eye, Katherine saw the soulful, mahogany eyes of a passionate woman set in symmetry on a porcelain face. Framed by a mass of raven curls, the familiar face of her mother caused a sense of comforting warmth to wash over her. She closed her eyes and felt the smooth satin of her mother's aqua dress as she was enveloped in her loving arms. Smiling, she opened her eyes to witness the rise of the morning mist revealing the rose-gold sunrise over the still water. She had faced her fear and her faith had been restored. She was ready to return to the island.

Bardo Thodol

"Can you tell me what you are saying?" asked Peter, the regression therapist. "I can hear you but I can't understand what you are saying." Katherine appeared to be chanting words in a language he did not recognize. Failing to respond to his request, she continued with her quietly respectful repetition of the foreign words. Peter knew that she was completely absorbed in the memory she was revisiting. He allowed her to continue for a little while longer. When the chanting ceased of its own accord, Peter quickly intervened, asking, "What is happening around you?"

"It is over," Katherine replied. "She is gone and now we can celebrate."

"Who is gone?" asked Peter. "And why would you celebrate her leaving?"

"It is the 49th day," Katherine explained. "The lama has prepared her conscious spirit and the monks have completed the purification rites so now we have to let her go. There is a bonfire burning and we are all to join together to dance around in a circle and sing until dawn. Now we are free to cry and wail our great sadness at her passing." Tears trickled from beneath the lashes of her closed eyes.

"Who has died?" Peter asked gently.

"My beautiful mother, Nima," she replied.

"And what is your name?" asked Peter.

"I am Pema," she answered quietly through her tears.

"Can you tell me more about your mother? What happened to her, Pema?" Peter asked politely.

Katherine proceeded to describe the events of the past seven weeks of her life. "I returned to the old village in the mountains when my mother died. It was important for me to be with her at this time. I wanted to assist whilst the lama guided my mother's spirit."

Peter asked her what she had been doing to help and Katherine explained how she continued to fill a bowl of food twice daily for her mother, whose body lay in the house. She described how the body was placed on the right side and covered to the crown of the head. She emphasized the importance of placing barley and butter on her mother's head and of creating a shrine of deities to assist with the deceased's journey towards rebirth. As she spoke, she breathed in deeply and then described the strong scent of burning incense.

Peter wondered where he was going to lead Katherine with this memory. He knew she was hoping to have returned to her 12th-century Welsh existence and had been very surprised to hear her voice a different name. He felt intrigued and was eager to proceed with this new memory. There was undoubtedly a reason for its timely surfacing. He noted that once again, albeit in a different lifetime, Katherine was experiencing the loss of her mother. However, Peter's imagination was fired up at the details of the ancient Tibetan traditions that Katherine was describing. He wanted to establish their authenticity.

"So you believe your mother's spirit will be reborn?" he asked cautiously.

"Yes," Katherine replied, "with our assistance she was guided through the six stages of the shadow realm until she reached the state of luminous mind. Then the nature of her rebirth was determined. Now the 49 days have passed, and we know she has been transformed, we will pass into mourning. Tears for loved ones can flood the path of the dead. Our moans are like the sound of thunder to them, and our cries cause them pain and confusion."

"How will you know that she has been reborn?" he asked, pushing a little further.

"We will now visualize our loved one smiling as she turns and walks away from us, and we will ask Buddha to fill our broken hearts with pure love and light once more," she responded.

Peter thought that it would be good to bring Katherine to the end of this incarnation on such a positive aspect of her memory. As she paused, he interjected, "And as you see her walking away enveloped in light and love, so you too can move forwards to the last days of this life and find yourself facing your own death, bathed in the same golden glow."

Peter watched as Katherine appeared to enter into a deeper state of consciousness. Her breathing slowed and she relaxed into the reclining chair; he noted the serenity of her expression. He continued to sit and watch, waiting for an indication that she was ready to speak again. However, when her face became expressionless and her breathing so shallow that he feared that her soul had become disembodied, he knew he had to make contact with her and somehow bring her back into her body.

"Can you hear me?" he asked gently.

"Yes, I can hear you," she replied and Peter let out a breath of relief.

"Where are you?" he continued.

"I am at home, looking out through the trees," Katherine responded with a smile, although her eyes were firmly closed.

"Who are you with?" was Peter's next question.

"I am here with my children." Once again tears trickled from her eyes. "They have brought me to the bamboo tree house, where we have spent many precious hours together. I love this place. Over the years I have come here to play with the children and when they grew up I sometimes came here to be alone, to have some peace and to think. There is nowhere else I want to be."

Peter asked her to further describe what she could see around her.

"I am sitting in my old wooden chair, with cushions and a warm blanket. The girls are fussing over me, but I'm fine. It is June so there's a warm sun and a cool breeze. I can see the sky, my beloved mountains and the lake in which the kids used to spend many hours splashing around. We are waiting for the midsummer sunset which we can see at this time of year through the break in the mountain ridge in the distance. It is the deepest crimson red. I am happy to rest here forever. I have so many happy memories and have shared so much love. My daughters are both grown women and our eldest has a family of her own. I am a grandmother to four fine, young men. I can breathe easily here, amongst the Scots pine and larch trees. I have asked them to bury me here on the family land, in the hills amongst the foxgloves and the purple moor grass overlooking the lake." Katherine spoke with both great pride and tenderness in her voice. "We have had so many happy years living here, building our home and raising our family; although it's been harder these last seven years, coping with the farm and the business on my own. Now it is the turn of our son and daughters and grandsons to carry on with the farm and the woodlands. We did the right thing, learning the traditional skills and teaching them to our children at a time when the economy went into freefall. When the international monetary system finally broke down and Ireland went back to the use of the old punt, we had much more to barter with in the local community."

Peter knew this was not the end of the life that Katherine had previously depicted. He was sure that she was experiencing another existence. There was no mention of Tibetan traditions or the spiritual beliefs she had so eloquently described just a matter of minutes ago. He had suggested to her that she move to the end of her life, and now it was clear that this was a recall of the end of a third previous existence. Peter wanted to know more. He asked her, "What are the names of your children, those who are with you at this time?"

Katherine smiled through closed eyes as she introduced her family to him. "Niamh and Tomas, the twins, are here with Aislinn, my eldest daughter, who has been at my side for a long time. They are sad because they know our time together is short. My son, Tomas, is choked with grief but I am happy as we have shared many precious years together. It is time for me to go."

Peter had two more questions to ask. "Tell me your name," he gently implored her.

"It's Katherine; Katherine Walsh," she replied.

"And what is the date?" he asked. He was stunned into silence by her reply,

"It's my 79th birthday; Midsummer, June 21st, the year 2061."

Peter started to shake. Katherine had just described the final scene of her current life. In his many years of experience as a past life regression therapist, no client of his had ever seen into his or her own future. He was wishing that he had misheard the date. However, the realization was ringing out rudely in his own conscience. He could not just ignore it. He was fighting the greatest of temptations to find out more about the future. His imagination was running wild in the fields of possibility as to his own future existence in 49 years' time.

As Katherine had described her life on earth, it had reassured him that all of the doom-mongering about the demise of the world amidst global warming and warring nations was a misguided fallacy. He had a millennium's worth of questions for her about life in the middle of the 21st century. However, he was also compelled to remain true to his professional ethics. This was not about his curiosity; he first and foremost needed to consider his client's wellbeing. Thinking more clearly, he decided that when she was fully conscious, he would check to see how much of the vision had permeated her waking consciousness and he would destroy the recording. Feeling less panicked, Peter breathed deeply and counted her back to full consciousness. On opening her eyes, Katherine felt herself without words to describe the all-pervasive sense of peace and deep level of calm she was experiencing. She continued to just smile serenely at Peter, despite his repeated questions asking how she was feeling.

State of Grace

Katherine glowed. Her hands tingled and there was a sparkle in her eye. She was energized and yet feeling comfortably relaxed at the same time. She could now think of her past life loves and losses with sadness, yet she was happily in harmony with the present day. Almost halfway through her retreat, she was feeling far more positive about her future. She believed the regression therapy had helped her resolve some unconscious issues which must have been blocking her view. She was confident that she could reconcile whatever the future was to release onto her path and still focus on the wide open space, signposted, *'freedom'* which lay ahead. It was as if clearing out the clutter of negative experiences and emotions from her past had released the energy she had been lacking to propel herself forwards in her life.

It was with this newly found sense of confidence that Katherine started to think of the practicalities of her future. In just over three weeks' time she would be leaving the island and the lighthouse keeper's cottage that she called home. It was here that she had realized and learned to respect her real values. The insight had served to strengthen her sense of self, who she was at the core, and what she wanted to do with the rest of her life. She had decided to pursue a path back into academia, or at least some form of teaching, where she would hopefully be able to share her time and thoughts with more like-minded people. And there was Fin...

With the realization that his stay on the island was drawing to an end, she felt a flourish of excitement and decided that she would have to say or do something before they ran out of time. She ventured to the retreat house to track him down. Gently tapping on the door of his room, her constant rehearsing of what she wanted to say left her with a tension headache and a dry mouth. She need not have worried however, Fin was his usual warm and welcoming self and she felt relaxed within minutes of entering the room. He was clearly in the process of packing up to move on. He motioned for her to sit down and she found a space to sit on the bed.

"I didn't bring many things," Fin explained, "but I have acquired a few extra things over the weeks." Katherine noticed a book on the foliage native to the island. She picked it up and flicked though the pages.

"I read that some of the trees weren't native to the island and I want to learn more about the nature and history of the more hardy of the species," he explained. "The climate in Wicklow is similar to here and I'm hoping to add a greater variety of trees to the area."

Katherine was interested to know more about his plans. "So when you leave here, will you be going to Ireland?" she asked.

"That's the plan," Fin replied. "I have arranged for some things to be shipped over, although I got rid of a lot of unwanted stuff before I came to the island."

"Yes, me too!" Katherine joked, as an image of Darrel flashed into her mind and momentarily she wondered how he had responded to the divorce petition. She doubted if the solicitor would have any news for her yet and filed the application in the back of her mind as items to deal with on leaving the island. Her phone could remain switched off for a little while longer.

"You're looking much better," Fin commented. "Have you recovered from whatever it was that was causing you to pass out?"

"I guess so," replied Katherine. "I'm feeling fine, thank you. And thank you for your help at the castle the other day, and the pub. It was all very chivalrous of you!" she said with a smile.

Fin laughed, "Well, I don't want you to get the wrong impression of me."

"No, not all," she replied hastily.

"I'm not always that well-behaved," he laughed. "But I wouldn't take advantage of a sick girl!"

It was Katherine's turn to laugh, albeit nervously. She was wondering where the conversation was headed. Fin had a sparkle in his eye as he explained that the next day and night were to be his last on the island. "How would you like to spend the day?" Katherine asked tentatively. "We could meet for lunch, maybe?" she ventured.

Fin grinned. "I would like that. Perhaps we could take a picnic to the lighthouse?" he suggested. Katherine was pleased. She did not really want to lunch with the other members of the group tomorrow. There would be plenty more opportunities to mix over the next few weeks if Fin was no longer around. She wanted to make the most of the remainder of her time with him.

The Lighthouse

Katherine woke with a flutter in her stomach. Her first thought was to clean the cottage. Fin would be coming over at lunchtime with a picnic for them to take up to the headland. After a manic hour of dusting, sweeping and general tidying, she turned her attention to her own appearance. The dark circles under her eyes were less noticeable and she had a bit more colour in her cheeks which she reasoned was probably down to the excitement she was feeling. Her hair colour had faded now to a softer shade of red and hung in loose curls around her shoulders. She played around with it, twisting and holding it high on her head whilst checking out her profile in the mirror. She wanted to lie in the bath and pamper her skin with oils, however she was running out of time and so she took a shower. Gently moisturizing herself with her favourite lavender and ylang ylang lotion, Katherine noticed that her breasts were a little tender to the touch. Feeling a little perturbed, she quickly turned her attention to her wardrobe and rifled through her drawer for a matching set of underwear, selecting a fresh, white bra-and-brief set edged with grey, silky piping. Ensuring her arms and legs were fragrantly moist, she pulled on a pale-blue camisole and a pair of jeans. As she was securing the zip, she heard a tap at the door. She came out of the bedroom to see Fin turning to close the door behind himself and her heart rate rapidly accelerated.

"Great day!" he exclaimed, placing the picnic basket on the kitchen table.

"What's the weather doing?" Katherine asked, reaching for a white cotton sweater.

"You won't need that," Fin assured her, "it's warm and sunny."

She hesitated and then replaced the item on the kitchen chair. Looking longingly at her strappy high-heeled sandals, she knew they would be totally impractical for the walk across the headland and so slipped her feet into a pair of pretty denim blue pumps. "Okay, I'm ready. Do we need anything else for the picnic?" she asked, looking at the basket on the table.

Fin opened the lid to reveal some fresh bread, smoked salmon, soft cheese, rocket leaves and cherry tomatoes. Katherine also noticed two bottles of sparkling wine and a box of Swiss chocolates. Feeling pleased, she picked up a woollen blanket from a chair and they headed out for the short walk around the headland to the site of the lighthouse. As a recommended viewing spot, the lighthouse had a couple of picnic benches and a pay-per-view public telescope. Katherine hoped it would not be busy with too many tourists passing by. As they approached the lighthouse she could see that one of the benches was taken up by a family and suggested to Fin that they head to the sheltered patch of grass on the furthest side of the disused building. Here they found some discarded scaffolding and workmen's tools.

"It looks as if the outside surface of the building has recently been treated with some weatherproofing material," commented Fin.

"Have they forgotten their tools?" wondered Katherine. "Or perhaps they haven't finished the job?"

Fin scanned the newly coated surface of the tall building. "It looks like a good job to me," he said, rubbing his hand gently across the freshly treated exterior. Katherine was struck by the range of Fin's skills. He spoke of a background in corporate management and yet it seemed he was also able to raise a practical hand when necessary.

They shook traces of sand from the red and brown checked blanket and laid it out on the ground. It still felt a little damp from the wet sand on the beach but they knew that it would dry out in the afternoon sun. To Katherine's surprise, the conversation did not flow as easily as usual and she found herself biting her bottom lip during awkward moments of silence. To remedy the tension, she poured them both a large glass of sparkling wine and sipped to soften the silence. In-between bites of his bread, Fin offered comments and Katherine responded with as much enthusiasm as she could muster. However, she became increasingly frustrated as it became obvious that the afternoon was not going the way she had hoped. The chat was a contrived mix of polite manners and awkward silence. Katherine started to wonder if she had read the situation wrongly, and poured herself another glass of wine. Finally mustering up the courage, she asked him if he was feeling all right. "It's just that you don't seem your usual, upbeat self," she commented.

"I'm sorry," he said, "I suppose I don't relish the thought of leaving here..." As he spoke, the sunlight had dimmed and they both looked up to the skyline to see rainclouds approaching the island.

"It will be fine," she replied, not really knowing what else to say. *What did he mean?*

The uncomfortable silence resumed. There was so much that she wanted to say. She felt that they had grown closer over the last couple of days, but he was leaving very shortly and she had no idea of how he was feeling or what he was thinking about her.

The truth was that Fin had first noticed her on the quay in the rain, and from the moment the boat had landed he had sought out her company on the island. He had not been expecting to find someone so intriguing, so attractive, at the retreat. Following a succession of failed relationships, and a planned relocation to Ireland, the last thing on his mind was to embark on a romantic interlude; or so he had thought. Now he felt torn. The notion of returning to the family farmstead had felt complete for him, until he met Katherine. Now he felt that something was missing from the picture. She invoked a passion within him. When they were together he felt so excited, energized, so alive. Yet they hardly knew each other and he had no idea how she felt about him. Should he risk rejection and humiliation by telling her how he felt?

As the sun disappeared behind the dark clouds and raindrops ran from the edge into the centre of her empty plate, Katherine suggested they should pack up and head back down to the cottage.

Fin looked up the sky around, trying to assess whether the clouds were likely to pass over, when they both heard a distant rumble of thunder over the sound. "I think we are about to get soaked, unless we can find some shelter close by," he said with a disappointed expression on his face.

She bundled up the contents of the basket whilst he walked around the lighthouse. Then she heard him call her name.

"Katherine! There's an open door. Bring the basket around here; we can take shelter in the lighthouse."

"I didn't think the building itself was open to the public," she replied, peering inside the open door of the building.

"It's not meant to be," Fin explained. "They must be restoring the interior too. There are pots of paint and brushes in here too."

"So you think they'll be coming back?" she asked.

He shook his head. "I guess they listened to the weather forecast and didn't expect any tourists to be around today!"

A curious Katherine followed him in through the open door. Stepping into the circular space which spiralled high overhead, she felt a little dizzy. "Wow!" She opened her eyes wide, trying to trace the trail of the wrought-iron steps leading up to the lantern. "Shall we climb up?" she asked, excitedly.

Fin was looking around, admiring the ornate mosaic tiled floors and bead-board panelling adorning the walls. "They're doing a great job of restoring the original features," he commented.

However, she was already halfway up the staircase. Fin followed her up to the gallery, a platform wrapped around the lighthouse, which afforded them a 360 degree view over the island and into the sound beyond. They watched in awe at the approaching storm, sweeping in over the sea and heading towards the harbour. They witnessed the waves turning anthracite grey, reflecting the heavy clouds; the wild wash merging with the heavy downpour from the sky. Above the gallery stood the lantern room, a metal and glass structure sitting at the top of the whitewashed masonry tower. Fin pointed to the astragals, the diagonal glass storm panes, and explained to Katherine how the keeper would have used the handrails for safety when he climbed out of the tower to clean and polish the glass.

"Until the late 1700s the light would have been an uncovered flame," he explained, "exposed to the elements, until the invention and production of glass. Then the first lamp, the Fresnel lens, was created by a French physicist and fuelled by sperm whale oil." Katherine frowned in disbelief and dug him in the ribs with her elbow.

"It's true!" he asserted. "When that resource became scarce and too expensive, the Europeans turned to colza oil. Guess where that came from?" he teased. She shook her head with a wry smile.

"Wild cabbage," Fin announced. "These guys were the way ahead of the times with their use of biofuels. Then, of course, there was kerosene and eventually electricity."

"Talking of electricity," Katherine said, "just take a look at the lightning!"

He looked over the sea. "It looks as if the wind has changed direction," he announced. "I think the storm is heading this way." She gripped his arm, fearful that the lighthouse, the highest building on the island, might be struck by lightning. As a peal of thunder crashed overhead, she jumped and turned to bury her head in his chest. Fin took great delight in wrapping her tightly in his arms. She felt paradoxically scared and safe at the same time; his chest felt warm to her face and his embrace was comfortably firm.

"Don't worry," he assured her in soft tones, "the dome is metal but it's fitted with a lightning rod which channels the power of the strike away from the building."

As the whole of the gallery became illuminated with electric blue, Katherine shrieked and wrapped her arms tightly around his body. She felt a slight shock of excitement and heard the word *trust* echoing through her mind. Fin felt her softness and warmth and reassured her, "It will pass over in a few minutes." He was enjoying her scented heat and let his arms drop gently to the base of her back. She looked up at him and he leaned in to kiss her mouth. A shot of desire passed through her and she closed her eyes as her moist lips met his. Fin's tongue gently traced the outline of her lips before entering her mouth and with a surge of passion her tongue joined his in a gentle exchange.

The pure intensity shocked Fin; it had been a long time since he had kissed anyone. Katherine felt the firmness in his trousers and he pulled away self-consciously. She reached her arms over his shoulders to pull him back towards her and in response his hands dropped down to grasp her denim-clad rear. Lost in exhilaration, she felt as if she would never need to come up for air. As the kisses and the clutches became more urgent, Fin pulled her away from the storm panes of the gallery by her shoulders and the two dropped on their knees to the floor. He reached out to cup her breast and she yelped in unexpected discomfort. He pulled away and she interrupted the kiss to say, "No, don't stop," pulling him back towards her.

"Not here," he said and stood up to lead her out of the gallery.

Holding her hand gently, he led her down the spiral stairs and leaned himself up against the whitewashed wall of the tower. Katherine ran her hands over the shirt covering his chest and slid her fingers in-between the buttons. As her fingertip brushed a nipple, Fin felt a jolt in his loins and leaned forward to kiss her once more. His hands searched urgently all over her body and their mouths were locked once more in a passionate kiss. They were interrupted by the sound of voices trailing through the open tower door. It was the workmen, returning from their break. She shook with excitement, feeling like a teenager about to be discovered in an intimate embrace with her first boyfriend.

"We have to go," said Fin, and they headed towards the door.

"Just sheltering from the rain, mate," he said apologetically, holding his palms up towards the sky. "Looks like its passing over now, so we'll head off." The workman smiled knowingly, having noticed the couple's flushed cheeks.

"What about the picnic basket?" asked Katherine when they were out of earshot of the workmen; food was the last thing on Fin's mind.

Blue

The couple headed urgently over the headland and down to the cottage. Once inside the kitchen door, Fin lifted Katherine's damp top and kissed her breasts. She felt a warm, moist sensation spreading between her legs and her breathing became laboured.

Once again his tongue was in her mouth, searching more firmly now and she reached out her hand to massage the bulge in his jeans. He broke away to unbutton his shirt, throwing it on the floor before unzipping his jeans. Taking Fin's hand, Katherine turned to guide him into the bedroom. Inside, she removed her soft cotton bra as he unbuttoned the stud fastener on her jeans.

"Do you have anything?" she whispered. Fin's hand stopped instantly.

"Dammit!" he cursed, red-faced and agitated.

"No worries," said Katherine, "I do," as she pointed him in the direction of the bathroom.

"It can wait," said Fin, smiling as he lay Katherine back on the bed and removed her jeans. Lying beside her in just a pair of white shorts, he worked his way down from her excited nipples to the moist cleft between her legs with his insistent tongue. Katherine caught her breath as its warm tip teased her, its lightest touch sending the strongest of sensations of pleasure to her core. All thoughts melted from her mind and she started to feel in shades of blue. Midnight blue was the first hue generated from deep within her. She felt its power and intensity spread out from her abdomen. Her heart started to race and she fidgeted in anticipation of the sparks of electric blue that were about to explode in her body. She came in showers of silver sparkles, like fireworks piercing a midnight sky.

Fin rose from the foot of the bed and went into the bathroom. She watched, unmoving, wanting to retain the feeling in her body for as long as she could. However, the colour changed once Fin was above her, hungrily kissing her neck and pressing himself passionately inside her. Katherine became enveloped in an amethyst haze. She was confused. This was not one of her colours. Then she realized that it was the hue of *his* energy she was sensing, and she trembled with the thrill. There were no words until he shuddered to a halt, rolled over beside her and whispered, "I can't stay the night. I have to catch the early morning boat."

"I know," she whispered in return.

Fin slept until dawn, when she roused him gently, rubbing his bare chest.

"You have a boat to catch," she reminded him.

Katherine felt a strange sense of despondency as she walked back to the cottage from the water's edge. Fin had taken her mobile telephone number and promised to text her with his address when he arrived home. She had been invited to visit him in Wicklow when she left this island and she knew that the offer was genuine. Even as they parted on the slipway, she had felt happy and buoyant after their night in the cottage. However, a heavy gloom was descending and she started to experience a dull ache in her legs. On reaching the cottage, she started to feel short, sharp, stabbing pains low in her abdomen. She was bleeding, but her menstrual cycle was not due to end for another week. She sat on the edge of the bath and looked at her feet in confusion. Just hours ago she had felt so high, so connected, so happy. Now, again, she was empty and alone.

Week Four

Positive

"Yes, the pregnancy test result was positive, Mrs Hewett. What was the date of your last period?" asked the female doctor, looking closely at the exhausted expression of her patient. Katherine's pale face was drawn and her eyes looked tired as she explained that she had bled just three weeks previously, although it had been very light and lasted only two days.

"That sounds like an implantation bleed," explained the doctor. "This happens in a third of pregnancies. It can happen at the time the fertilized egg implants in the uterus, on average between six and twelve days past ovulation. The present level of the hormone hCG in your urine sample indicates the existence of a pregnancy for more than fourteen days. However, only a blood test or an ultrasound scan can determine the exact gestation. Are you happy to leave it for a few days and take another test, or would you like me to take some blood today?"

Katherine had explained that she was on holiday in the area and that the retreat director had told her about the drop-in health clinic. She was not sure how much longer she would be staying on the island. She was confused. The only possible opportunity for her to have become pregnant during the last month was the night she had spent with Henry. But he had undergone a vasectomy. How could she possibly be pregnant?

"I'd rather be sure," Katherine replied. "Can you take some blood now?" she asked.

"Yes, if you're feeling well enough," the doctor smiled reassuringly.

"When will I get the results?" Katherine queried.

"You can telephone the clinic tomorrow after two p.m. if you don't want a further appointment," the doctor informed her.

With the telephone number for the clinic and a clutch of information leaflets in her pocket, she left feeling disoriented and depressed. This was new territory to her; a wholly unexpected situation and she had no idea where she was headed, sensing only that she should be treading lightly. The pain and the bleeding has stopped again, however she knew that there were changes happening inside her body over which she had no control. Sensing that the confirmation of the pregnancy had shocked Katherine, the doctor had also advised her of the failure rate of first pregnancies and suggested that she seek immediate medical attention if the bleeding became heavier and the pain returned.

As she stood alone, waiting for the boat ride over the sound, feelings of anger at the unfairness of life, and in particular at the hand of cards she had been dealt, were slowly washed away with the heavy downpour of rain. *At least the weather will keep the tourists away,* thought Katherine.

There was only one place she wanted to be and was in no mood for the company of others.

For the next few days she sat alone in the lighthouse keeper's cottage, pondering her future. Thoughts of the distant past were no longer occupying her mind. She had been forced into the here-and-now by her own body, and the landscape of her future seemed to be changing by the day. Although she had no appetite, the nausea became unbearable when she failed to eat something for more than a couple of hours. Having read the pregnancy advice leaflets, she threw the remaining soft cheese into the rubbish bin and guiltily emptied the dregs of wine down the kitchen sink. She rested during the day, telling herself that she had no choice but to accept whatever was meant to happen to her.

However, her ambivalence was playing out a daily dance in her mind. If, as the doctor had warned, she were to miscarry this unplanned pregnancy, then life as she knew it would continue. If she was to make it past the 12-week stage, then she would be having a baby.

A baby! Another bout of nausea sent her into the bathroom, but even after retching there was little relief and she sat on the floor with tears streaming down her face, wanting it all to end. She had always believed that she would have children, a family, in the way that such scenes featured happy, smiling people in films and television programmes. She could quite easily imagine lively families chatting and laughing around large dining tables. However, she clearly had no concept of how being in the situation would actually *feel*. She had certainly never expected to feel this way. She was tired of the sickness and irritated by the soreness in her breasts.

At times, she felt as if she had woken up in someone else's body. One morning she actually wondered if her body had been invaded during the night by some alien creature. Replaying the image of the fertilized egg embedding itself in the lining of her womb, permeating the walls of her arteries and veins and diverting her blood flow into its rapidly dividing cells, she pondered on the notion that her bodily tissue was becoming interlocked by way of fast, finger-like branches of the developing tissue of a whole new being and she felt a momentary sense of revulsion. She had not even planned this. What did any of this have to do with having children? No one had told her it would be this way. She had considered only the cuddles and smiles and clean-smelling baby clothes.

This led to her theorizing as to her future. Maybe she was destined to spend her life with Henry? He must have had second thoughts about the vasectomy. Perhaps he decided that it was too final and that at some time in the future he might want children...and now he had the chance... The proposed vasectomy had been the catalyst for her flight from Henry; she had left without even discussing the issue with him, believing his decision to have been final. Then it had been Darrel's selfish and controlling arms which held her back from her dream of being a mother. Now, set free from her marriage, she decided that logically her next step had to be to go back to Henry who was, after all, the father of this child. However, the words in Katherine's mind just did not fit with the rhythm of her heartbeat. As she imagined herself happily standing next to him, another image surfaced. It was one of her feeling small and isolated whilst he was in the company of other women. She quickly closed it down. Things were different now. These relapses into victim-like thinking were becoming less frequent. She had a sense of newfound strength; probably acquired during her retreat, she guessed. She could now close down the painful, negative images which no longer served any purpose for her. Instead, she told herself that this sort of news was worthy of a face-to-face conversation. She would travel back to Henry's place and let him know the good news. She was sure that deep down he would be pleased. After all, it was only just under a month since they had last been together and created this new life now growing inside her.

An hour later, having packed her small rucksack and tidied up the cottage, she stood on the threshold and glanced wistfully back into the cottage. This had been a sanctuary. On one level she had found some peace here, and yet she was leaving with unanswered questions. She would remember her time here as one of self-restoration and exploration. Having come here with the intention of making a change in her life, she was now leaving to pursue a new path, albeit one that she had not anticipated. She had written a note for the course director and another for the counsellor, Shirley, thanking them for their friendship and wisdom. However, she would have to leave her secret memories of the time spent with Fin, inside the cottage. Closing the old wooden door, she said goodbye to him. However, on turning the key she felt a sharp pang in her chest; one that forced her to stop and catch her breath.

Henry

With just an hour of the train journey remaining, Katherine rummaged around in the bottom of her rucksack for the phone she had placed there a month earlier. Annoyingly, it would not power on. She wondered if keeping it switched off for this length of time would have resulted in the battery power discharging. She could call a cab from the public telephone at the train station to take her to the university campus. Once there, she would know where to find him.

However, the note on his office door simply stated, 'Away'. Katherine doubted it was referring to any location off campus and so she headed over to his garden apartment. The curtains were closed, yet the door was open.

"Hello! Anyone home?" she called as she let herself into the entrance hallway.

There was a shuffling of papers and a croaky voice from the study down the hallway answered with a surprised, "Yes?"

Inside the study, she found a dishevelled Henry poring over a pile of documents. "Henry! Why didn't you answer the door? Didn't you hear me knock?" she asked as Henry looked up at her in surprise.

"Katherine! I wasn't expecting anyone..." He was staring at her, in a daze.

"Henry, what's wrong?" She walked over to the desk. She wanted to hug him, he was looking so lost. "Are you ill? Henry, what's happened?"

"No, I'm not ill," he replied. "I've just had a bit of a shock." He gathered himself together and stood up, opening his arms to greet her. "Katherine, darling, let's go and get a cup of tea." He was trying hard to be his usual charming self, but as they walked into the kitchen she could feel that something had changed. "So, you've finished your retreat?" he asked, distractedly stirring the sugarless cup atop the breakfast bar.

She paused before replying. Something told her that she was not the only one with news. "I've had to cut it short. I've got something to tell you," she replied, "but first I need to know what's going on with you."

Henry took a deep breath and leaned on the surface of the bar between them. "There's been a claim made against me," he explained.

"What sort of claim?" she asked.

"It's a load of nonsense, really, but the university say that they have to be seen to take it seriously and to investigate it thoroughly. I've been suspended from teaching until further notice." Henry coughed.

"Henry?" was all Katherine could say. The only thing that immediately came to her mind was that he had been accused of plagiarism. What else could so seriously affect an academic?

Henry knew he had to explain the details to her. "It's a claim of sexual harassment. A student has claimed that I pressurized her into sex with the promise of a place with university funding for the Masters programme. It's not true. She's just not Masters material," he said flatly.

"Did you sleep with her?" Katherine cut straight to the point.

Henry grimaced before answering. "Yes, we went to dinner and one thing led to another, as it does between adults."

"Just the once?" Katherine asked.

Henry sighed before replying, "More than once."

It was Katherine's turn to sigh.

"She's just a desperate young woman," he continued, in an attempt to justify his position. "Up for it when she thought it might help her career. She had no real feelings for me. She was just using me and, when she didn't get what she wanted, well she turned nasty."

Katherine knew this was not good for Henry. She was well aware that his reputation had long been the subject of salacious speculation. Just the fact that the university were prepared to take the complaint seriously meant there was bound to be some fallout. Professional misconduct was one thing. However, a claim of sexual harassment was much more serious.

"And, what's more," Henry continued, "the bitch is saying that she's pregnant and that I'm the father." Katherine felt as if her life was being sucked into a black hole located somewhere in her lower abdomen. The room started to close in on her and she sat down sharply on a stool at the breakfast bar, fearful of fainting.

"It's not mine," Henry carried on, oblivious to her state of weakness. "She says she's about three months. I know she was sleeping with others, younger men, so it's far more likely to be one of theirs," he reasoned.

"So you never had a vasectomy?" Katherine asked quietly.

Henry stood up and looked straight at her, as if he had just remembered she was in the room. "No," he confirmed.

"Why not?" She had to ask.

"After you left, there was really no need," he said, stumbling over the words.

"So you wanted children, just not with me?" She fired the question directly at him.

"No, no! I never wanted children. I just figured that once you left the issue would never arise again. I wasn't planning to have children with you or anyone else. I just thought that the opportunity left with you. I knew how much you wanted a family."

Katherine was confused. "So if I had stayed, you would have gone through with it to make sure we didn't have any kids? And once I left, you thought you would just leave it up to chance; or the other women, I guess."

Henry shrugged and said, "I wasn't planning on having any

new relationships."

"Not one that lasted long enough to talk about the future, obviously." Her scathing criticism was conveyed in her sharp tone. Then she burst into tears.

"Katherine?" Henry seemed genuinely confused at her outburst.

"I'm pregnant." She managed to squeeze out the two words in-between sobs and gulps.

Henry's face paled. "Is it mine?" he asked quietly.

She nodded. All she wanted was for him to wrap his arms around her and tell her that everything would be okay. All Henry could think was how bad it was going to look for him when this news got out on the university campus grapevine.

Steadying himself on the bar, he impulsively asked her, "Are you sure? Who else knows about this?"

Katherine continued to cry.

Terminus

Whilst she sobbed herself into exhaustion, Henry unpacked her bag and made up a bed on the sofa. When she finally stopped, he assured her that he would support her in whatever she chose to do, although he was not sure what physical use he could be as a father.

"I'll help out financially, as long as I have a job," he offered, seriously. "But men my age are usually playing the role of grand-father," he added. "And I'll support you if you decide not to go ahead with the pregnancy. Although I don't think it will be wise for you to stick around here too long; whilst the investigation is going on, that is."

Typical Henry! His concern is first and foremost for his own reputation! thought Katherine, as she managed a weak smile of irony. She had no idea what she was going to do.

"I can't think straight at the moment," she explained. "I'll probably be able to make more sense of things after some sleep.

I'm tired," she added, making her way into the bedroom where she curled up in the comfort and familiarity of Henry's bed and drifted off into a deep and dreamless sleep.

She was woken by the early morning sun shining through the opening in the curtains. As the realization of her situation dawned on her, Katherine's body became heavy and the now familiar gnawing sensation in the pit of her stomach returned. In-between the loud clanging of questions in her mind she could hear only the hypnotic rhythm of Henry's snores from the sofa. What had she been thinking? Had she really believed that Henry would make good father material? Was her judgment impaired by her condition? Or was she just feeling desperate?

A bout of nausea forced her out of bed and Henry stirred as she rushed past him. When she returned from the bathroom she found him making a pot of coffee and placing some croissants on a tray to warm in the oven.

"Just some weak tea for me," she requested in an apologetic tone.

Henry looked into her small pale face and said, "I'm sorry. If I thought there was any risk of this, I would have taken precautions. I thought that at my age there was a low risk and that as you were married you probably had it covered anyway."

"And I thought you had gone ahead with the vasectomy," Katherine told him.

Henry shrugged and leaned over to place the croissants in the oven. "Do you think you could manage one of these?" he asked, and she nodded. "Now that the initial shock has worn off, hopefully we can talk about things," he added cheerfully.

Katherine knew that there was no room for her and a baby in Henry's life. He had no intention of changing anything. And who was she to expect it? Neither would she be satisfied waiting on the sidelines until the game was over. Things had moved on and her romantic dream of playing happy families with this man was just that; a romantic notion based in a time that no longer existed.

"I have been feeling rather poorly," she explained to him. "The doctor explained that, as this is my first pregnancy and that I'm experiencing bleeding, the chances of it succeeding to full term are quite low anyway. If I get more pain or heavier bleeding, she suggested that I go to the hospital. I'm only about four weeks, so a miscarriage at this stage would not be unusual or dangerous. However, if I decide on a termination, it would also be quick."

Pouring himself a cup of coffee, Henry sipped as he listened. He did not wish Katherine to feel any pain, but he felt no connection to this new life. For him, this situation was one to be resolved in the most pragmatic of ways.

"If you decide to make an appointment at the hospital in the city, I'll take you," he volunteered. "Not that I'm pressuring you," he added hastily. "It's your decision and I'll help out as best I can. Just let me know what you decide and I'll be happy to do whatever you want."

It was not long before Henry found himself doing just that. After breakfast, Katherine had decided to lie down and Henry took himself back to his paperwork. A scream brought him running to the bathroom, where he found Katherine doubled over in pain. A few minutes passed before she could breathe normally and she looked as if she might faint.

"Come on, let's get you to a hospital," he said.

The drive to A & E took less than 20 minutes but, to Henry, it seemed like forever. Every red traffic light, every bus decelerating to a stop and an elderly man and his tiny Jack Russell walking over a pedestrian crossing seemed to take a year. Even the A & E seemed to be working in slow motion and then finally Katherine was attended to: a busy nurse perfunctorily requesting Henry to provide them with her name, age, address, and next of kin.

"I'm just a friend...she was visiting..." he mumbled in response to the question about his relationship to the patient.

"We will need a home address and next of kin," the nurse persisted.

Katherine responded on his behalf, volunteering his name and address. "I'll be staying there for the foreseeable future," she told the nurse.

Henry plonked himself on the edge of a gurney and closed his eyes, relief flooding him now that the unexpected and awkward administration was taken care of. Exhausted, Katherine was slipping in and out of consciousness. The nurse put aside her chart and proceeded to take her patient's blood pressure and check her temperature. Eventually, a young doctor breezed into the cubicle, shone a light into each of her eyes and eased a spatula into her mouth to examine her tongue and throat.

"Rehydration...intravenous..." he instructed an attentive student nurse.

Henry was directed to a coffee dock down the corridor and the nurse helped Katherine into a hospital gown and onto a bed. A second nurse tended to the intravenous rehydration line. Over the next two hours, intermittent urine tests monitored her falling hormone levels.

On Henry's return, the doctor briefly reappeared to inform him that Katherine would be admitted as an inpatient overnight for observation purposes, and would be taken for a TVU scan the following morning. Henry sat at her bedside until she fell asleep.

As he drove home alone in the early hours, he reasoned with himself that the decision was now in the hands of the gods and he was feeling rather relieved about handing over the responsibility. He would look after Katherine for a while. She would probably need to stay at his place for a few days, at least. After that, he had no idea what to do about her and soon his thoughts reverted to his own tricky situation.

There was no way that the harassment allegations were going to be resolved as spontaneously as the current state of affairs with Katherine. He would have to work out a way to minimize the fallout if he wanted to continue with his valuable tenure at the university. He was far too comfortable to up sticks and move his show on at this stage in his career. The bedrock of Henry's world had been blasted high and wide by the recent revelations in his private life and his instinct was telling him to take cover until all of the dust had settled.

Limbo

Katherine stood at the hospital entrance, waiting for Henry's car to pull into the parking bay opposite. Ignoring his questioning expression, she sat silently in the passenger seat beside him. The atmosphere continued to intensify for the duration of the journey home. On arriving at his place, she took herself into the bedroom and firmly closed the door. Not knowing what else to do, Henry busied himself in the kitchen rummaging for the ingredients to cook up a meal for her. Sitting on his bed, Katherine found herself replaying her conversation with the sonographer.

"There won't be much to see," she had been advised by the technician. "At this stage, all we expect to find is the gestational sac." She had shifted uncomfortably as the woman in the white coat adjusted the probe, not sure whether or not she wanted to see anything.

"Ah! There, can you see a round dark shape?" the woman had asked Katherine, pointing to a small, round, dark patch visible amongst the blurred, grey background on the screen. "This is usually visible from four to five weeks."

"Is there any more you can tell from the scan?" Katherine had asked.

"I'm afraid not. It can confirm the pregnancy, but at this early stage there is very little else we can see. We won't be able to pick up a heartbeat until the sixth week." The sonographer's response had been sensitive but firm.

At dinner, a red-eyed Katherine sat opposite Henry picking at his peace offering of poulet basquaise.

"Do you need any medication, or just a chance to rest?" he asked, chewing his last mouthful.

"I don't know," was all she could bring herself to say.

"Well, you can stay here for as long as you need," he said, placing his knife and fork on the plate. In his mind, this pregnancy was already over. Although relieved that he would not have to face any more difficult decisions, he was also keen to tread carefully with any suggestions for the future. Any talk of what was to happen next was clearly off the agenda until her mood lifted. All she could see was the stark image of a black hole, on the screen of a hospital monitor.

Investigations

The next few days played out in a downbeat rhythm, in which Katherine read magazines about motherhood whilst Henry had buried his head in a pile of papers in preparation for his disciplinary hearing. They faced each other with painful politeness at mealtimes, only to retreat to their respective corners as soon as possible to tend to their own personal preoccupations.

Their turgid trance was broken by a telephone call from the police. Henry peered around the bedroom door with the telephone in his hand. "It's the police," he announced softly to her. "They're asking if I have any news about the whereabouts of a Katherine Hewett."

"The police! Why...? How..." What could they want with her?

"What shall I say?" he whispered, although he had pressed the mute button on the handset.

"What do the police want with me?" A heavy sense of dread and fear began to creep over her.

"Will you talk to them?" he asked gently.

"Do you think I should?" She was looking for some indication from Henry as to what to do.

"They said that they found this contact number amongst your hospital records from your recent admission to A & E, and that they have been looking to get in touch with you for some time," Henry said, shaking his head and shrugging. "That's all that has been said. Shall I say you are resting?"

Henry turned away from the bedroom door to respond to the call, and then returned a few moments later with an earnest look on his face.

"Katherine, darling, they need to speak with you. They have some news for you. I've given them this address. They will be calling round shortly."

Henry was sitting on the sofa in the lounge with his arm around Katherine's shoulder when the two young officers in uniform knocked at the door. The female officer seemed to take the lead role, advising Katherine to remain seated and asking her how she was feeling. At Henry's beckoning, she took a seat opposite them. The male officer hovered awkwardly, his eyes seemingly scouring every inch and corner of the room.

"I'm afraid we have some upsetting news, Mrs Hewett. It's about your husband, Darrel. I understand that you have separated. However, your husband was reported missing by your housekeeper, Mrs Jenks, some three weeks ago. We have since found one of his cars abandoned and we now fear for his safety."

Katherine found herself unable to speak.

The officer continued, "Technically, you are still his next of kin and we have been trying to contact you since the day he was reported missing. Your disappearance has caused us some consternation."

Katherine cleared her throat. "I've been away, on a sort of holiday; a retreat where contact with the outside world is not a priority," she explained weakly. "I haven't been in touch with anyone. Well, except for Henry."

"We had a mobile telephone contact number for you," the officer continued. "It was the only contact stored in Mr Hewett's phone. He had deleted everything else. We left messages for you to contact us as soon as possible."

Katherine cast a glance at her phone which had remained switched off whilst charging for the last few days. Her action was noted by the young male officer who spoke up.

"We need to know if you have had any contact with Mr Hewett over the past three weeks."

"N-no. No, I haven't," Katherine stuttered in response, feeling a wave of guilt wash over her. "What has happened to him? You said you fear for his safety?"

"As we've said, it's been over three weeks since anyone has seen or heard from him," explained the officer. "Can you tell us exactly where you have been staying during that time, Mrs Hewett?" The male officer's formal tone startled Katherine and she automatically relayed the name and location of the island retreat.

"And if we contact the proprietors of this establishment, they will be able to confirm your claims?" the officious officer continued.

"Yes!" She was feeling distinctly disquieted by his line of questioning. "Yes, they will confirm I was there," she assured the female officer who had started to take notes. "Do you think I have something to do with Darrel's disappearance?" she asked in disbelief.

"We just need to know the last time you saw Mr Hewett, Katherine," the female officer chipped in to soften the tone. "We are just trying to piece together the events of the days leading up to his disappearance."

Katherine took a deep breath and spoke her thoughts aloud. "The last time I saw him, he was leaving for work. It must have been the Monday, no, the Tuesday morning. We'd been sleeping in separate rooms and we didn't speak that morning. I saw his car pull off the driveway. Then I got my things together, ready to leave."

"What car was he driving?" the male officer asked.

"Oh, it was the black Fiat, I think." She seemed unsure.

"Where did you go?" The question was fired by the male officer.

"I came here," Katherine replied. "I stopped off on the way to the retreat."

"Can you confirm that, sir?" the female officer asked Henry.

"Yes," answered Henry, without hesitation. "She arrived here on the Tuesday evening and left the following morning."

"And if you don't mind me asking, how do you two know each other?" the officer continued. Both Katherine and Henry attempted to answer at the same time. He volunteered that they were 'old friends' and she added that she had once been a student here at the university.

"And between the morning that you left your house and today, you have not seen or spoken to your husband?" The male officer's tone was firm and direct.

"Yes, that's correct," answered Katherine. "I knew I would have to face him at some point over the divorce, but to be honest I was avoiding it for as long as I could. I thought that he might cool down after he had a few weeks to get used to the idea."

The officers looked at each other before the young man walked over to pick up Katherine's phone.

"Would you be willing for us to take a closer look at your phone?" the woman officer asked.

Katherine nodded in agreement.

"Is she implicated in the disappearance?" Henry wanted to know.

"At this stage, we are conducting a missing person enquiry," explained the male officer, "and we would be very appreciative of any assistance you may be able to offer."

Despite Henry's attempts at further questions, neither officer would be drawn to provide any more information.

"Will you be contactable at this address until further notice, Mrs Hewett?" Katherine looked at Henry before answering that she would be staying there for the next week or so.

"We would appreciate it if you contact us before you leave," requested the young female officer. "We will be in touch if or when we hear something further and we will return your phone as soon as we can."

"What was that all about?" Katherine asked as Henry closed the door behind the two officers.

"Am I a suspect? Do they think I'm involved in some way with Darrel's disappearance?"

"What's happened? What do you think he's done?" Henry asked.

"I have no idea," she responded. "The lawyer advised me not to speak to him after he issued the divorce petition to minimize the opportunity for conflict. Why have they taken away my phone?"

"You could have refused to allow them to take it," advised Henry. "But at least they will be able to see you've not been in touch with him, if that's the case."

"Of course it is!" she protested.

"As *is* the case," he corrected himself. "Hopefully they'll turn something up soon," he reassured Katherine. "I expect they have been monitoring his banking and other online accounts."

Katherine shivered at the invasion of privacy. However, she knew that none of their investigations would show that she had been in touch with Darrel. "Do you think they know why I was at the hospital?" she asked. *Dammit!* she thought, wishing she had thought of these questions before they had left.

"They'll be in touch," Henry said emphatically. "Is your husband the type of man to do, well, anything stupid?"

"Stupid? No!" She frowned. "He's a very manipulative man. He hates the thought of things being outside of his control. I can't imagine him ever voluntarily relinquishing his power. No, I can't see him doing away with himself. I'd say it's more likely that he's off on some quest for a new wife or a business opportunity. He's so arrogant. He wouldn't have given Mrs Jenks a second thought. I'm sure if the police speak with his colleagues in the city they're more likely to find him."

"There must be a reason they are concerned about his disappearance," replied Henry. "I suspect there is something they haven't told us. And you disappearing around the same time must have raised suspicions."

"Well, they know where I've been, and that I've got nothing to hide. And I'm sure Darrel will turn up," Katherine concluded.

A long silence ensued. The incident had leveraged each of them to view their situations from fresh perspectives. Henry had been forced to looking over and above the campus walls for the first time in decades and Katherine realized that her past was not yet content to be laid to rest.

Uncomfortable Truths

A few days later Henry woke her early in the morning with a cup of tea. "Darling, I have a meeting with the disciplinary committee. I'm hoping we can resolve this unpleasant business without it having to go outside the university walls. I've decided to play ball and see if the department can offer her something of an olive branch. I won't mind her sticking around if she withdraws her complaint. Hopefully one of the others will offer her a place on another Masters programme," he explained.

"What about the baby?" she asked.

"I don't think there is a baby. Or, at least if there is, it isn't mine," Henry replied thoughtfully. "I think all talk of a baby will disappear if she gets offered a place. I'm sure she won't turn down the offer of a bursary, but we'll have to wait and see. All I can do is support her application to the department."

"And what about *this* baby?" Katherine asked quietly.

Henry took a deep breath and his voice took a different tone as he said, "That's a whole other issue. Can we talk about it when I get back? There's no rush, is there?"

Katherine sighed. It was still early days and anything could happen with her pregnancy.

Midway through that afternoon, Katherine was roused from

her nap by a rap at the apartment door. Looking around for Henry, she realized he had not yet returned from his meeting, and she answered the door to the police.

"Mrs Hewett, we have come to return your phone," announced the same young male officer she had met at the start of the week.

"Yes, thank you. We are very grateful for your cooperation," added his female colleague. "Can we come in?"

Katherine offered them a drink and tried to focus her thoughts whilst brewing herself a pot of green tea. Today she was the one looking for answers.

"So is there any more news on Darrel?" she asked, placing the cups on the coffee table in the lounge. Both officers were seated this time and seemingly more open to sharing some information.

"We have spoken to his parents in America, friends, and the colleague for whom he left the only voicemail message, and I'm afraid we are no further forwards in this investigation," the young man explained, placing Katherine's phone on the table.

"We were hoping that you would have some idea," explained the female officer, "but it seems that there has been no contact between you both via your mobile phones and we have confirmed that you had a booking at the island retreat. We have spoken to people who can confirm your movements there." An uncomfortable feeling welled up inside Katherine and an image of Fin momentarily flashed into her mind. She wondered to whom they had spoken and was starting to feel resentful that her privacy was being unfairly encroached upon.

"Has Darrel done something wrong? I don't understand why you think he's missing. He's a man of means; he can travel at the drop of a hat. Have you checked airport departures?"

She was still unsure why the police were interested in him.

"Most missing persons tend to show up within 48 hours of their disappearance, Mrs Hewett, and one of his cars was found abandoned."

"Where?" she asked.

"On the beach at Godington Gap," was the reply.

"The beach?" Katherine's concern heightened.

"Yes, the car had been driven, or pushed, from the cliff and was found on the rocks," explained the lady officer. "No body has been found," she hastened to add. "However, there was the one voicemail message left on a friend's answerphone which might suggest he was not in a good state of mind. And that is the last that anyone seems to have heard from him."

A horrified Katherine could not believe her ears.

"What did it say?" Katherine needed to know.

"I can't recall, exactly," said the female officer, "but it was words to the effect that he was sorry that things hadn't worked out."

"And you think he's killed himself? Oh, my God! No, not Darrel!" She was finding this hard to believe. "Why?" she asked. "Was it because of the divorce?" Suddenly a wave of fear and guilt hit her, and feeling nauseous she had to leave the room. The officers could only sit patiently and listen to the sound of retching from the bathroom.

When the sickness subsided she returned to the room and the questioning continued.

"Mrs Hewett, is there anything, even the smallest detail that you can recall, that might give us an idea as to what happened or where Mr Hewett might be?"

Still fighting the nausea, Katherine recounted events of the last few days she was in the house. "I had spoken with my solicitor on the Friday and finalized the details for the divorce petition. He advised me that if I was going to leave the matrimonial home it would be better to do it sooner rather than later. Darrel and I, we signed an agreement before we married that in the event of a break-up I would not be entitled to any of the assets he had accrued before we met. The solicitor said that after seven years of marriage, the agreement would be less persuasive in court if I wanted to fight for any of them. I told him I no longer wanted any part of that life. I just wanted my freedom, and so he advised me that to stay at home whilst the court hearings were going on could prove very difficult. That's when I finalized the booking on the retreat." She stopped for a sip of tea in the hope of settling her stomach before continuing. The police officers waited once more.

"There's no way that things were ever going to work out between us, but I never thought he would do anything like this, like suicide. I would never have gone to the lawyer if I thought it would have this effect. I would have just left…" She started to cry.

The female officer leaned forwards over the coffee table and took Katherine's hand. "These events are hard to predict and even harder to prevent," she explained. "If it's any consolation, we found the divorce petition amongst the other unopened mail. We don't know if Mr Hewett was even aware of it. And it was only your contact number we found stored in his phone. But you believe he was aware that you intended to leave him?"

"Yes," replied Katherine. "The relationship had been in difficulty for some time. We had been sleeping in separate rooms and he knew I had resigned from my job. He was out of the house for most of the weekend, but I have no idea where, and you said you've spoken to his friends and work colleagues? Darrel had a wide network of people around him, and lots of women," she added.

"So, when was the last time you saw or spoke to him?" The male officer was getting impatient.

"As I said, it was the Tuesday morning. I saw his car pull off from the driveway."

Katherine then asked if it was the black Fiat that had been found on the beach.

"No," was the officer's reply. "We recovered a black Ferrari Barchetta, but as we have said there was no trace of Darrel at the scene."

"When did you find it?" she asked thoughtfully.

"Mr Hewett was reported missing by the housekeeper on the Friday morning and we traced the car to him quite quickly," replied the officer. "So, we believe he went missing sometime between Tuesday and Friday, and the car was discovered washed up on the rocks after Saturday morning's high tide."

Unsettling

"That was exhausting," said Henry, looking washed out. "Emotionally exhausting, I mean."

"Yes, I can imagine," Katherine said wryly. "Having your most private details dragged out in public is very uncomfortable."

Oblivious to her inference, he continued with his diatribe. "She was there, of course, to gloat over my squirming; playing the innocent, the injured party. Perhaps I should have played the victim. I wonder what the outcome would have been if I suggested that *she* had seduced *me*? And all in the interests of getting a place on the Masters programme?"

"But you're the authority figure in this particular scenario," she reminded him.

"It's not as if I ever promised her a place," he continued. "Sex is sex and work is something else. Why mix it up?"

"Maybe our emotional experiences are an inextricable part of our lives? Perhaps we don't all separate different aspects of our lives into convenient compartments?" Katherine suggested.

However, Henry was simply not listening. "The committee decided that there is no need to refer the complaint outside the university and the little bitch gets her bursary for a Medieval History Masters. So our paths shouldn't cross again in the future. The warning will not have any real effect on my career, but it did give that dried-up old bag from Women's Studies the pleasure of looking down her nose at me."

Katherine was all too familiar with the rivalry between Henry and this particular colleague. Mary Brooke was a staunch feminist and she and Henry had clashed at many interdepartmental meetings. The truth was that they were both actually very much alike in temperament and ambition.

"So you're in the clear?" she asked.

"Yes, things won't be going any further," he confirmed, with a sigh of relief.

"And the baby?" Katherine asked with caution.

'Well, if she is pregnant, you couldn't tell," Henry replied dismissively. "I don't think we'll hear any more about that." However, he was consumed with the indignity of his own situation. His reputation had been ridiculed and his ego had been trashed. The truth was that, for others, nothing had changed. They merely continued to think their private thoughts about Henry. The only difference was that now he had been called to account for his actions and he had been faced with the contempt of his counterparts. He had been forced to see himself through the eyes of his colleagues and was disquieted at the view. To her, he appeared withdrawn and became somewhat circular in his conversation. It seemed as if he was shutting himself off from the prying, judgemental eyes of the world.

Katherine once again found herself in a state of limbo, having to wait around to discover the consequences of the actions of the men in her life. She delved deeper into her own pregnancy, developing a particular interest in the biological details of the developing foetus. The minutes she spent pondering the changes in her body turned into hours of research and she became awash with awe at the exact timings and the tiny details of the process of conception and development. She read that at six weeks' gestation, the heartbeat registered as a faint flicker in-between the black and white dots on the screen of the ultrasound monitor. She also learned that the gender of the baby is not determined until the seventh week of the pregnancy, the time at which the pineal gland instantaneously appears, nestled in a nice central location, underneath the midpoint of the brain. She marvelled at the magic of the creation.

What if it was true that the soul did not enter the body of a new being until it was seven weeks old? Where was the soul lurking until this time? Katherine's thoughts turned to the notion of reincarnation and her own personal experiences with past life regression therapy.

What if the soul chooses its own destiny? She wondered if there was a waiting list of souls eager to find a body. Would her new baby have a new soul? *Are there any new souls, or are we all on a recurrent cycle of death and rebirth?* She was finding it hard to imagine the life inside her as a person. However, she knew that she wanted it to be a unique and unencumbered individual; one whose soul could sing in happiness, not one struggling under the weight of negativity carried forwards from other lives. Katherine longed to share her thoughts and fears with Henry. However, his state of self-absorption persisted.

A few days had passed without hearing anything further from the police and Katherine called her solicitor to clarify her position as to her legal standing in the event of the failure of her estranged husband to show up. She was advised that the lawyer had received no response from Darrel in relation to the petition, and that the divorce could not proceed whilst he was missing. She told her solicitor that she believed that he was not dead and would turn up at some point and was assured that if he resurfaced she could resume proceedings. However, should he remain a missing person he would be presumed dead for legal purposes after a period of seven years.

Her heart sank when she realized that until he showed up, dead or alive, her current marital status would remain unchanged. She was stuck, again. Her sweet taste of freedom had been quickly soured by some unexpected events. The fun and pleasure of the last month of her life had been consigned to a dreamlike status. Her memories of Fin which she had reluctantly stored behind the cottage door were now fading fast into her subconscious, as she was having to face up to the rather grim and gritty realities of life.

Week Five

A Sort of Homecoming

One week earlier, Fin had disembarked from the late afternoon ferry at the port of Rosslare with the entirety of his life's accoutrements packed into the boot of his jeep. Having rationalized his need for all the belongings he had acquired over time, he figured that if he had inadvertently discarded something important, he would now undoubtedly learn to live without it. He had been working towards this move for a few years, always keeping a low profile and managing to adapt to the changing circumstances which had cropped up from time to time. Now was the moment of truth. There was no more planning, and no turning back. It was time for him to step up and assume his status as the proprietor of Spring Well Farm. Although he knew how to avoid every pothole in the mountain roads leading to the family farmstead where he had drawn his first breath; paradoxically his future here was still largely an unknown quantity.

As he drove north, along the eastern coast road, Fin had reflected on the changes in his own life and those of the people he knew from his childhood. Most had married, some divorced, many had borne children, and the majority had moved away or died. During the seven summers he had spent working on the farmhouse, Fin had re-established only a few old family connections, including his closest neighbour, Dan Brien, whose dairy farm was situated at the end of Lusmore Lane. However, he had not been readily accepted back into the fold. People who moved away from the mountains were traditionally regarded with suspicion on their return, especially if it was to reclaim old land with new ideas. Fin had come to realize that as much as he was a product of this environment, his relationship with it was at best tenuous. His house, land and community were not there to prop him up. He had realized that he needed to painstakingly reinvest his time, money and attention to create a sense of homely comfort in the space.

Not knowing how he had been living his life since he left the mountains for university some 25 years previously, the imaginations of his neighbours and distant relatives as to the person he had become in this time and space had gloried in open season. Fuelled further by way of fleeting visits for family wakes and weddings, snatches of overheard conversations and concealed whispers had created quite a colourful existence for Fin, only the barest of elements of which held any truth about his life. There was speculation that the lack of general information about his career was evidence in itself that he was in the employ of the intelligence services. Fin alone knew only of the banal truth of his corporate experiences.

During the hour's drive, Fin had realized that in coming back to himself, reclaiming his own life, he could not depend on any time or place to cushion his fall. Having cut himself adrift from the life that he created, for the first time he began to see that, in essence, it was a work of fiction. The names and faces of the people with whom he had spent countless hours in boardrooms and bars, doing business, on behalf of some faceless corporation, had faded over time. The days spent on endless train journeys with his head lost in a screen of balance sheets and financial strategies, punctuated with late-night city stops, now flashed by him on a high-speed track to the past. His vista was now one of great open spaces, green fields and tall pine forests. The city smog had been replaced with the sweet mountain air and the roar of traffic had been replaced with the evening birdsong amidst the trees, as he had pulled up, high in his beloved Wicklow Hills.

Before unpacking the jeep he took a tour around the place, checking all was as he had left it the previous autumn. It had been a relatively mild winter and he was here now, at the start of the summer. It was time to put all his plans into action. The refurbishment of the stables was complete and he had put out feelers for owners and trainers looking for somewhere from where they could offer riding lessons. Fin felt that riding was just one of many activities which would draw the holidaymakers to the log-cabin village he had planned for the woods, which lay to the west of the farmland, far enough away not to interfere with life at the farmhouse, yet close enough to keep an eye on things.

Both the farmhouse and the old barn were ready to open to the public. It was Fin's dream that those curious of how living and working on a hill farm in Ireland in the late 1800s would have looked and felt could visit for an authentic experience. He wondered why the knowledge of ancient farming methods resonated so strongly within him; how the understanding of the techniques came to him so easily. His education had been solely from within the four walls of school and university buildings. He pondered whether it was genetically passed down the generations, along with the general family afflictions and affectations.

There was also a beautiful lake here and Fin was torn between the desire to open it to guests for holiday and recreational purposes and keeping it for his own private use.

Having unlocked all of the doors, he had made the most of the fading sun, and taken a look around to make sure everything was in place. If he was quick, he thought he may be able to catch the last of the summer tourist trade in the hills by hosting some open days at the farmstead. Then he could concentrate on completion of the other planned facilities in readiness for the following spring. Realizing he would never be able to manage all aspects of the business himself, Fin knew that now was the time to re-establish relationships in the hills over the next few months, but at this point he had a pressing, personal ritual to perform.

At the edge of the woods, overlooking the lake amongst the Scots pines and larches, there was a majestic, sessile oak tree. From here, if you climbed high enough, you could glimpse the last rays of the midsummer sunset through a break in the distant mountain ridge. Fin's father had first shown the boys how to climb the solid old tree to catch the view, when they were just old enough to walk, much to their mammy's chagrin. Later, Fin and his elder brother learned to use the tree as an escape from their mother when she was displeased with them over some childish mischief. It was their play den, their safe haven, their resting place, their home. As Fin approached the edge of the woods, a last trace of the golden sunset danced momentarily on the gently rippling surface of the lake, before the sun dipped behind the mountain ridge. He stopped to admire the magical moment, before looking for the tree. He remembered that if he climbed high enough in midsummer, it was possible to watch the colour of the setting sun deepen into crimson, through the gap in the horizon, as it sunk a little lower in the evening sky. Standing admiring the great oak, he realized that there were only a couple of weeks to wait until he could, once again, capture that magical moment.

Irish Eyes

During the first week back at the farmstead, Fin immersed himself in the memories of his childhood. Rooting through the old family photos which had just been left to rot in a damp cardboard box, he had salvaged the best offerings and intended to use a high-quality scanner to create copies and thereby preserve the precious few remaining images of his parents and grandparents. As he looked closely at the faded black and white faces he was reminded of the warmth and kindness of his mother; he followed the curve of her smile which pushed her cheeks up to wrinkle gently at the corner of her eyes. And with a sudden laugh of recognition he saw some of his own features and expressions in the frown of his middle-aged father. He was now seeing himself, and his life, through new eyes; ones that had been present and overseeing for all time.

Feeling cold and alone with his heritage, unsure if the dampness in the newly renovated cottage was due to the soaking into the stonework of some 200 years of rain or the newly plastered walls, Fin had taken to lighting a peat and log fire in the evenings and reflecting over a glass or two of Tullamore Dew. He was settling back into his own skin, and into the fabric of his family home. The part of him he had left behind when he left Ireland had been reborn anew. He felt a greater sense of wholeness and identity and yet, paradoxically, for the first time in his life he was aware of the overwhelming uncertainty of his future. He smiled at the recognition that none of the high-powered jobs he had held, relationships invested in, or any of the homes he had acquired, were still in existence. It was now clear to him that the certainty he had believed in was all just a grand illusion. On reflection, he could now see that nothing had ever been enduring, that all aspects of his life had been subject to constant change, and yet he had been so focused on just one element at a time, the beauty of the grand design had eluded him. For the first time he could see how tenuous life could be, how something that weighed so heavily on his mind one day could bear no significance just a few weeks later. He could now for the first time appreciate the fragility of the human experience, and particularly the delicacy of relationships. Regardless of vows, agreements, ceremonies, or rings, the life blood of love was in the precious time spent sharing unique experiences with people. Fin could see that now. Any part of it could have been taken away from him at any time, indeed some of it had. Other parts of his life he had thrown away willingly, shaking off the people and places that constrained him. He had a few regrets. However, they were now far behind him.

When the Dew ran dry, Fin ventured out to spend his evenings at one of the local hostelries. He reasoned it would be good for him to touch base again and ask if he could leave some leaflets advertising his open days at the farm for the tourists. 'Doyle's of Dunealy' had belonged to the same family for as long as he could remember; although old Declan Doyle had passed away some six years previously. Since then, the place had been in the hands of his Italian widow, Drina, and their eldest son, Liam, who was a couple of years older than Fin, having been a friend of Fin's older brother, Cillian. However it was Rosa, his younger sister, with whom Fin had been more familiar. The two had been secondary-school sweethearts, which proved an ongoing source of tension between Liam and Fin, until, much to Liam's delight, Fin passed the Leaving Certificate exam and left for university.

His long-distance relationship with Rosa had limped on for a few months. However, Liam had taken every opportunity to create a wedge between them and Fin had finally admitted defeat. He stopped calling. Some years later he heard that Rosa had married the son of a local farmer. Fin had only seen her once since he had left the hills. Against the local wisdom and intentionally flying in the face of convention, she had attended at the funeral mass of his mother, whilst heavily pregnant. He was now taken aback to see her familiar face smiling at him from behind the bar as he walked in with an armful of leaflets. She had managed to conceal the shock she had registered on recognizing him.

"Fin...? Fintan Byrne? Well, it's been a while! Must be six or seven years since your ma's..." Rosa stopped short of the word 'death' and continued, "Well, it's great to see you. What will you have?" She continued to chatter away as they both waited for the Guinness to settle. "Are you home for a holiday? Or is it some family business you're attending to, maybe?" Fin explained that he was staying at the old family farm and would be there for the foreseeable future. Rosa's deep, brown eyes flashed her interest from beneath two deeply arched, dark eyebrows as she fixed her gaze on him and he felt a familiar stirring.

"How are things with you? Jack and the boys are doing well, I'm sure," he spoke stiffly.

"Yes, there're all grand. I have a daughter too, Orna. She's recently turned seven, going on seventeen, if you know what I mean," she smiled, as she served up the glass onto the bar between them. Fin smiled and continued their conversation,

"So, you're working here now?"

"Only whilst Ma's away. She's in the hospital. Liam takes her into Dublin for treatment and she's always a bit rough for a few days following the chemo, so I'm sort of on standby, as and when, you know?"

"I'm sorry to hear that," Fin replied. "I hope they've caught it in time."

Rosa shrugged her shoulders and forced a smile. "She's still got that hot head about her! I'm sure it's what keeps her going. There now, can I get you anything else?" She was looking at the leaflets Fin had set down on the bar. "Do you want to leave those here with us?"

Fin animatedly explained his plans for the farm, whilst Rosa listened with interest. He spoke about his plans for the construction of eco-cabins in the woods and about his vision that people would be attracted to the place as a safe and friendly family holiday. He wanted to use the best of new environmental technologies and fuse them with the more traditional farming and land-management methods to create a unique experience.

"I want people to enjoy the land and the lake," he explained, "but not at the expense of the soil, the trees, or the animals." Fin went on about how he wanted to offer riding lessons for holiday-makers and asked Rosa if she knew of any local instructors who would be interested in some seasonal work. Meanwhile he said he was happy for the stables to be used for the benefit of his friends and neighbours, so he could learn the ropes.

"So you have stables for rent? I've been looking for somewhere for Orna's pony. She's just started riding and the new mare we have for her is nervous around the other horses on the farm."

"Then you must call round and take a look at the place," he offered. "Of course, there's a lot more work to be done, but I'm hoping that there will be people interested in helping me establish and build the business."

There was an awkward silence and then Rosa responded with warmth. "It's good to have you around again." It was with great reluctance that she turned her attention to a flock of hungry new customers appearing at the bar, enquiring as to availability of tables in the restaurant. Alone again, Fin finished his drink a little too quickly and managed to catch her eye with a wave as he left the premises.

The Ould Chap

Although feeling grounded whilst wandering around the farm clearing spaces for his planned ventures, outside his safety zone Fin was finding it much harder than expected to make progress and find other people who would help and support his efforts. He regularly checked his phone for messages from Katherine, reasoning that she was sure to be in touch soon. Happy to pay for people's time, skills, and ideas, he had factored these costs into his business plan for the place. Now he just needed to sense some interest, from someone – from anyone.

However, finding himself alone for long stretches of time, he concentrated his attention on the finer details of his business plan. He used the time to source suppliers for the rainwater harvesting and grey water systems he was intending to install in the eco-village and to finally plan the work on the drainage system for the forest-based village. He intended to make the best use of the area's natural resources, and rainwater was a given.

The use of solar panels for heating was posing more problematic. He did not want to sacrifice any more trees to clear a greater space for light and his mind started to wander as to other alternative sources for bringing light and heat into the forest. He thought that perhaps the use of biofuel might be the way to go, having recently read that bamboo was now regarded as the main 21st-century timber as a sustainable substitute for tropical hardwood products in an era of mass deforestation and exploding population. It was recognized as having a myriad of modern applications, including use as a biofuel, a fabric for clothing, and a source of food. Fin learned that if he was to plant bamboo at the farm, for a fixed investment for an eight-year period, he could rely on an annualized return of at least 18 per cent profit. The US Timber Trade Federation forecast stated that the global forest industry was to increase in value 53 per cent, and would be worth trillions of dollars by the year 2020, with bamboo offering a sustainable solution for the boom in demand.

Fin was also researching the names and functions of the ancient farm equipment he had saved from abandon. Some of the pieces of machinery had been hanging around for as long as he could remember – some rusting in the fields, others sequestered away in the dark, unused corners of the courtyard. They included a Wexford Engineering drill plough with double moulding boards used for earthing up the potato crops and an asses cart with high-sided creels for transporting turf, along with a traditional wooden slatted turf barrow. He also restored a winnowing machine. It took him a while, as the simplicity of the device initially misled him. However, this large, hand-cranked machine used for removing chaff and weed seeds from the corn harvest was soon back in full working order, when he realized that by pouring the corn into the opening on the top of the wooden hopper, the chaff and weed seeds would be separated and simply blown away by the action of the large fan rotating inside the hopper. Once he had the information, he was able to restore the pieces, where possible, to some form of working order, to paint them for further preservation and to label them up for inquisitive visitors to the exhibition in the great barn. Fin was enjoying the challenge of the fusion of the old and new in his life. He liked the notion of reworking the old machinery and traditional methods, whilst incorporating new ideas. After all, the intention behind them all was the same: the sustainable use of natural resources with the lowest impact of pollution or destruction on the environment.

Standing in the only empty field, situated between the farmhouse and Lusmore Lane, wondering how to best utilize the uneven area, he recalled the annual ritual of gathering of black-berries from the bramble hedge with his mammy. Momentarily, he was transported back to one sunny August of his childhood, when his only concern was choosing the juiciest berries to please his kind and gentle mother. Closing his eyes, Fin could feel the sun on his cheeks and the soft warmth of his mother's embrace. As the memory faded, he opened his eyes to find the face of a stranger leaning over the gate in the hedge. Startled, he held up his left palm to shade his eyes from the midday glare and addressed the man. "Can I help you?"

The stranger removed his brown, woollen cap and wiped his brow. He was an old man, the sweat on his brow suggesting that he was struggling in the heat of the midday sun. Fin asked if he would care for some refreshment, extending the invitation by opening the gate to the field.

"That would be grand," replied the grateful man, replacing his hat. "A drop of water would be very welcome." As he stepped into the field, Fin noticed he carried a large leather satchel which seemed to weigh heavily on his left shoulder, and surmised that he was peddling wares. Leading the way across the sloping field he stopped and turned around intermittently to allow the man to catch up, assuming he was struggling with the pace. However, the old man had begun to whistle cheerfully to himself as he took in the scenery around him, strolling nonchalantly over the field. Feeling discomfort in his stomach, Fin tried to dismiss his anxiety; surely he had nothing to fear from this old pedlar? However, there was something very odd about him. Arriving in the courtyard, the 'quare' chap stopped, and waited politely for Fin to fetch some refreshment from the kitchen of the cottage. Fin quickly returned with a glass of water, as requested, to find the old man standing, cap in hand, amongst the whirling leaves whipped up by a sudden summer breeze.

"Thanks a million," he said, taking the glass from Fin who for the first time got a good look at the man's face. A swarthy and heavily-lined complexion suggested a life lived largely in the open air. Also, a stooping gait made him appear aged. However, Fin was struck by the youthful spirit in his striking, green eyes.

"So, what is your business around these parts?" Fin asked, his gaze drawn towards the pedlar's old leather bag. For a moment he felt transported back to the hills of a hundred years or so years ago. Unperturbed, the old fellow continued to steadily drink his water.

"Ah! There's nothing like a glass of Spring Well water," he exclaimed on draining the glass, handing it back to Fin. "It's been a while since I've tasted it, and it's still good!"

"Oh, you know the place? When were you here? Do you remember my parents?" asked Fin, absentmindedly taking hold of the empty glass.

"People, they come and they go," replied the old man. "It's the hills, the trees, and the lakes that guide my way and call me home. Now tell me, do you have any plans for this here field of yours?" he enquired.

Slightly taken aback, Fin responded that at present he was unsure of exactly what to do with the land, although he was considering a couple of options.

"Well, I'm looking for a safe home for some horses and that field would be a grand place, just off that quiet boreen," the old pedlar stated cheerfully.

"I'd be happy to come to some arrangement, for just a season or two," Fin explained, thinking in terms of an unexpected increase in his cash flow. "However, I do have plans for that field, in the longer term..." He felt a sense of vagueness descend over him and he was struggling to verbalize his thoughts.

"Ah! It will just be for the one season," replied the old man, "and I would be very careful as to any plans you might have. That field has a life of its own, you know, and it might not take too kindly to your plans." Fin wanted to ask him what he meant but found himself unable to formulate the words. His mind seemed strangely empty and he could only watch whilst the old man reached into his bag and took out a very old book, its cover stained brown by turf smoke.

Handing it to Fin he explained, "It's as well to know your past before you go stumbling into the future. You wouldn't want to be stepping on anyone's toes now, would ya?" With a wink and a knowing smile, he thanked Fin once again for the water, stated how glad he was that they had reached an agreement, and turned to leave. Holding up a hand to shade his eyes, Fin wanted to question the man further. *What agreement?* He did not remember talk of any money changing hands. *Other people's toes! What on earth is he talking about?*

He was feeling faint, confused, as if all his energy had been drained out along with the water in that glass. Weakly, he managed to ask, "When will you be bringing the horses around?"

"They'll arrive before the midsummer, and will be leaving before midwinter," the old fellow answered, and continued on his way. Fin watched open-mouthed from the courtyard, asking himself, *Who is this man?* From behind he appeared a much more sprightly soul, seemingly becoming taller and taking larger strides as he walked away into the distance. Fin squinted in an attempt to focus more clearly, thinking that the strong sun must be playing tricks with his eyes.

"What about hay and food?" he finally managed to summon the energy to shout, fearing the old guy who was now halfway across the field would no longer be able to hear him.

However, the man continued on until he reached the gate, and just as he was about to step into the country lane beyond, he turned and waved before vanishing from sight. Fin looked down at the old book in his hands. *What the hell is this?* Flicking through the aged pages of the thin, pamphlet-like book he had been handed, Fin saw a series of what appeared to be poems or songs, written in Irish and illustrated by a selection of roughly hewn woodcuts. What was he expected to do with this? *Is this my payment for letting out the field?* he asked himself. *What the feck...!* He found himself laughing at the whole bizarre episode. *Crazy old fool! I'll probably never hear from him again!*

Rosa

"Can I call up later? Is that okay with you?" Rosa sounded on edge.

"Of course," replied Fin. "What time can I expect you? It's just that I might be in the woods or by the lake and I might not hear you arriving."

Fin wondered why Rosa's tone had been hushed, and their telephone conversation had felt a little abrupt. However, they had arranged to meet by the stable block at two o'clock, so that Rosa could see if the facility was suitable for her daughter's pony.

Her cheeks looked a little flushed as she stepped out from the family's car and Fin watched as she brushed down her burnt-orange, silky skirt, smiling to himself as she loosened her glossy, brown curls with her hands. She was still not confident about her own appearance, he thought, even after all these years. Since kindergarten, Rosa's beautiful face had intrigued Fin as she stood out from the crowd with her exotic looks. However, he also remembered the taunts and jibes from the other kids, all of which had served to make her feel like an outsider in her home village. Her brother, Liam, had experienced less of the bullying as he had taken matters into his own hands, resolving the issues with his fists on more than one occasion. However, it was different for girls. Rosa's confidence had been chipped away, insult by insult, the constant references to her olive complexion forced her to hide her face despite her desire to blend in, until she learned that to be not seen or heard was the safest option. As a result, she had passed many an hour hidden away in the pub's kitchen, learning her mother's vast array of culinary skills and was able to produce many authentic Italian recipes. Fin had enjoyed many an evening at the kitchen table with Rosa, studying science or history, and being comforted with a bowl of pasta carbonara or a slice of garlic ciabatta.

"Hello! And welcome," he gestured, stepping out of the shadow of the stable block.

Rosa smiled and looked around before commenting, "I haven't been here for years. You've transformed the old place!"

"Yes, these are the new stables," he explained. "They are built on the site of the old block, but as you can see there is much more room inside for storage. I've secured the field behind so the animals can graze, and there's more land to be used in the field below, if it's needed."

Rosa gazed around with an air of admiration. "It's so much cleaner and organized than our old place," she sighed.

"Yes, but yours is a working farm," Fin was quick to placate her. "This place will change quickly with the passage of hooves and muddy boots, I'm sure."

Keen to show her around, Fin asked if she would like to see what he had done with the great barn and the restored farmhouse. Rosa obliged by accompanying him on a tour of the buildings fronting onto the courtyard, consistently complimenting him on the transformation he had effected.

"And where do you live?" She looked straight into Fin's eyes as they stepped back into the courtyard.

He indicated the small cottage which stood alongside the great barn. "It still needs work," he explained, somewhat apologetically, "but it's habitable, for me at least, for the moment." There was an awkward silence before they both started to speak again at the same moment.

"Would you..?"

"Could I...?"

Neither finished their sentence in respect of allowing the other to speak, and so Fin motioned with his head in the direction of the cottage, before walking off towards the small wooden door at the entrance. Rosa followed close behind. Both felt their pulses racing; hers with excitement, his more out of apprehension. Rosa had found her marriage stifling of late, and the future was looking uncertain. With the deteriorating health of her mother always on her mind and the future of the family pub to consider, she sensed change in the air and was welcoming it. Life in this rural backwater had left her with a sense of disappointment and great frustration as she was tired of having to renounce her own desires to forever please someone else. Perhaps this was her time, she thought.

Fin had felt the pleasant stirrings of youthful memories on first meeting up with her again. Although he knew that what had passed between them could not be conjured back into existence; too much time had passed and too many other people stood in the space between them. As they stepped into the open-plan lounge of the cottage Rosa looked around, noting the stained, curved, wooden staircase opening onto the untreated floorboards, running up to a large, open fireplace. Fin had yet to properly furnish the place, and was using pieces of his parent's old painted furniture until he could acquire his own. Rosa imagined how the place could look, with the magic of a woman's touch.

"It only has two rooms downstairs," he explained, opening an oak door to reveal a newly fitted oak kitchen which ran the length of the cottage and had a large table placed in the centre of the room. Another fireplace contained a log-burning stove and the pretty window positioned over the sink allowed a view into the small, private, walled garden to the rear of the cottage.

"Do you remember playing hide-and-seek in the garden?" Rosa asked, turning to look out the window at the ivy-clad stone walls, two blossom-filled apple trees, and the old weeping willow. Fin smiled as he recalled the happy childhood memories.

"Liam was so infuriated when he finally found us both there, hidden behind the apple tree, he stomped off home in a temper and I had a right telling off from Ma." Rosa laughed. "We were only young; it was all so innocent. But neither Liam nor Cillian would see it that way."

It was true. At that age, their friendship was marked by innocent childhood pastimes. However, the time spent together continued well into adolescence and both families looked on as Fin and Rosa became closer. To the couple, it was a natural progression. They had always spent many hours in the company of each other and were a little bemused by the change of attitude towards them. However, as they entered secondary school, it was Rosa who had initiated romance into their friendship. A somewhat bemused Fin had finally accorded by consummating their romance in the forest at the foot of the farmstead, late one summer afternoon, when they were sure that the family were busy harvesting the hay. Although the fear of discovery, or unplanned pregnancy, had plagued the young couple who were living in a predominantly Catholic community, the desire to be together was greater and their relationship continued into their late teenage years. Fin's cheeks flushed now at the memories and wondered if the same thoughts were going through Rosa's mind. His intuition was correct. Rosa still had her back to him and was leaning over the sink, with her chin in her hands and her elbows resting on the windowsill. Fin couldn't help but feel attracted by the soft curve of her body. Rosa knew his eyes were firmly fixed on her posterior and an awkward silence ensued, until she released the tension. Turning around to look straight at him, and with a wry smile on her face, she asked, "So, Fin Byrne, who are you playing with in the garden, these days?"

Fin floundered. He wanted to say there was someone, but suddenly he was not so sure. Katherine had not responded to any of his messages or returned any calls. Face to face with his childhood sweetheart, he found his memories of Katherine fading fast. Rosa's face was etched in his mind: a fixed image, becoming animated with new life. He warmed to the familiarity of her beautiful face, her dark eyes now speaking with the life experience gained during the twenty years which had passed since they were last together.

"I'm here on my own," he replied. Rosa glowed as she walked towards him.

"And you're married with three children," he added.

Her expression darkened. "Yes, I'm married with three children and have a husband who shows no interest in me. When Liam and I inherit the family pub we are going to run it together, despite what Jack thinks. I've been at home too long. The kids are old enough now. They don't need me around all the time. I've got plans for that business." Rosa took Fin's hand and led him to the foot of the stairs. "Are you going to show me upstairs?" she asked. Fin hesitated and her expression softened. "If it's a problem…" she started to say.

"No, no problem," he replied. "There's just not much to see: the bathroom and one bedroom."

Rosa stood her ground, gazing up at him from beneath her beautifully arched brows, and so Fin gestured an invitation for her to walk up the stairs in front of him. Passing the open door to the bathroom she walked straight into the sparsely furnished bedroom. As she looked around, Fin hurriedly retrieved some discarded clothes from a chair placed next to the bed.

However, Rosa had no intention of sitting on the chair. "So, this is where your grandparents slept?" she asked, walking towards the end of the bed.

"Yes. When Cillian and I came along they swapped homes with my parents, allowing them the use of the space of the farmhouse whilst they lived here."

"And now there's only you?" Rosa asked once more.

"Well, there's Cillian in the States, of course. He's married, with children."

"Yes, he keeps in touch with Liam," Rosa said.

"I had no idea!" exclaimed Fin, who only heard intermittently from his elder brother.

"Yes, he's kept his ties," Rosa noted. "He and Liam speak a couple of times a year. Liam keeps saying he will go over to the States to visit, someday."

"Has Cillian been here since my parents' funerals?" Fin asked.

"No, not to my knowledge," came the reply. "So, Fin, all these years and you've never married?" Rosa sat herself on the end of the old, wooden bed.

"No, no marriage for me." Fin delivered his answer in a light-hearted joking tone, in the hope of diverting the direction of the conversation. "No kids either!" However, he knew that his efforts were in vain. Rosa was determined to find out if there was a romantic interest in his life.

"So, how have you managed to escape the clutches of holy matrimony for so long?" she asked, joining in the joke.

Fin shrugged and apologetically offered a half-baked explanation, "Mainly due to work commitments, I'd say."

Rosa knew she wasn't going to get any further with her enquiries and changed tack. "So this farm renovation is a solo project?"

"Yes," Fin confirmed. "Of course, both Cillian and I inherited equal shares in the farm but he made it quite clear that he had no interest in the old place. He's washed his hands of the farm. I started work on it the year after Ma's funeral. I wasn't sure how it would turn out. I guess I was thinking of renovating it to make it more saleable. My life, my work, was in England at that time. It's only the last couple of years that I thought of coming back here to live. That's when all of the business ideas started occurring to me, and here I am."

"Well, I'm glad you're back," Rosa said. "It's really great to see you again, Fin."

Standing up, she took a few steps towards Fin and threw her arms around his neck, nestling her cheek into his shoulder. Unsure of how to respond, Fin stood somewhat stiffly with his arms at his sides.

"Seeing you again brought back so many memories," she continued, whispering her words into the curve of his collar bone. "Do you remember how happy we were? I know we were only kids, but we were so close." Fin felt her warm breath and the moisture of her soft lips as she kissed his neck. "As soon as I saw you over the bar, Fin, all my feelings for you came flooding back."

Fin's arms were around Rosa now, and his lips were touching hers. He felt a shock of pleasure at their sweet, moist softness and his body reacted by pulling hers harder against him. Rosa let out a low moan of pleasure and explored his mouth with her tongue. Fin's hands moved to her lower back and drew her in closer. He could feel the cushion of her breasts against his chest and his hands traced the curve of her buttocks, slightly lifting her silk skirt with each circular motion. Rosa's tongue became more insistent, demanding, and he felt as if he was starting to lose control of himself.

A sense of helplessness washed over him and he closed his eyes; she dropped her arms from around his neck to tackle the fastening of his jeans. He was telling himself she was a married woman; she was his past, not his future. However, the thoughts weren't communicating with the further extremities of his body.

Then it was his turn to moan as Rosa slipped her hand inside his shorts and gently rubbed his firmness. Fin grasped her breast, his fingertips seeking out her nipple, which firmed immediately at his touch. With one hand still stroking his penis, Rosa opened her blouse to reveal both breasts through a sheer, pink balconette bra, and placed her hand on the back of his head to encourage him to free her erect nipple with his tongue. Rosa's moves were confident and Fin reacted eagerly at first. But as her movements became more bold and her desire more urgent, Fin started to feel as if he was the submissive partner. Losing control was not a comfortable feeling for him; he sensed some danger and sought to restore the equilibrium of energy between them.

His mind wandered back to the woods, on that summer afternoon where they had first made love. It had happened spontaneously and he could not recall any sense of urgency, only the sensation of something so new and pleasurable, the secrecy fuelling to the excitement.

However, Fin was not feeling the same pleasure, just a demanding urgency on Rosa's part. As she dropped to her knees in front of him, he knew he did not want things to go any further. Her sweetness was turning a little sour and with every action she was making, in his mind, he was pulling further away. The feel of her tongue on his manhood felt like an electric shock that travelled up his spine, leaving a cold trace and piercing his clouded mind. Pushing her head gently away, he said, "Rosa! No, we can't do this!"

Ignoring his protestation, Rosa pulled him back towards her and tugged at his jeans and shorts, in an attempt to render him bare.

"No, this is wrong!" he exclaimed, grappling defensively with his clothes.

"Shh!" said Rosa. "Just enjoy!" Convinced he was just being a little bashful, she was intent on being successful with her endeavours. "I don't love my husband. I love you. I've always loved you," she said reassuringly.

Fin was now torn. This wasn't how he remembered Rosa. He couldn't deny the attraction, but there was no sense of familiarity once he had got past her beautiful smile and the lilt of her voice. She was different now. She was a stranger to him. The other women he had been intimate with over the years had relegated his memory of Rosa to that of an innocent young girl at the time of his life when he had been an innocent boy. That moment had long passed, and it felt wrong to Fin to pretend otherwise. Neither of them was still innocent, or young. Grasping her firmly by her upper arms, he forced her to stand on her feet.

"I can't do this now," he said, looking apologetically into her downcast face.

Rosa's long, silky, brown locks were partially covering her face and as he tried to gently push them aside she shook herself loose from his grip.

"Who is she?" Rosa asked, her eyes flashing angrily at the rejection as she wiped her sleeve across her mouth.

An image of Katherine flashed into Fin's mind. "There's no one…probably. But there might be," he responded, aware of how confused he sounded. However, he was seeing quite clearly and it was the face of Katherine Walsh that was foremost in his mind's eye.

Edge walking

Fin had been back at the farmstead for two weeks and he had not heard a word from Katherine, despite his numerous jokey texts and voicemail invitations. He was fast running out of novel ways to basically say the same thing: '*Please call me, I want to see you again.*' However, he had no idea where she was or what she was doing. In a moment of desperation, he had phoned the retreat house in Wales to ask if they could pass on a message to her, only to learn that she had left the island the previous week. *She could be anywhere.* Although Fin realized that he knew very little about her, there was still some part of him which felt, quite paradoxically, greatly comforted and very excited when he closed his eyes and thought of her. However, unless, or until, she contacted him he was powerless to do anything else except to continue with his farm project.

Summer was now beginning to unfurl its longer, lighter evenings in the mountains and he was spending more time about the farm. The boggy patches of land around the lake were drying up and he decided that a wooden walkway was needed, so the periphery of the lake could be accessible all year round. If he wanted to encourage springtime fishing breaks at the lake, then it would be necessary to provide better facilities. The mountain spring which gently eased its way out from between the rocks at the top of the farmstead flowed furiously during heavy rains, providing a generous source of fresh mountain water for the lake. Fin had spent two summers clearing the lake of much of the stranglehold of weeds which had taken root, and now he was seeing lilies appearing on the surface of the pond. The area was rife with frogs and water boatmen so he felt confident that the ecological balance of the water life was being restored. He learned that largely due to the waterways of Ireland being geographically isolated during the last ice age, the range of naturally occurring types of freshwater fish were largely limited to char, eels, brown trout and salmon. Although other species such as perch and bream had been introduced over the years, pike and salmon were still the fishermen's favourites. He was keen to replenish the stock in his lake. However, he was not interested in competition fishing, Fin wanted to provide his holiday guests with both a source of entertainment and a high-quality, country-living experience. He would start by creating a walkway with lakeside seating areas for fishermen.

After sketching a plan for the design, he estimated how much timber would be needed and ordered a delivery of materials. It was time for some good old-fashioned labouring! The work would occupy his mind and help him channel his energy. Fin knew and loved the sense of satisfaction he felt upon completion of a job. He was willing to try most skills, although he was also happy to defer to expert knowledge when he realized the need. He had spent some of his winter evenings in woodwork classes where he had learned basic joinery techniques. However, the timber supplier pointed him in the direction of a local carpenter who was happy to assist him with the project. It was now mid-June and the fine weather conspired with the longer days to help him make great progress with his water's edge walkway. Fin was finally starting to feel that he was mastering his challenges.

It was late one evening whilst he was on his hands and knees, nailing the few remaining timbers into place, when his mobile phone suddenly vibrated on the wooden bench behind him. The signal on this part of the farm was intermittent so Fin was surprised to hear it. At the initial thought that it might be Katherine returning one of his many messages, he jumped to his feet. However, stepping closer to the phone he hesitated, wondering if it might be Rosa calling again. He had been avoiding her calls. As he looked at the display, a faint recognition of the number flickered through his mind, and sheer curiosity caused him to answer.

"Fin...?" It was Cillian's voice.

"Yes it's Fin, who....?"

"It's me, Cillian." Then there was silence. "Where are you?" he asked.

"At home, in Ireland," Fin explained. "Where are you?" He wondered if his brother was in the country.

"Oh, I'm at home, upstate," answered Cillian, who lived on the banks of the Hudson River, a few hours' drive from New York. Fin felt suspicious as to his reason for calling. It had been a while since they had last spoken.

"I'm just wondering how the work on the old place is going." Cillian's comment answered his question.

"It's going well," Fin responded warily. *Why is he asking now, after all these years?*

"So when will it be ready to market?"

Fin, feeling as if a heavy blow had been delivered to his chest, was unable to respond immediately.

"Fin? Have you advertised the place for sale?" Cillian was insistent. "We did agree to sell..."

Fin squeezed out his response, "That's not how I remember it..."

"What do you mean? You don't remember that we agreed to sell?" Cillian's tone became harsh and menacing.

"We talked about selling, and you decided that the old place wasn't worth anything." Fin spoke slowly and surely.

"Yes, that's why you started work on the old place, right?" Cillian's tone softened a little.

"No, I've poured my life savings and my soul into this place. I've renovated and restored it, and I've created a business," Fin replied. "It's not for sale."

He was not sure if the signal had failed or his brother had hung up, but the line went dead.

Fin's head was spinning. *Why now? Seven years on?* Cillian had been quite clear at the funeral: he wanted nothing to do with the farm or the land. Well, if he thought Fin had toiled over the years just to sell the property now and pocket the profit, he would have a fight on his hands. Fin would never have a good rate of return on his investment if they sold now. He acknowledged that Cillian legally owned half the property but Fin had been hoping to buy his share once the business had turned a profit. This was his home, and soon to be his livelihood. It simply was not for sale.

Gathering his tools, Fin made his way back to the cottage, checking his phone for more calls or messages. However, he sat in silence for the remainder of the evening, his mind raging with angry thoughts and words for his brother. *How dare he!* He resisted calling back. He would need to gather his thoughts before he had another conversation with Cillian.

An early morning rise followed a restless night for Fin. In the cold and lonely early hours, he started to doubt himself. What if this was just a pipedream? Had he got it wrong? Did he really think his brother would not be interested in his share of the family inheritance?

Fin had no intention of taking any more than was rightfully his. However, perhaps he had been a bit naïve in believing his brother would never call in his share. Fin had every intention of giving Cillian his half, as soon as he could raise the cash. However, if he insisted on calling it in now, all of Fin's efforts would have been in vain. Even if they could find a buyer for the land, all of the work that Fin had put into developing the place into a viable business would be wasted. He was woken at dawn by a text from his brother simply stating: *'I'm catching an early morning flight.'*

Glancing at the time, he worked out that it must be about midnight in New York. An Internet search informed him that the first flight out was scheduled at five a.m. from Newark. Good! The time difference gave Fin a head start. He would head into Dublin and seek out some legal advice. He needed to know what he could do, if anything, to safeguard his future. Following a couple of timely calls, he was able to secure an appointment at Kelly and Sons in Dame Street, and by midmorning he was walking towards Temple Bar. The practitioner, whose online profile stated that he was *'experienced in resolving probate disputes between beneficiaries of family estates,'* was an old-school lawyer sporting tired pinstripes with braces. He lifted his chin and looked over the top of his spectacles at Fin, before reclining into the high back of his well-worn, leather chair. With his steely eyes firmly fixed on Fin, he asked, "So, the actual will is with the family solicitor in Wicklow town, you say?"

His deeply furrowed forehead suggested displeasure.

However, his words were delivered slowly and in a pleasant tone. Fin explained the provisions of the document, but it was clear that the lawyer wanted to see it for himself.

"The principles of the 1965 Succession Act are clear," he explained, "but I would need to read the terms of the will itself."

Fin explained that Cillian had, in effect, renounced his executorship in relation to the grant of probate required to prove the will. He had stated that, due to the fact he lived on the other side of the Atlantic Ocean, it was impractical for him to be involved in the business, leaving it all up to Fin. As far as he knew, no further action had been taken nor had an Assent been drafted which would have been required to transfer the ownership of the property into the brothers' names. Essentially, all Fin wanted to know was if his brother could now force a sale some seven years later. Rather apologetically, Mr Kelly was unable to provide reassurance against such action and suggested that Fin make further enquires of the Wicklow solicitors. It was with a heavy heart that Fin made his way towards the River Liffey and trudged along Wellington Quay, cutting a sad and lonely figure amidst the fast flow of the river and the city bustle. He stopped and turned away from the grey smudge of suits walking briskly past to stare into the grey rush of the waters below him.

Taking out his phone, he called Keenan and Quinn in Wicklow Town. They had dealt with the Byrne family's legal matters for as long as Fin could remember. The elderly receptionist informed him that Frank Keenan was not available and asked if he wished to make an appointment. When Fin confirmed his name, the friendly lady commented that she had been very pleasantly surprised to have already spoken with his brother calling long distance from the United States.

"Cillian has booked you an appointment for tomorrow afternoon," she stated, in the mistaken belief that they would be attending together. "We shall see you both at 4:30!"

However, Fin knew that Cillian had intended to speak alone

with the solicitor. He now realized that his brother was serious about selling the farm. Chiding himself for his naivety, he wondered, *Why did I think I would be left alone to follow my dream? Life just isn't like that, people aren't like that.*

He had spent the previous two weeks believing that he had escaped the rat race, only to have caught his foot squarely in a trap laid by his own brother. Driving home into the mountains, Fin was distracted with the 'hows', 'whys' and 'what ifs' of the situation. Why had Cillian decided to get involved now, seven years on? How did he know Fin was back in Ireland, and why did he want to sell the farm now? Had he heard about the renovation work? If so, who had told him?

As he drove past Doyle's he was reminded of something Rosa had said that day at the farm; a throwaway comment about Liam and Cillian still being in touch. What if Liam had told Cillian about his plans for the farm? Fin had not spoken to Liam during the previous two weeks. However, he had left some leaflets advertising the farm at the pub, when he had first met up with Rosa. An uncomfortable feeling welled up in the pit of his stomach. What if Rosa had asked Liam to call Cillian out of revenge? He had rejected her advances, she was married, and it just hadn't felt right. But surely she hadn't taken it that badly? Fin's foot hit the brake and he pulled off the road onto a grass verge. There was only one way to find out. Turning around the jeep, he headed back towards the pub.

Old Wounds, New Salt

Rosa looked up as Fin strode into the bar. His stance informed her he was not just calling in for a quiet pint or two.

"Rosa, can I have a word?"

She looked straight past him with a bored expression on her face. He tried another tack. "Rosa, is Liam around?"

"He's in Dublin," she replied coldly.

"Oh, how is your ma?" Fin enquired respectfully, on recalling that Drina Doyle had been in hospital in the city.

"Ma's quite comfortable, thanks for asking," Rosa said with a smirk. "She's in bed, came home from hospital yesterday. Liam's picking up a friend from the airport." Fin knew she was referring to Cillian. So his suspicions were correct! It was Liam who had contacted Cillian and informed him as to Fin's progress and plans for the farm.

"Why, Rosa?" he asked. "Why did Liam feel the need to contact my brother, behind my back and inform him about my work on the farm?"

Rosa slowly finished pulling a pint of stout and placed it on the bar beside Fin before answering his question.

"Well, why don't you ask him yourself?" She nodded towards the entrance as she spoke. Fin turned to see Liam entering the pub, holding the door open for a jaded Cillian who stepped in behind him.

"Hello, Cillian! Come on in and take the weight off your feet. How was the flight? I'm sure you are keen to see your bed! Your room is ready for you." Rosa's disingenuous greeting grated on Fin. He knew there was little love lost between them.

When Liam saw Fin he bellowed, "What the hell is *he* doing here? Go across yourself, Fintan Byrne!"

Fin was stunned. He had met with Liam, albeit fleetingly, over the previous years on visits to the hills, at weddings and wakes, and he had never behaved this way. They had always traded pleasantries, not insults. What had changed? What was this all about? Shocked and confused, he looked questioningly at Rosa.

"You should go," she nodded. Fin looked at Cillian.

"I'll settle my things and call over the farm to see you," Cillian addressed Fin in an awkward manner, as he walked stiffly through the bar, with his overnight case in hand.

Fin was anxiously clock watching. If Cillian didn't turn up soon, he might as well go to bed himself. He reasoned that the jetlag might have got a grip on his brother, in which case he would not see him until the following evening. However, Cillian was anything but tired. Hearing the displacement of gravel by tyres on his driveway just before midnight, Fin knew there was only one likely caller. He just hoped that he would be alone. Cillian saw his younger brother standing in the open doorway to the cottage. Approaching, face to face, the elder brother spoke first. Always wanting to appear reasonable, Cillian smiled and gestured with open palms.

"Fin, I don't want any trouble. Can we talk about this?"

However, Fin had learned that when his brother flashed that smile, there was trouble brewing. He was reasonable, until he was denied his own way with circumstances and people. Then things would get ugly. It was all or nothing with Cillian who, more often than not, had achieved most of the goals he had framed for himself in life. However, he had never quite conquered the free will of his younger brother. Cillian harboured jealousy of his younger brother's happy nature. As the eldest, he was the serious son of the family. Hard on himself, he also sought to inflict his relentless drive on others around him. Happy to glory in his own success at forging a new life in the US, he still felt an irrational sense of failure when Fin triumphed closer to home in the UK. Cillian felt it unfair that Fin's achievements were not as hard won as his own. And now he felt as if the family home was to be unfairly taken away from him too.

"I'm sure we can come to a fair arrangement," he stated, sensing Fin's resistance.

Fin stepped back to allow him to enter the cottage. Cillian looked around, failing to comment on what he saw.

"Fin, things are different now." He was trying a different tack. "The global economy was very different seven years ago. My business was thriving. It's not so good now and since Maria and I divorced, well, she took a big chunk of my assets. I only want what I'm entitled to."

Fin was shocked. He had no idea that Cillian's marriage had fallen apart. Suddenly the gulf between them widened further. Fin realized he actually knew very little about his brother. What would their parents think? Their mother had always tried desperately to ensure that the two got along, despite the overt sibling rivalry. A knot of guilt constricted him at his core. Looking at Cillian, Fin could see the strain in his expression and felt the tension increase between them.

"Give me some time. I'm just about ready to launch the business," Fin implored. "I've spent so much time laying the foundations for this business. It just needs the chance to succeed. A couple of good seasons and I will be able to buy your share of the farm."

"I can get a court to order the sale immediately," warned Cillian.

"Can't you just give me a chance? I'll pay you half of the full market value. It will be worth much more as a going concern," Fin pleaded to his brother's business sense.

Cillian was torn. "But you don't belong here," he said through gritted teeth.

"What on earth are you on about?" Fin was confused. "I was born here! I've spent the last seven years working on this place."

"You're not welcome here any longer," said Cillian. Fin felt an uncomfortable lurch in his stomach.

"Who said I'm not welcome?" he asked with loud deliberation.

"We never though you would come back," said Cillian. "The Doyles thought you would be selling up and staying in England. They don't want you here."

"Who...Liam, or Rosa?" asked Fin.

"They both want you out of here," was the reply.

"Well, I'm not so sure Rosa would agree with you on that!" Fin retorted with a wry smile.

Immediately he was transported to another dimension where

events played out in slow motion. Cillian's face had turned a deep shade of crimson and his clenched fist appeared to grow larger as it loomed large in Fin's face. The heavy punch floored him, his head hitting the wooden floor beneath their feet and he blacked out. A few minutes later, Fin found himself lying on his back, looking up at the ceiling through blurred vision. Slowly returning to his senses, he could feel a dull ache emanating from his right cheekbone and could hear his brother's voice, but as he tried to speak he felt pain shoot into the back of his skull. Sitting up in slow motion, he raised his hand to wipe the blood that had started dripping from his nose. He looked up at Cillian in utter confusion.

"That's for Rosa," followed the explanation.

Fin tried to ask what he meant, but he couldn't form the words, his coordination was still impaired. He tried hard to focus on his brother's face and realized the reason for his shrinking range of vision was due to a fast-swelling eye. Cillian looked closely at his brother. Now he was in shock. Why hadn't Fin put up a fight? He just hadn't seen it coming.

"You didn't know, did you?" Suddenly, the picture was becoming clear to him.

"You had no idea of the mess you left behind? Did you? Oh my God, Fin!" Cillian bent over and helped his stunned brother to his feet. "It's about Rosa. She was three months' pregnant when you called it off with her. Liam wanted to come to England to smash your face in..." Cillian became acutely aware that he had unwittingly carried out Liam's wishes, albeit some 25 years later. Again Fin tried to speak, but the pain prevented the words and he could only shake his head.

"You never knew!" Cillian realized Fin had no idea of what had happened after he had left the hills for university life in the UK.

"So no one told you? Not Rosa? Not Liam?" Again Fin shook his head in response. "Jaysus! Liam said you knew and that you turned your back on her."

Fin was struggling to make sense of what he was seeing and hearing. Cillian led him through the open door to the kitchen and sat him at the table. Then he went to the sink and filled a glass from the drainer with water. He looked around and finding some kitchen paper he placed both on the table in front of his brother.

"Here..." He wiped the blood from Fin's face and pushed the glass of water towards him. "So you never knew Rosa was pregnant? And so Liam was lying to me? I was so pissed off with you! I thought you knew and didn't give a toss."

Fin was now in a dull fog. A deep throb had taken over the right side of his face and head but his comprehension was clearing. "Liam told me that Rosa didn't want anything to do with me," he explained slowly, painfully. "He wouldn't let me speak to her on the phone and she never returned my calls. I never knew about the baby..." The words conveyed his sadness. "If I had known...I would have come back, or taken her with me. I would never have just left her." Fin had a new pain, one deep in the pit of his stomach. It was a sense of emptiness, of sadness, of loss. Then his mind sprang forward into action as he thought of the children who had accompanied Rosa and Jack to the Byrne family funerals. Fin frowned in confusion as he tried to work out which child was his.

"Was it...did she...?" he managed, eventually.

It was Cillian's turn to shake his head. "There was no child. Liam made sure of that. He arranged for her to visit an abortion clinic. Old man Doyle and his missus never knew. Liam and I kept it between us. We had no choice, all those years ago."

Fin was now starting to piece together the puzzle. All these years had passed with such allegations being whispered, unbeknown to him, behind his back. Fin felt sickened and he retched. Cillian reached for a bowl that was placed in the middle of the table and placed it under his brother's chin. When he was done, Fin asked, "Why didn't *you* say something to me?"

Panicked by the sight and smell of vomit and overcome with guilt about his actions, Cillian asked if he should call the doctor. Fin reassured him that he would be fine, but he would be happier if the Doyles knew the truth, or in the very least he wanted Rosa to know the truth. He had never abandoned her or their unborn child. It was Liam's misguided machinations that had led to their separation and her pain. Fin wondered why Liam had chosen to make it that way. As he voiced his concerns, Cillian's actions became manic.

"Let me take you to the hospital. You hit your head when you fell. You blacked out. You need to see a doctor. Let me get you some treatment. You could have concussion."

Gingerly, Fin shook his head and checked to see if the nasal blood flow had been stemmed. "I'm okay. I just need some ice for my eye. Could you could get some from the freezer and wrap it in a cloth?" he asked Cillian. The estranged brothers sat at the kitchen table, facing each other; both wondering how the hell things had come to this.

"I don't understand *why*," Fin started the conversation. "Why you never said anything to me about this?"

Cillian fumbled over his words, before offering up a poor explanation. "You were away at university and Liam told me you refused to come home and asked for my help. What could I do? I couldn't let Ma know. We didn't want anyone to know. I was left to clear up your mess. Liam asked me, how could I refuse?"

"And you believed him? Why would you choose to believe him without even checking it out with me?" Fin asked.

There was silence. The question echoed around the minds of both brothers. *He wanted to believe it.* The realization suddenly dawned on Fin. His brother had wanted it to be true. It was that old sibling rivalry spilling over into adulthood, and he was sure that Cillian still felt the same way towards him now despite them both heading for middle age. He had always jibed Fin for being a mammy's boy. It was all just an expression of his jealousy, the resentment he felt towards his younger brother for just existing.

Fin got up and started rooting around in the kitchen drawers for some pills to kill the pain in his face. Cillian continued to sit in a subdued silence. Nothing he could say could justify his behaviour. He felt the strong discomfort of defeat. Shaking, Fin left him in the kitchen as his search for medication took him to the bathroom upstairs, where he thought a cool shower might help soothe his burning face.

As he stepped into the bathroom he heard Cillian's voice from the foot of the stairs, "Do you have any Bushmills?" Fin told his brother to help himself to the bottle in the cupboard, before becoming immersed in the cool, refreshing spray of the shower.

The Truth in the Trees

Fin woke around five a.m. when the sun crept in through the curtain-less bedroom window. At first he was unsure as to the events of the previous evening, and he was not sure how he came to be on the bed. However, he was soon reminded, courtesy of the return of the painful throb to the right side of his head. He listened, but could hear no sign of movement from the kitchen below where he had left his brother a few hours ago. Rising too quickly to his feet, Fin was stopped in his tracks by the pounding in his skull. It felt as if he had drunk a whole bottle of whiskey.

He trod tentatively to open the bedroom window to breathe in some fresh morning air and saw Cillian's car still on the drive. Fin thought he must have fallen asleep where he left him at the kitchen table. He struggled into the bathroom to take more painkillers and lay back down on the bed, thinking that he would let his brother sleep off the booze and speak with him later on that morning. Cillian had to tell Liam and Rosa the truth. It needed to come from him, and then perhaps if Rosa wanted to talk about it Fin would be up for a conversation with her. However, with Liam, it was a different story. He needed more time to work out how to deal with him.

Fin was woken up around lunchtime by the scrape of tyres leaving the gravel driveway of the farm. Cillian had gone. He had left without another word. Fin knew he wouldn't be back, at least not for a long while. He felt saddened at the thought of his brother stuck in the same old cycle of resentment and discontent. However, he recognized that it was all of his own making. One day he might finally face up to the fact that it was not always someone else at fault and start taking responsibility for his own life. However, Fin's mind was full of his own conflicting thoughts. The shock revelations about Rosa and her pregnancy were reverberating wildly within his psyche. He could have been a father, for all these years, without knowing; or perhaps it would have been different if Rosa had told him about the pregnancy. Fin mulled over the many possibilities. His life could so easily have changed course as a result of one event. Looking back, he could see how tenuous it all really was; how one decision could cause waves and ripples in so many other lives. He reasoned that in a twisted way, Liam was probably trying to protect his sister. He could see no other reason for him acting the way he had. However, it did make Fin feel a little paranoid at what other people around the area might think of him. What other lies had been spread around about him during his absence from his homeland? Well, he was back here to stay for as long as he could make a success of the business and he would do whatever he could to make good with the Doyles. He now viewed Rosa in a very different light. Perhaps he had come back for a reason...Rosa had said she still loved him, Fin, despite being married to Jack, he thought to himself as he examined his facial injuries in the bathroom mirror.

To escape the ruminations of his mind, Fin cleaned up his face, put on his working clothes and headed down to the woods. Just as he always had, from childhood, he found great peace amongst the trees. Maybe it was the oxygenated atmosphere, but he found he was able to breathe more easily and the fog started to clear from his mind. Amidst the peace he was able to focus on his latest project. Using the timber that was left over from the lakeside walkway he started to build a tree house in the branches of the grand sessile oak, where he and Cillian had played during their childhood. Fin realized that whereas he could not control the events of the past or the lives of those around him, he could be responsible for creating his own future. He just needed to go back into his past to be the person he had always been, without questioning his own motives or second guessing his own choices. He was here, now, for a reason and he had plans that would help him move forward. Regardless of whatever else might happen around him from now on, he believed he would be okay as long as he remained true to his roots.

Week Six

Face Off

Katherine and Henry had fallen into a routine. He was quietly getting back to work, refusing to acknowledge any signs of fallout from his sexual indiscretions. She was delving deeper into the practicalities of pregnancy and the meaning of motherhood, still experiencing great ambivalence and uncertainty about her situation.

She found that the best way to deal with the daily nausea was to eat more often, eschewing large meals for regular snacks. As she felt obliged to make more traditional dinners for Henry each evening, she experimented with new recipes during the day, in-between naps. It was whilst she was chopping up some ginger root, and watching the breeze-brushed roses through the open kitchen window that she saw a woman approaching the door to Henry's garden flat. Noting the contempt with which she flicked the gate closed behind her, Katherine sensed this visitor was not calling in for a friendly chat. The abrupt rap of clenched knuckles on the door confirmed her supposition.

A young woman in her early twenties, with a shock of blonde tresses, stood on the step, her otherwise pretty features set to a snarl, which quickly disappeared when she saw Katherine.

"Oh, I'm looking for Henry," she said, glancing away in the direction of the rose bushes.

"Henry's not here," Katherine replied. "Can I take a message for him?"

The pale, blonde girl looked past Katherine and into the hallway of the flat.

Stepping back, Katherine asked, "Do you want to come in? Henry's not going to be back until this evening, he's got a late afternoon lecture scheduled."

The young woman looked Katherine up and down before raising her chin as she spoke, "I just wanted to let him know that his little mistake will be sorted out, I can make it go away, but he will have to pay for it." Katherine could see her lips tensing, as if to add, 'and it's not up for discussion'. She noted the tired look in the girl's eyes and sensed her underlying distress.

"And your name is?" Katherine didn't really need to ask.

"Just give him that message. He'll understand," the girl snapped.

Katherine wanted to say something, but she dared not divulge the fact that she knew about the girl and about 'Henry's little mistake' as she risked hurting her. Henry's actions had already humiliated her when he callously dismissed her claim that he was the father of her unborn child. And how would she feel if Katherine were to tell her that she carried a sibling? It could so easily have been Katherine on the doorstep, some nine years previously. Her own belief in Henry's proclaimed support for her slipped and she felt vulnerable. The girl's hostility and rage were palpable but Katherine was quick to notice the slight bulge of her abdomen on her small frame. Subconsciously the young woman pulled together the sides of her grey linen jacket and tied the loose belt.

"Tell Henry that I'll be in touch, shortly," she said, and with a defiant toss of her head she flounced off back towards the gate, her cockiness faltering only when she failed on the first attempt to replace the latch.

Katherine watched as she walked away. She looked so young and Katherine sensed how small and powerless she actually felt, despite the big attitude.

At dinner, Katherine waited while Henry poured himself a glass of dry Muscat wine to drink with the tuna Nicoise salad before announcing, "*She* came here today."

"Who?" Henry asked nonchalantly.

"She's having an abortion, Henry, and she wants you to pay for it," Katherine said.

Henry flipped; his eyes widened and his voice rose to a shout. "She's only interested in the money! How much more will she try to milk from me before she moves on the next unfortunate fucker?" Henry rarely swore. Katherine realized that he was greatly angered. "Well, if it means she'll finally leave me alone, I'll be more than happy to pay," he growled. "What a joke! I'm told not to approach her for any reason and she has the cheek to show up here, at my home."

Henry took up his wine and wandered into the lounge, consumed with his raging thoughts. Katherine ate in silence, trying to get her head around his willingness to write a cheque to pay to extinguish the life of his own child. She was chilled by his cold disdain but even more disturbing was the thought that the young mother could destroy her own child. Suddenly there was something else rising to the surface of her awareness: a consuming guilt about her ambivalence towards her own pregnancy. She had been putting on a brave face, telling herself that the situation would resolve itself shortly. However, the visit from the young girl had made her thankful that she wished to go ahead with her own pregnancy. She knew in her soul that she had made the right choice.

Heartfelt

Katherine had slept for only a few hours. Not sure whether her light-headedness was down to lack of sleep or excitement, she was happy to remain quietly sitting in the hospital waiting room, sipping bottled water. She was scheduled for an ultrasound scan at 09:50 and she found herself blinking to erase from her mind the memory of the gut-wrenching black hole from the previous scan.

Finally, the sonographer appeared. "Ready, then?" she smiled. Katherine watched the black and white pattern of dots on the screen.

"Of course, it won't resemble anything like a baby at this stage. This pulse here, this is her heartbeat," explained the sonographer.

"Her?"

"Just a figure of speech, I'm afraid," the sonographer replied. "It's much too early to determine the sex. That won't even be decided for a few more weeks. But you will be able to see when you have the next scan."

"So you think this baby is going to live?" Katherine asked tentatively.

"At this stage in non-subsisting pregnancies, we usually see an empty amniotic sac floating about. Here we can see a lively little figure."

"What about the blood I've lost?" Katherine enquired.

"Ah, here you can see the placenta," explained the sonographer as she moved the sensor lower on Katherine's abdomen. "It's lying low in the uterus, very close to the cervix, and is probably the cause of the bleeding. If the placenta moves higher, as often happens, the bleeding will stop."

"So I'm going to have a baby!" Katherine's own heart seemed to skip a beat. This was now very real to her.

"There are no guarantees," explained the sonographer. "However, everything is looking just as we would expect at this stage."

"Can you tell how many weeks' pregnant I am?" Katherine asked as she peered intently at the screen.

"The general size would suggest you are about six weeks and two, maybe three, days. Do you have any more questions?" Katherine smiled and shook her head as the technician removed the sensor from her abdomen. Sitting up in readiness to get off the bed, she felt a strong head rush. The sonographer noticed her trying to steady herself and advised to sit there for a further few minutes and fetched a cup of water from the cooler.

"How are you feeling now?" she asked as Katherine handed back the empty cup.

"Fine," Katherine replied with a big smile. "Absolutely fine!"

She made another appointment for a routine follow-up scan for ten weeks' time and left the hospital. Walking out into the sunlight, she noticed the tulips dancing in the hospital garden beds. Taking a deep breath, she tasted the sweet, fresh breeze on her tongue and suddenly felt an urge to celebrate. She had stepped safely into new territory and was energized, as if she was walking on a new layer of the world; one which felt softer to the touch and sweet-scented. However, there were thick clouds passing quickly over the sun and she sensed there might be rain. Nevertheless, she spent the rest of the day in the city centre, wandering around department stores full of baby clothes and accessories. She browsed the maternity and motherhood sections of the bookstores and bought herself a large supply of folic acid pills from the health food shop.

And whilst she sat in the coffee shop of a shopping mall sipping a cinnamon latte which had just taken her fancy, she became aware of the sheer number of mothers making their way past her pushing prams or walking about clutching the hands of their toddlers. Quite paradoxically, she felt a weird kind of kinship with, and a concurrent sense of disconnection from, these women. It was as if she was glimpsing a world into which she had not yet been granted permission to enter. As she slowly scraped the milky froth from the edge of the cup with her spoon, Katherine deliberated on her newly discovered horizons. She was now seeing things very differently. She wasn't sure if it was down to the retreat or chemical changes taking place in her body that accounted for the psychological shift, but she was definitely seeing life through a different lens. Her status in life had changed: no longer someone's daughter, wife or girlfriend, she was now a mother-to-be, and the balance of power in her world had shifted. She was the only person who would now chart the course of her own future and that of her child. Watching the other people around her going about their daily routines – shop assistants, waiters, office workers grabbing a quick coffee during a break, delivery men – she pondered the logistics of having to allow for the needs of another person; a little person who would be completely dependent on her. She realized that, from now on, almost every, if not all, aspects of her existence would be permeated with the consideration of his or her needs. Before she began any practical adjustments to her lifestyle she needed firstly to ensure that she had enough room in her mind for two.

Leaving the mall, she chose the 20-minute walk over the bus journey back to the university campus. It gave her time to think about breaking the news to Henry.

Summer Rain

She found him in the front garden tending to the yellow rose bushes. He looked up as she approached. "I was wondering when you'd be back," he said with a smile, and holding his palms towards the sky. "You're just in time. I think the heavens are about to open. Have you had a nice day?"

Katherine explained that she had been at the hospital and his expression immediately darkened. "Things are looking more optimistic for the future of the baby." She spoke quietly, fearing that her words might float on the breeze and in through the open windows of the neighbouring apartments. "The scan showed a strong heartbeat and the size of the foetus suggests I'm just over six weeks' pregnant," she confirmed.

Henry looked at the ground and staked the prongs of his fork into the freshly turned earth of the flowerbed. Resting his right forearm on the handle and wiping his brow with the back of his left hand, he sighed deeply. "So you're having this baby?"

Katherine was taken aback by his bluntness. "Well, I have to get past the 12-week stage, and then I can be sure. If the foetus, the baby, makes it that far, its chances of survival are greatly improved. Then the 16-week scan can detect or rule out any potential developmental problems. Although none of the tests are one hundred per cent accurate."

"So *you* want to have this baby? What about my career, your career?" Henry's manner had not softened and Katherine was hurt by his cold disconnection.

"Yes," she said, "I am having the baby, but you don't have to worry yourself about it." As she spoke the words, she was surprised by the strength in her own voice. This was another shift, the end to the perceived constancy of a male and her acceptance of reliance on any man. It was she who was the singular consistency in the dynamics of her life. That was how it had always been. Now she could see that the rights and the responsibilities of her existence rested solely with her, unless she chose to hand them over to someone else.

At that moment, she vowed never again to hand the responsibility for her physical, mental and emotional wellbeing to another person, male or female. It did not mean that she would seek to control anyone else's life – not even her child's life – she was merely reclaiming the right to run her own life, free from the constraints imposed by others. Her rational mind was telling her that this might be an over-altruistic or downright naïve concept, but in her heart she could sense a knowing that what she wanted was a fair deal for everyone.

"This is my child. It's clear that it's not your wish to bring up a family," she told Henry. "I respect your choices, and in return I think you need to respect mine."

"Don't I have a say in all of this? What about my rights? What is it about you women? Aren't you happy unless you're screwing a man, complicating his life, trying to force him into doing something he doesn't want to do, being someone that he's not?"

Henry ranted. He threw down the handle of the garden fork. "Women!" he growled through gritted teeth and stormed inside.

Katherine felt the soft summer rain fall on the crown of her head, and closed her eyes. For the first time in her life she felt grounded, steady on her feet, yet light enough to float. Energized by the sweet, fresh scent of vegetation on the vapour of the early summer rain and reassured by the soft breeze, she smiled to herself and whispered to her unborn child, "This is about you and me. You will always be the most important person in my life, and we'll never be apart, I promise you."

Inside, she could hear the shower running. She selected a packet of herbal tea from a new range at the health shop and as she waited for the kettle to boil she unpacked the rest of her purchases. Henry showered, changed and looked less heated by the time he emerged from the bedroom.

"I'll get my things together," she volunteered.

"Oh, Katherine, there's no need..." He sounded exasperated. "I'm just not sure what's happening any more. Things are changing all around me and it's all so fast..."

"This isn't about you, Henry," she sighed, "...or me. This is about the new life that we have created. A child deserves two committed parents, people who are prepared to put its interests first, each and every time. To be able to do that, both parents need to have the room in their minds, as well as their hearts, for someone else."

"I don't want you to think I don't care about you or the baby," Henry protested with a pout. "It's just that I'll need some time to get used to the idea, the changes."

As he spoke he scanned the room. Katherine knew exactly what he was thinking: *There's no room here for three.*

"Henry, there's no need for anything in your life to change," she told him. "I have no intention of living here or asking you to move off campus."

Indeed, she had often wondered lately if Henry could actually function in the world outside of the university. After all, he had been there for nearly 40 years. Since she had known him, his visits outside of the university were mostly to other educational establishments and always for the purposes of attending academic conferences or conducting research. She suspected that Henry would struggle to live any other life now, even if he tried.

She was correct in assuming that leaving his campus flat had never crossed his mind. Henry's body may have been that of a mature, middle-aged man. However, his mind functioned on another level. Despite being the age of most grandfathers, his psychological development had peaked somewhere in his twenties, probably at the same time he was awarded his PhD, and was now highly unlikely to progress any further.

"I'm not asking you to give up anything," Katherine continued. "In fact, I'm not asking you for anything at all. I'm telling you that I am going to have a baby. And that's all."

She knew now that he did not want to be a father, but neither did he want to be seen to do the 'wrong' thing.

"I'm not going to stop you playing a part in her life, Henry," she said, "but only if you get involved out of a sense of love and not duty or guilt." Henry was taken aback by this new assertiveness.

"Her?" he asked.

"Just a figure of speech," Katherine replied. "Can I stay until I get a research position lined up? I'll move out as soon as I know where I am going."

"Of course you can stay," he said with a quizzical look on his weary features. "Yes, you must stay until you arrange a position. I'll help you look. I'll ask around and see what's available here."

"I will be looking further afield," she told him, "but of course I'll have to take the first position offered to me, given my situation."

"I'll help you with the finances," he said lamely. She gratefully accepted his offer.

As if by Chance

Katherine felt she was now entering a new and exciting chapter in her life. Sometimes, on first opening her eyes in the morning, she felt an overwhelming sense of expansion; a belief that life was opening up and about to offer her new and rewarding opportunities and experiences. She would rise with a smile and give thanks for her currently cramped circumstances, safe in the knowledge that they were only a temporary arrangement. On other occasions, she woke with a feeling of dread and anxious thoughts buzzing around in her head like the irritating buzz of a dying wasp trapped in a room. Amid this teetering from elation to unease, she knew she needed to focus on her quest to find a funded research project in a university with crèche facilities.

As high summer approached, she gathered together some academic journals lying around the flat and began searching. She had particularly enjoyed Classical Greek philosophy and had been commended on her rather creative account of the trial of Socrates. Finding that precious little had actually been written by Socrates himself, the recording of his words being left in the hands of his students and contemporaries, Plato and Xenophon, to be enshrined in the form of dialogues and replies, Katherine had taken the opportunity to hypothesize creatively about the great thinker and his scribes, and thought she might like to revisit her earlier study and approach it with the benefit of a greater range of life experience.

As she trawled through the lists of research projects available from the various university history departments, she found her attention increasingly drawn to the ancient history of Britain and, more specifically, Wales and Ireland in the 12th and 13th centuries. For the first time in weeks, she sought out the historical notes she had hastily scribbled following her past life regression experiences at the island retreat. Flicking through the pages, she transcribed a few key dates, names, and events and headed off to the university library with Henry's pass to use the

Internet, and began to research possible projects in universities around the country. After a few hours of browsing, she started to see both her opportunities and her desires far more clearly. She was not interested in combining history and archaeology, or economics. She wanted to delve into words and pictures, into the moral details of the lives of her ancestors. She wanted to learn about their beliefs and actions, to discover how they made their choices and lived their lives. However, as with her Classical history studies, she had chosen a subject about which very little had been recorded.

Casting her mind back to her now fading memories of the regression sessions, she wondered how anything was recorded amidst all of the childbirth and warring of the ruling classes in 12th-century Wales, the classes that would have received an education. Then she recalled something about her past-life son Gerald Cambrensis becoming a man of the cloth and a scholar, recording contemporary life in Wales and Ireland.

She typed in 'postgraduate historical studies in Ireland' out of sheer curiosity. What she unearthed immediately captured her imagination:

'The Irish Kings' Court Project 1144 – 1509 is seeking to recon-struct the records of the Medieval Irish Kings' Court, some of which were believed to have been destroyed in a fire at St Mary's Abbey in Dublin in 1304. However, some were also said to have been kept in the tower at Dublin Castle after 1309, others surviving until a further fire at the Four Courts in 1922. The creation of a calendar of the court's letters has been proposed in an attempt to reconstruct the documents which contained the details of the moral judgements and remedies offered by the chancellor, the keeper of the king's conscience, in cases where common law could not offer any relief. It is believed that these recovered and reconstituted documents will provide a rare insight into the lives of the Irish people in the medieval era, a time of turmoil and invasion, when many saw their land seized by conquering forces. These records could document the names of the estate owners and note the

dates that the substantial lands of the South and East, along with their contents, came into the hands of the Cambro-Norman invaders.'

Katherine felt a rush of excitement and yet quite paradoxically, also a sense of calm as she read on, eager to glean as much information as she could about the university and surrounding area. The smiling face of Fin flashed into her mind when she read the advertising blurb for the university *'situated just an hour or so from the Wicklow Mountains National Park'* and then she quickly closed down the image. There was no room for men in her projected plan for the immediate future. That would be far too complicated a prospect at this stage. Her thoughts turned to the unread text messages and unheard voicemails she had received from him, all but one of which she had deleted from her phone. She had made the right decision she was sure. She told herself that meeting him had been just a coincidence. She could have struck up as strong a friendship with any of the other retreat members; it just so happened to be him. And he just so happened to be in the east of Ireland, along with a few hundred thousand or so others 'only an hour or so' from Dublin University which just so happened to offer the one course she wanted to pursue.

Finding an email contact for the admissions department of the university in the name of Esme Walsh, she was reminded of one of Fin's first comments to her informing her that her surname was Irish. She quickly wrote a message to her namesake enquiring as to the application procedures and possible funding arrangements for the research project. It was relatively late in the academic year to be applying but she would still be one step ahead of those undergraduate students waiting on their final exam results. She also half-heartedly applied for two other programmes. Then she typed her own surname into the search bar and read all she could about its origins.

Over dinner, Henry listened as Katherine relayed the unearthed history of her family name.

"Did you know that the Irish family name of Walsh actually came from Wales? Apparently they arrived during the time of the Cambro-Norman invasion, landing at Bannow Bay in County Wexford. They made a name for themselves by helping the King of Leinster to reclaim his kingdom before Henry II of England arrived in 1171," she announced.

Henry looked up quizzically and continued to chew a slice of roast chicken. She continued, "I've learned that the early Welsh and Irish had much in common, both being of the same Gaelic stock. For example, they both practiced tanistry as a system of selecting rulers; both sides sought refuge in their neighbouring countries at times of tribal conflict. The current version of the name can be traced from Philip Brenagh or Breathnach who arrived at the same time as the legendary Strongbow in 1170. He's said to have distinguished himself in a naval engagement against the Danes at Cork and was rewarded with land and property in Kilkenny, and then later further afield. It seems that the Walsh fortunes were intertwined with those of the Fitz-Geralds. They seemed highly influential until Cromwell's men marched onto the scene and massacred them all in the 1700s."

"I didn't know you had any interest in medieval Gaelic history," Henry commented.

"I picked up some bits and pieces when I was at the retreat in Wales," she replied, "and I would like to find out more about my grandfather. My father was born in Hampshire and his father was also a naval officer in the early decades of the last century when Irish nationals formed some 200,000 members of the British military ranks. He may have been Irish. If not, I'd be interested in tracing the family history to find out if I do have any Irish heritage."

Henry waited for her to finish, nodded in acknowledgement and then asked, "Darling, is there any more roast chicken?"

Katherine was not bothered by his lack of interest. Over the following days, whilst waiting for a response to her email enquiry to the university in Dublin, she found herself distracted by intruding images of Fin. Her mind was filled with the memories of their time on the island and of wonder as to the farmhouse in the hills. In quiet moments, she would catch a glimpse of the familiar sparkle of his crystal blue eyes and feel a burning desire to be close to him.

Seat of the Soul

Katherine endeavoured to occupy herself whilst waiting to hear about her university applications, by turning her attention once more to books about babies. She felt that the more information she could have to hand at this early stage the better she could prepare for motherhood alone. She was convincing herself of her innate practicality and reassuring herself that she would have no problem balancing the demands of a new baby and her need to earn a living and yet, delving deeper into the nature and implications of motherhood, doubts crept in.

It was whilst researching the milestones of development during pregnancy, in an attempt to work out how she could fit her condition into the academic calendar that she found herself again caught up in the details of the developing foetus. She read an article explaining that the actual gender of a child is not determined until the seventh week of gestation, the same time that the pineal gland appears in the brain. Sifting through the medical information, she noted further that the pineal gland is independent of the brain, residing outside the blood-brain barrier and is largely responsible for the production of melatonin, the body's natural sleep-inducing chemical. She learned that it is regarded as the individual's body clock, regulating sleep and reproductive growth by measuring time in relation to periods of darkness and light.

Then she noted a cross reference to the belief of Descartes, the well-known 17th-century philosopher and mathematician, who referred to the gland as the 'seat of the soul'. Feeling drawn to explore this notion further she came across various other metaphysical assertions of the functioning of this single, pea-sized gland as a 'third eye' enabling psychic abilities. She reminded herself to take whatever she read with a pinch of salt as all theories were human interpretations and, as such, probably based more on irrational belief than actual scientific fact. Nevertheless, she was intrigued and read on, finding a wealth of spiritual claims about the functioning of this tiny, human body part.

She learned that in Hindu tradition the gland is associated with the third eye of extrasensory perception, illustrated clearly in the religion's portrayal of the God Shiva with a visible third eye painted onto his forehead. She found that the pineal gland is linked with the sixth, or crown, chakra also called 'the Lotus of a Thousand Petals', functioning as a nexus of energy from the metaphysical universe into individual human consciousness. She also read of the emergence of new paradigms of thinking which were looking to reconcile some of these scientific stances and metaphysical beliefs of the functioning of the pineal gland concerning its alleged production of a chemical similar in structure to DMT, a powerful hallucinogen.

However, the conflicting notions of science and the spiritual worlds left her with a distinct sense of dissonance over what she really believed.

Additionally, she recalled the details of a discussion she had with Fin over dinner at the pub, the Mill on the Pond, some three weeks previously when the issue of reincarnation had once more raised its head somewhat uncomfortably for Katherine. At the time, she did not know why. Now, she remembered some talk about the period of 49 days during one of her past life regression sessions and began to look for her notes and the recording that the therapist made of each of the sessions. But she was unable to locate all the documents and concluded that in her haste to leave the island she must have left some of them behind.

Scanning the calendar, Katherine worked out that her baby would reach the 49th day of gestation on Midsummer's Day, her own 30th birthday. Where would she be, and what would she be doing on that day?

After dinner, she told Henry she was having an early night and once in bed she drifted off to sleep. Her conscious mind had mulled over the information. In sleep her unconscious processes provided her with a most fearful perspective on matters. In her dreams, she was arguing with Henry who was holding the key to an old wooden door that Katherine needed to open and he was refusing to unlock it for her. In sheer frustration, she grabbed the key from him and turned it in the lock. As the door opened in front of her, she saw the smirking face of Darrel, her missing husband. He was holding something that resembled a swaddled baby in his arms and goading her that without him she would never achieve what she wanted in life. She screamed out but heard only silence and as he turned to walk away with the baby in his arms she found herself paralyzed, unable to move, unable to reach out and take the baby from him. She could only cry helplessly as he walked away until she heard another voice calling her name. Through the doorway she could see the side profile of an older, bearded man.

He turned to look at her, revealing eyes ablaze with anger and she heard these hurtful words from between the cruel curl of his lips: "You are a worthless woman! Yours is not the right to speak to me in that manner. Learn your place, wife, let me show you what your life is worth to me."

Katherine heard herself begging him, William, for mercy, for her life. She whispered between stolen breaths, as his grip tightened around her throat. "William, please, for the sake of the children."

However, he continued to berate her, "You are but a useless woman with no right to interfere in the business of men, of great men such as me and my warrior sons."

Through closed eyes and with fading consciousness she heard his ranting, telling her that the ship would sail without her and she would be left at the castle to fend for herself. She felt the final pressure of his thumbs against her throat, and then she knew only blackness.

She woke coughing and gasping for air. Sitting up in bed, eyes wide open in the dark, she found the bedclothes drenched from her cold sweat. Her breathing was reluctant to return to a steady rhythm; her whole being awash with the fear that this man was still alive. As much as she could reason that he had died many years ago, she could not deny the feeling that he was still around. She retched at the notion that his spirit or soul was lying in wait for a chance to hurt her once more and then she had to rush to the bathroom and vomited in fear at the thought that his black soul might be destined for the unborn child within her.

Feeling empty, Katherine sat alone in the early morning light, huddled on the floor, clutching her knees to her chest, the dead weight of the dream still weighing her down. Why could she no longer intervene in her dreams to save herself from harm, as she had been taught by her childhood therapist? She knew she had to act; to do something, anything, to ensure that this cycle did not continue. Her dark mood lingered for a few days. It did not go unnoticed by Henry who thought it easier to ignore rather than attempt any engagement with her. It was only when she picked up the email inviting her to a university interview in Dublin that her mood lifted. After the initial rush of excitement, she was left with a huge sense of relief. This was her chance! A pathway had opened up in front of her and she needed clarity if she was to take full advantage of the opportunity. Casting off the cloak of doubt and dread she concentrated all of her energy on her plans, beginning with a trip to Ireland.

Eager to finalize the practical details of her journey as soon as possible, her thoughts turned to arranging travel and accommodation. The ferry from Pembroke and the train from the port of

Rosslare to the city was by far the most cost-effective option; she just needed to work out how long she would need to be in Dublin to get a feel for the place and find out if it was the right move for her. Looking around the university campus would be the easy part; trying to work out what other facilities would be available to her was another issue. She would definitely need to make very good use of whatever pastoral care was offered at the university. She informed Henry about her interview and impending plans to travel to Ireland. He looked a little taken aback at first. However, he said that he would make a few phone calls to find out who he could speak to in the history department of the university. He would, of course, be happy to give her a glowing academic reference. However, the residual feelings following the nightmare still nagged at Katherine and amongst the documents and items she needed to take to Ireland with her she made sure to include the notes and recordings from some of the past life regression sessions. She sensed a need to resolve issues from her distant past in the hope they would not echo into her future.

St Davids

Katherine paused at the top of the stone steps leading down to the cathedral grounds, feeling heady. She needed to catch her breath and survey the scene before her in the 21st century. It was not hard to imagine how it would have looked in the 12th century as it had a timeless atmosphere: very quiet and still, despite the tourists buzzing about below her. She yearned to know more about her past-life sons and had made the pilgrimage to the Pembrokeshire cathedral en route to Ireland.

Instinctively she headed for the nave, the oldest part of St David's Cathedral. She had read that a screen built by Gerald de Barry and Bishop Peter de Leia in the 1100s still remained at this location. The walls at the west end of the building were now leaning outwards, and the original vaulted stone ceiling, which had been destroyed during a 13th-century earthquake, had been replaced by a wooden structure. The walls of the nave were lined with carved wooden arches and the space was now filled with empty wooden seats. Pleased to find herself alone, she stood, closed her eyes, and breathed in slowly and deeply. She felt the slight shift of the ground beneath her feet and stumbled forward a little before regaining her balance. Around her, the air grew cooler. She could hear only the sound of hushed whispers and felt the swish of the ecclesiastical robes of the clergy as their procession passed her by. She was back to another time. Since engaging in past life regression therapy, her dreams had become more detailed and waking experiences such as this were increasing in frequency. She wanted to breathe in the air, to absorb the atmosphere of the time when her son Gerald had walked this way with his learned friends and colleagues. She knew there was some speculation as to whether his body had been buried at his beloved St David's, as was his wish. Katherine had no doubt that his body had rested here. Whether or not his soul was still wandering was her concern. If human genes carried the chemical imprints of past lives, perhaps emotional memories were also carried through the generations in this manner and she was well aware of the possible implications for her unborn child.

All too soon, her concentration was broken by an influx of other visitors and she felt obliged to move on. Still hungry for knowledge of her peace-loving past-life son, in whose life this cathedral had featured so prominently, she headed for the bookshop to see what further information she could find to read on her journey over the Irish Sea following in the footsteps of the rest of her kin: her warring, past-life husband and sons.

Sea Change

A weary Katherine boarded the night sailing at Pembroke Dock bound for County Wexford. She had believed she would experience less sickness on this sea, so renowned for its rough crossings, if she had the opportunity to sleep during the journey, and so she had booked a cabin where she could lie down. Curled up on a functional bunk, with a cup of tasteless tea and her books, she delved deeper into the history of the De Barry family and their exploits in Ireland:

'Two of the sons of William Fitz Odo De Barry, Philip and Robert, were amongst the initial phase of the 1169 invasion of Ireland, when three ships carrying some four hundred men set sail from the port at Milford Haven, landing on the island of Bannow, on the shores of County Wexford in the early days of the month of May. With the support of the Irish King of Leinster, Dermot MacMurrough; the Earl of Pembroke, Richard De Clare, also known as Strongbow, and King Henry II of England, the party was led by Robert Fitz-Stephen and consisted mainly of skilled archers. The longbow was the national weapon of the men of West Wales, with the Welsh being renowned for their skill in penetrating three-inch-thick branches of oak with their arrows and their ability to inflict mortal wounds on their enemies through the thickest of armour. Thus, combined with the efficiency of the organized Norman cavalry, the Cambro-Norman forces proved a most fierce and flexible force. Subsequently merging with a force of some five hundred Irishmen under MacMurrough, the combined army marched toward the Norse-Irish seaport of Wexford where battle began outside the walls of the town. Following assaults on the city, the Norse army retreated behind the walls and called for peace. The aforementioned Philip De Barry, regarded by his learned and honourable brother Gerald as "a man of prudence and courage", obtained large estates in Buttevant, County Cork, in reward for the part he played in the conquest. Whereas Robert, described by his own brother as "a young knight, that for his worthiness cared not for his life, and was rather ambitious to be really eminent", earned himself the cognomen, or citizenship, of Barrymore. He later fell in battle at Lismore in 1185.'

Piece by piece, the picture of her past-life ancestors was becoming clearer. As the facts were unearthed, the map was becoming more illuminated and the signposts aiding her quest were beginning to reveal themselves. Angharad had been left behind in the 1100s whilst her family conquered and eventually settled in Ireland. Being of mixed Welsh and Norman heritage, she had felt no desire to leave her beloved Wales and head for unknown shores. Her soldier sons had not inherited their conquering desire and lust for power from her and had been happy to blood-let for the land and wealth of others, under the guidance of their father and uncles.

In the writings of Katherine's past-life son Gerald, he described in detail both his life in Wales and his travels in Ireland. She felt exhilarated and profoundly privileged to have an invaluable insight into the lives of her ancestors from the unique perspective of her own past-life son. Feeling a little closer to her destination on this journey of discovery, she bedded down for the remaining hours of the sailing.

However, her sleep was wracked with unwelcome images of archers firing arrows and soldiers on horseback. The pounding of hooves over rough ground formed the soundtrack and she felt as if she was being dragged along unwillingly by the rampaging hordes, driven by bloodlust and power. Her dream perspective then shifted to the top of the high stone walls of a city where she was holding out her arms and watching helplessly as a rock thrown from the battlements hit the face of her son. She cried out silently in her sleep as she watched him fall to the ground, landing on his back in a ditch; a torrent of crimson blood flowing from his mouth, a gaping wound in his cruelly handsome face. Then, she found herself alone in a moonlit clearing where the silence of the night was broken by the ringtone of her mobile phone.

Startled, she opened her eyes and remembering that she was still in the ferry cabin reached out in the unfamiliar surroundings for her phone. In the darkness, she could just about make out a text message received from Fin.

It read, *'Farmhouse cottage finally fit for human habitation, let me know if you're ever here.'*

Without hesitation she typed, *'On the night sailing to Rosslare, arriving in approx. 3 hours.'*

Week Seven

Reunion

Fin was feverish. Since receiving Katherine's text he had been visibly skittish, unable to concentrate on anything, and reduced to clockwatching from the foyer of the Ferry Port Motel. He had left the farmhouse almost immediately and headed for the coast. With the roads empty of traffic he had completed the journey in just over an hour, travelling from West Wicklow down through the Ferns, passing the Augustinian abbey at dawn. There he had joined the main Dublin to Wexford road which had taken him to the port at Rosslare. The motel was the only portside establishment which catered for the night sailings and the lounge area was quite comfortable, despite there being only vending-machine refreshments available so early in the day. Breakfast was served from seven and Fin had decided that if the boat was delayed he would treat himself to a hot meal. It was due to dock at six-thirty and the queue of vehicles waiting to board for the outward journey had begun to build. He guessed the sailing was on schedule.

Not sure if she was driving or had made the crossing as a foot passenger, Fin didn't know whether to watch for a car or to offer her a lift. The many possible reasons for this meeting were rattling around in his head, refusing him any peace of mind.

The sun had risen and Fin watched the dockside preparations for the arrival of the ferry. He knew that the foot passengers were instructed to leave the boat before the cars were allowed to drive off. However, he would not be able to see from the lounge window if she walked off. He decided to wait just a little longer before texting. After all, she might not know he was here. Suddenly he could just make out some movement, a line of people through the semi-transparent walls of the tunnel through which the foot passengers disembarked. He would text her, just to make sure that they actually met up.

Fuck it! he thought to himself, and clicked on 'call mobile' rather than 'SMS'.

Hopefully they were about to meet face to face. Why was he feeling so nervous about speaking to her?

"Fin!" a breathy Katherine answered, sounding pleased to hear him. His heart thudded. "Hi, yes I've arrived! I'm just leaving the boat."

Emerging from the cover of the tunnel, she looked around her. Fin explained that he was in the lounge window of the motel on the hill; the modern-looking, single-storey building overlooking the harbour and that she was just a dot in the distance. She scanned the skyline and located the motel building.

"I'll come and pick you up," he suggested. "I've brought the jeep. I thought the space might be needed for your luggage," he joked, embarrassed at his own enthusiasm.

"You're here? Great! No, I'll walk," she responded. "I can wheel my luggage and the exercise and fresh air will help!"

"Rough crossing?" he asked.

"Hmm, sort of! I'll explain when I see you."

"Katherine," Fin said just as she was about to end the call, "what will you have for breakfast? I'll order it now and it will be ready for when you get here."

With a rush of warmth, she was reminded of his thoughtfulness. "Just some tea and hot buttered toast, thank you," she replied gratefully. Fin's mind shifted gears into a positively manic looping mode. He had been trying to contain the shock he had felt when she responded to his text message. Now mayhem was let loose in his mind.

She was here! Why was she here? Why hadn't she been in touch? Why had she not responded to any of his other messages? Had she even received them? Why was she here now? Was it to see him? If so, why hadn't she called earlier? What had happened in the four weeks since they were last together?

He checked himself.

Why was he so hung up on someone he hardly even knew?

Katherine hoped she had done the right thing in letting Fin know she was arriving on his shores. She had not expected him to be at the port to greet her, although the sound of his voice had been very reassuring. She had an hour or so to pass before the train left the port for Dublin and was pleased to have some company and hopefully some useful advice about the practicalities of her trip. She used the walk from the harbour to the motel to try to clear her mind which always seemed rather fuzzy these days. She was sure of what she needed to do whilst she was here in Ireland and had resolved not to say anything to Fin about the pregnancy. She was grateful for his friendship but she kept telling herself that anything more was out of the question, given her current circumstances. It was imperative that she got to the interview at the university and that she kept her mind firmly on practical matters. However, her excitement at seeing him again fluttered annoyingly in her throat, causing a tickly cough. As she reached the top of the hill, a nauseous warning prickled at the back of her throat and she knew it would be wise to eat something as soon as possible.

Fin jumped to his feet as she appeared at the entrance to the motel foyer. She smiled in recognition and he stopped short of hugging her, not sure of how he should react. Her cheeks were flushed red from the early morning exertion and Fin's wide, fixed grin was refusing all his attempts to relax and be cool. For a moment each stood with their gaze fixed firmly on the other, with Katherine lowering her eyes first. Fin grabbed the handle of her luggage and led her over to a sofa and low table in the corner of the room.

"Breakfast is ready," he announced. "We can take it here, or in the dining room."

Katherine said she was happy to eat from the lounge table and sank into the sofa. The uphill walk had proved something of a challenge and she was happy for the opportunity to rest, if only momentarily. She watched Fin as he walked across the lounge and disappeared into the dining room to collect the food, the wide smile spreading across her face showing just how pleased she was to see him. Minutes later Fin returned with a tray full of warm buttered toast with a selection of jams and honey for her and a full Irish breakfast for himself. The awkward silences were soon swallowed up by Fin's attempts at conversation whilst enthusiastically chewing on the black pudding on his plate; the sight of which turned Katherine's sensitive stomach.

"How can you eat that stuff?" she asked, with an over-exaggerated look of disgust on her face.

"Well I can see that you, yourself, have not lost your keen appetite!" Fin retorted, watching her spread a thick layer of blackberry jam on her fourth slice of toast. They both laughed, now relaxed and enjoying the warmth, humour, and mutual attention. When the plates were cleared, Katherine sat back on the sofa and sipped on the sweet tea Fin had poured for her.

"So, how is the farm business coming along?" she asked.

"Well, it's been a challenging couple of weeks," Fin started to explain. "There's still a great deal of work to be done, but I'm making progress..." he trailed off before swiftly changing the subject. "And what brings you here?"

His face lit up when Katherine told him about the interview for the postgraduate research project at Trinity College.

"So you'll be based here in Dublin for a while?" he asked excitedly.

"Well, the train leaves in half an hour and if I don't make it I'll be on the next boat back!" she exclaimed. "I'm hoping that I'm in with a chance to work on this project; it sounds very intriguing. If I am successful there will be many practical issues to consider, but I'm sure I can work things out," she explained.

"I'll take you," offered Fin. "We can drive to Wicklow or Bray, park up and take a short train-ride into the city. It's much easier than negotiating the traffic and the university is only a short walk from the station. Plus you get a free personal guide into the bargain."

"I wasn't expecting you to take me to Dublin," replied Katherine, her face flushed red; a mixed hue of embarrassment and pleasure. However, she also felt very grateful for his assistance. Since becoming pregnant, she had experienced a heightened level of anxiety in relation to crowds of people and when in busy places. It was as if she, as a mother-to-be, had automatically switched into a mode of self-protection. After such a restless night she would be able to relax, feeling much safer with an escort by her side.

"I don't want to distract you from the farm," she lied, wanting nothing more than the pleasure of his company – all her resolve to maintain a sensible distance from him steadily draining away.

"I'll be glad to get away from the farm for a while." Fin's assurance was the truth. Since his fight with Cillian and his sudden departure from Ireland, he had become very unsure as to the course of his future. His motivation for the progress of the business was waning. He was pleased to have something, someone else, to think about for a while. His thoughts about Katherine were running amok in his head and ricocheting around the other parts of his body.

"If we leave now, we should arrive ahead of the train. That will give us more time to play with in the city. Once the interview is over, I can show you some of the sights?" he suggested, jumping to his feet in excitement.

Settling into the rhythm of the ride, Katherine once again

struck up conversation about the farm. Fin was surprised at how much of the detail she remembered from their conversations on the island retreat, some four weeks earlier.

"So you're interested in environmental issues?" he asked.

"I can't say I know much about them," she replied. "But yes, I am interested in the things you talked about." Fin wanted to blurt it all out, tell her how it all seemed to be falling apart. He wanted to let someone know how he was struggling to make any business connections in the hills; how his reputation amongst his peers had been so unfairly tainted, and how his own brother now wanted to sabotage his attempts at setting up a new future for himself. And on a national level, the days of the Celtic Tiger economy were well and truly over with the sites of many large-scale building projects now appearing as dusty, deserted ghost towns on the edge of struggling cities. However, something steered him away from that line of conversation. Perhaps now just was not the time. Instead, he asked Katherine to tell him more about the interview ahead.

She too found herself departing from her original agenda. Having set out with the intention of explaining her situation in a very factual manner, Katherine found herself softening into the comfort of Fin's company. Her excitement about the possibility of studying in Dublin proved contagious; Fin's mind raced with all the ways in which he could help make it happen. Listening to his soft lilt and sensing his keen enthusiasm, Katherine persuaded herself that the time was not right to tell him about the baby. After all, it really had nothing to do with him.

Glancing at his watch, Fin asked what time the train was scheduled to arrive at Wicklow. She checked the timetable and, satisfied they could still arrive ahead of the stop at Bray, he was happy to continue driving, enjoying the opportunity to reconnect with her. It had been a couple of weeks since his last disappointing encounter with an attractive female, and he was happy that his memory of Katherine had not distorted during that time. He was still entranced by her, and the thought of her living closer also raised the possibility of their lives maybe intertwining in some way. Even if things at the farm did not work out quite as he had planned, the options were looking a little more favourable, he thought to himself as they sat in silence; Fin stealing glances at his beguiling passenger as she gazed out of the window.

There was also something invigorating about being 'a stranger in a strange land' for Katherine. She was feeling lighter and freer than she had for years. Since landing on the unfamiliar shores, she had witnessed the unfolding of a new life path for her. The anticipated sea change had certainly begun to work its magic. Unconsciously, Katherine let out a deep sigh of relief, whilst Fin smiled from the depths of his soul. Feeling lighter, he pointed out the Sugar Loaf Mountain ahead.

"We're close to Bray," he explained. "I'll park up and from there we'll catch the DART into Dublin."

They watched as the train pulled up to the platform. As all the carriages were full, Fin and Katherine had to squeeze themselves into the standing area. With the swift acceleration of the train as it pulled out of the station the two were thrown together, Fin moving his arm swiftly to steady her momentary imbalance. The two remained close, Katherine's head leaning into his shoulder for the duration of the journey, watching the station signs flash by as the train traversed the harbour side at Dun Laoghaire and eventually pulled up into Pearse Street.

"This is where we get off," explained Fin. "It's one of the longest streets in Dublin, and we will be walking south to the university campus from here."

The Old Library

Whilst Katherine was being interviewed, Fin found himself mooching around the old university library. It seemed that the sun had lured the city tourists to Dublin Zoo in Phoenix Park on the other side of the city so he could amble in peace amidst the cool and quiet atmosphere of the old building. Surprised at how much history was stirred up from his memory, he lingered over the intricacies of the ancient texts subtly illuminated under cover of glass, and marvelled at the workmanship of the oak-barrelled ceiling and galleries housing over a hundred thousand books. Always having been one to look outwards and into the future, he found this warp of time a welcome respite from the relentless pursuit of career success and achievement. He wondered how the course of his life might have differed if he had stayed and attended university at home. Here amongst the pages of the past, Fin became grounded in his heritage, reconnecting with the images and artefacts of his culture. Amidst the words and pictures which had shaped his past, he started to piece together the remnants of history which had served to shape the psyche of his nation. Closing his eyes, he tried to recall the sound from an ancient harp, the national emblem, as he relived numerous church services and school concerts. Also he felt the stirrings of political passion whipped up by the words on the 1916 Proclamation of the Irish Republic. Ireland had a long tradition of losing its young people overseas. He wondered if the phenomenon would ever be reversed; whether more people would return, and what it would take for that to happen. His reverie was broken by the vibration of the mobile phone in his back pocket.

'I'm finished! Where are you?' read the text message from Katherine.

Fin quickly replied and made his way out of the library building and outside onto the cobblestone path. He was greeted by a beaming smile from her and an enthusiastic account of the successful interview.

"We spoke at length about the history of the 12th-century Norman Conquest of Ireland," she explained. "I'm feeling very excited about this! They said they will call soon to let me know whether there is a place for me on the programme. And what have you been doing to pass the time?" Fin informed her that he had been conducting some of his own historical research, and asked if there was anywhere else she needed to go.

"I would love to see the Black Castle at Wicklow on the return journey, if possible. The Fitz-Geralds were active in this area," she said. Fin readily agreed to take her to the castle, situated on the east coast and to the north of the old port town of Wicklow.

"That would be great! There's not much else I can do today. I don't want to jump the gun. If I get offered a place then I'll have plenty of opportunity to find my way around this place." Katherine looked around excitedly.

"So is there anywhere else in the city that you'd like to see, in the meantime?" Fin offered. "I was here just a couple of weeks ago; but for business, not pleasure." He was now firing on all cylinders, sparked up by her enthusiasm and motivated by his own reflections and realizations. Katherine shrugged and Fin took the opportunity to take control. "Well, we can head to Temple Bar for some food, if you like. I know a couple of great, traditional-style places."

Magical Music

Katherine watched as the band of pipers in the corner of the bar struck up a tune, each contributing their own individual parts, and all without the use of any music sheets. As the tempo changed, she saw one young lad lay down his whistle and pick up a bodhrán. Although the other diners seemed to be concentrating on eating, drinking, and continuing their conversations, Katherine was entranced by the performance. Fin returned to the table with a pint of Guinness, a glass of wine, and a menu.

"Okay, thanks, but just the one for me," Katherine said, taking the wine glass from Fin who sat next to her and opened up the menu for her to read.

"I chose my meal at the bar whilst I was waiting for the

Guinness to settle," he explained.

Katherine opted for a plate of salmon and creamy mashed potato from the traditional menu, and sipped sparingly on the wine whilst waiting.

"The music is amazing," she commented. "The musicians look as if they are having a great time."

"That's because they are!" Fin replied. "See the old boy there, in the red shirt? He's been playing for donkey's years. He probably knows every tune and every word off by heart. These guys live and breathe the music."

"Do you know these songs?" she asked.

"I'm recognizing one or two," Fin replied, adding, "I played the whistle, as a young lad."

As a solo guitarist struck up a tune, Katherine and Fin quietened to listen. With his long, wild curls tumbling over his shoulder, the musician played with great ease; his gentle strumming alternating with a gentle finger-style playing. The instrument almost appeared to become a part of him as the soothing sound flowed from the strings and resonated around the rosewood body, captivating Katherine's imagination. Despite being surrounded by strangers, she became absorbed in the intimacy of this melodious scenario.

"So how have things been with you since I left the island retreat?" Fin said, finally breaking her trance with his direct question. He sensed her reticence and tried to fill the uncomfortable silence. "Did you enjoy the rest of your stay? Were there any more revelations about your past from the regression therapist?"

Katherine hesitated before replying, "There were revelations, but not about the past. I left the island a few days after you."

Fin's eyebrows rose over his pint glass as he took another mouthful.

"I discovered something, and I had to find out whether something would work out," she continued. "But I was surprised to find out something else, well a few things, actually. I'm not making myself very clear, am I?" Fin's comical expression suggested he had not grasped the gravity of Katherine's situation.

"Clear as mud!" he joked. "Would you care to fill me in on any of the details so I can try to make some sense of it?" The conversation was interrupted by a welcomed round of applause rippling around the bar. The musicians announced that they were taking a break and would return after some refreshment, before they headed to the bar.

In the muted atmosphere, Katherine's voice fell to a whisper, "I'm still trying to make sense of it all! Well, I discovered that my divorce has not even got off the ground. I was informed by the police that my estranged husband disappeared before receiving the paperwork from the court."

"Disappeared?" Fin asked, looking perplexed.

"His car was found abandoned on a beach, and apparently he hasn't showed up at work or been in touch with any of his family or friends. The police are treating it as a 'missing persons' investigation, but so far they have drawn a blank. Apparently they were looking for me when I was on the island, as it seemed that I had 'disappeared' at the same time. When they found Darrel's mobile phone, it only had my number stored in the contacts. Then they took my phone away for examination."

"Why?" Fin asked.

"At first they suspected that I might know something about his disappearance, I guess," Katherine replied. "They were looking for any evidence of contact between us during that period."

"So, still no one knows where he is?" Fin said with a frown.

"No one knows where he is, and nobody matching his description has turned up. As I said, at the moment it's a 'missing persons' enquiry." She sighed.

"That must have been a shock," Fin reasoned, thinking aloud.

"Yes, it was a shock but I don't believe he's dead. He has lots of connections and money, so I'm sure he'll turn up when he decides to come back to face reality. He's not the type to do anything stupid. I just hope he shows up soon so we can sort things out!"

"Well, as long as you're not seriously concerned about his wellbeing, surely you can just carry on with your life?" Fin asked.

"The divorce can't go through until he turns up," Katherine replied. "So it's more a state of limbo than a case of moving on, in that respect."

"What if he never shows up? Does that mean you will have to remain married?" Fin's mind was starting to chart the consequences of the situation.

"If he didn't show up, then after seven years he could be declared legally dead and I would finally be free of him. Seven years!"

"But that won't stop you making your own decisions, about travelling and studying and things, meanwhile." Fin wasn't sure if he was asking a question or making a statement.

"It's just the uncertainty, the not knowing whether or not he'll ever turn up again," she answered. "It feels as if I have an albatross around my neck."

"You're still free to make all the other choices and decisions," Fin said, trying to lighten her load.

"Yes, I'm finally making all of my own decisions," she agreed. "But these days, it's not just about me," she announced, hoping her slightly raised voice would make her sound more confident than she was actually feeling. "In fact, soon there will be two of us to consider." Fin had no idea of what she was about to tell him.

"I'm pregnant," she said.

The colour disappeared from Fin's face as he drained the Guinness from his glass.

"But it's not yours," she quickly added. "I didn't realize, but I must have already been pregnant when we first met."

"Ah, so the bastard has disappeared, leaving you with a baby?"

"Oh no!" Katherine exclaimed, and now knew she had to tell him the whole story. "Darrel's not the baby's father. That's Henry."

"Henry?!" Fin questioned, his eyes arched in surprise.

"Henry was, is, an old boyfriend," she explained. "I called in to see him before I arrived at the island. I lived with Henry before I met Darrel. He's an academic, I met him at university. We broke up when he said he didn't want to have children. I left and went to the city, where I met Darrel. I hadn't seen Henry for some years and I only got back in touch when I decided to leave my job and Darrel."

"So how long, I mean, when is the baby due?" Fin asked, feeling as if he had just been cut adrift on dangerous waters.

"It's early days," Katherine explained. "I'm just about seven weeks, so there's at least another thirty-three weeks to go. That's why I'm trying to get everything sorted now: the research post and somewhere to live."

What a fool! She's not here to see me, Fin thought, trying desperately to tread water and contain his disappointment.

"So is Henry hoping to come to Dublin?" he asked, trying to sound practical, holding his chin above the surface, whilst really wanting to submerge into self-pity. "Or will you be sharing your time between here and there?"

"Henry's not interested in the baby," Katherine said bravely. "It wasn't planned and he doesn't want to be a father. He never has, that's why we split up. Ironic isn't it?"

"So you're bringing this baby up alone?" Fin had no idea where this conversation was going.

"Yes," replied Katherine. "That's the plan. Once I've arranged a research post I'll have to find somewhere to live and make some sort of childcare arrangements. I didn't think it wise to ask about crèche facilities in the initial interview."

"So you would come and live here permanently?" Fin asked with a faint glimmer of hope in his eyes. "Or at least for the duration of your university research?"

"Yes, I'd love to come here," she replied. "I just need confirmation from the university."

"That would be grand." Fin took a deep breath, feeling as if he had just reached a life-saving rock, and sat back in his chair. Both sat smiling, each relieved to have tested the waters and, despite the potential horrors lurking in the depths, to have found them invitingly warm.

An Caislean Dubh

Katherine leaned over the bridge in the late afternoon sun, watching the swans on the river; her attention drawn to one sleeping beauty with its eyes closed and its beak nestled under its feathers. She was struck by the peaceful serenity of the bird amidst the splashing of the neighbouring ducks.

"This footbridge is known as Parnell Bridge," Fin informed her, pointing to the plaque affixed to the stone wall. "Charles Stewart Parnell lived in a place called Avondale, about seven or eight miles from here. He was a member of the House of Commons where he made a brave attempt to establish Home Rule for Ireland. Unfortunately his career was scuppered when he took up with a divorcée named Katherine...and further down the Leitrim River there's the stone bridge," Fin continued, deliberately ignoring the startled look on Katherine's face whilst sporting a cheesy grin on his own.

"Wicklow is also home to a famous mariner, Robert Halpin. He was born over there," Fin continued, pointing to an old building now under renovation. A sign over the door said, 'The Bridge Tavern'.

"Have you heard of him?" he asked and Katherine shook her head. "He was the captain of the SS Great Eastern, a ship designed by Brunel. It sailed all over, laying the first telegraph cables which connected the world. There's an obelisk in his honour in Fitz-William Square, here in the middle of the town. Would you like to see it?"

"Do we have time?" Katherine asked, glancing at her watch.

"Sure," smiled Fin. "We'll take a walk along the harbour front to the castle and then wind our way back down through the town. That way you'll get to see the gaol!"

"The gaol?" Katherine spluttered.

"It's just a museum these days," Fin assured her. "Although I believe it has held a few of my relatives over the years! The O'Byrne's are amongst some of the notorious 1798 rebels."

"Who were they rebelling against?" asked Katherine.

"Well, after being sacked by the Vikings and invaded by the Normans Wicklow then fell under the enforced rule of the English so I guess they fought them all, over the centuries. Those who weren't hanged there or in Melancholy Lane were transported to the antipodean colonies in the 1800s."

Katherine shuddered. "I think I'd rather see the castle," she said.

"The *Black* Castle?" Fin laughed. "How do you think it got its name? There were plenty of similarly dark deeds carried out there!"

Katherine was intrigued. Her imagination had been ignited during the discussion with the historians during the university interview and she felt drawn to the site of the castle ruins on the cliff. Whereas she feared the thought of being trapped within the prison walls, at least she could breathe freely and feel the wind in her hair from between the stones on the windy promontory.

"On a clear day you can see the Welsh mountains of Snowdonia from here," said Fin when they arrived at the castle. The site was deserted and Katherine stood staring out to sea. Whether or not the history of the Fitz-Geralds in Wicklow was that of her past-life family, real people had lived and died in this place. Katherine did not experience any of the imagery she recalled from the cathedral and the castle in Wales, but she did experience a strong sense of curiosity. Yes, she wished to learn more about this place and its people. She had a deep desire to know what happened to the Fitz-Geralds, the brothers and sons of Angharad De Barry, once they had alighted on Irish shores in the 1100s. She was struck by the synchronicity that their greatest enemies appeared to be the O'Byrne clan, the ancestors of Fin. Tears started to flow down her cheeks. Blaming the keen wind on her face and the heightened hormone activity of pregnancy, she brushed them away. Turning around to speak to Fin, she saw him walking away from the castle ruins, along the grassy bank. As he turned to the side she could see that he was talking into his phone. Then he turned and paced along the verge, his facial expression turning from one of concern to anger and upset. Katherine waited for the conversation to end and headed over to him.

"Is everything okay?"

He shook his head as he slid the phone back into the back pocket of his jeans. "That was Frank Keenan, the family solicitor. He has received a request from Cillian to initiate proceedings against me." Fin's faced flushed red and Katherine could sense his distress.

"Who is Cillian, and what proceedings?" she asked gently.

"Cillian is my brother. He lives in the States and he wants to sell the farm," Fin explained through gritted teeth.

"Surely they can't...they won't..." Katherine started.

"Frank Keenan said he wasn't prepared to act for one brother against the other, but that's not to say that another lawyer wouldn't. He says he's advised Cillian to take the matter to another firm and he's advising me the same."

"Can he make you sell the farm?" asked a concerned Katherine.

"As far as I know, when Cillian refused to have anything to do with the farm and renounced his rights to manage the estate under the will, he should have signed a document transferring ownership of the land to me. Frank said he drew one up but that Cillian never signed it and so it was never executed. The farm is still in joint ownership and so he can force me to sell or to buy him out. And there's no way I could afford to buy him out." Fin was despondent. He had been able to forget his woes for a while but now they were back with a vengeance. "It's so unfair. I've poured all my money and seven years of my life into that place. I haven't asked him for anything and now he's going to flex his muscles and I will lose all of my investment."

"How could you lose it all?" Katherine asked.

"The current market value of the land and the renovated properties divided equally between us won't cover the cost of my investment. There's no way the business element can be sold as a going concern, and so I'll come out of it with no business and only half the value of the property." Fin's gaze dropped to the ground. "I'll just have to minimize my loss and start looking around for something else..."

Katherine hated seeing him appearing so defeated. "So you're just going to let it happen?" she asked.

"I have no other choice," he replied.

"You can fight it!" Katherine said, suddenly feeling fired up. "You can't let him take all this from you. What if you offer to buy him out at a future date, as soon as you can?"

"He's not going to go for that option," said Fin.

"Well, what if you just refuse to cooperate with the sale?" Ideas flooded into Katherine's mind. "If he's over the other side of the Atlantic, he might get tired of the fight and give up."

Fin grimaced and said, "When we inherited the farm, things were going well for Cillian. Now he's divorced and has lost his house and half his money. He's not going to give up easily on this fight."

"Well, you just can't just give up on this either!" Katherine's impassioned plea surprised him.

"Well, it's not as if I'm leaving the place today," he joked, feebly. "In fact, it's about time I got back. What time is the ferry?"

"It sails at ten o'clock and I need to check in 45 minutes before the sailing," Katherine answered. "Is there time to visit the hills before I head for the port?"

"It's just a half hour from here," Fin said, pointing in the direction of the majestic mountain range on the horizon. "I'll be happy to drive you there."

The Wicklow Way

Fin's mood lifted the higher he drove into the hills. He pointed out the Scots pine forests, explaining that they were essential for the survival of the red squirrel in the region. Katherine was taken with the contrast of the golden gorse, against the swathes of majestic purple heather.

"It's breathtakingly beautiful!" she exclaimed.

"Yes, it has inspired many artists and writers and is home to actors, musicians and some famous film directors," Fin replied, as they passed some grand iron gates and glimpsed stately houses otherwise hidden in the landscape of gently rolling fields and ancient trees. "It's the season for foxgloves and fuchsias which line these lanes."

They drove in silence for a while, Katherine soaking in the natural beauty of her new surroundings.

"Over in the west of the mountains you'll also see the ferns and white bog cotton flowers. They're edible, you know. We often had them packed in our school lunchboxes," Fin remarked. Thinking he was ribbing her, she delivered a light punch to his shoulder.

"It's true!" he protested. "Well, about the edible bit. We never actually got them in our sandwiches."

"Apart from the squirrels, what are the other types of wildlife?" Katherine asked.

Fin thought before answering, "There are foxes everywhere,

but the sika deer are probably the most prevalent of the wildlife; especially in the north of the mountains. And there are goats on the steep hills alongside the glacial lakes; for example, back there at Glendalough."

Katherine was sure they had been driving for more than half an hour. She felt as if she was being drawn deeper into the mountains. Soon all she could see was the tops of the ridges and the evening sky. As they reached the top of a narrow track Fin announced, "We are now venturing into Byrne territory, notorious rebels and bandits. But stick with me and you'll be okay." He winked when he made his last comment.

As they stopped at a crossroads, he continued, "When the British built the military road and the army barracks just south of here, they finally got the better of the rebels."

"What did they do for work, back then?" Katherine asked curiously.

"When they weren't fighting the settlers, I guess they farmed or worked in the mines," he answered. "In the valley we're headed to, Glenmalure, there's a history of the mining of iron ore, copper, and lead." As they descended into the valley, Katherine felt as if she was being driving back in time. She felt a slight sense of fear at the remoteness of the locality.

"You won't get a mobile phone signal for miles around here!" Fin laughed. "Unless you reach the top of Lugnaquillia there, being the highest peak in the Wicklows."

He pointed out the window as they drove along the bottom of a valley.

However, Katherine was more interested in a quaint building set back into the hill. "What's that place?" she asked.

"That's Wiseman's Lodge," Fin replied. "It used to be open to the public. Shall we see if we can get a drink there?"

The jeep turned off the road and up the dusty track, its potholes evidencing years of neglect. "Rumour has it that this place started off as a hunting lodge for the well-to-do, but was commandeered as the headquarters of the rebels. The original owner was said to have patronized the cause of the rebellion, using his respectable front to harbour wanted men and illegal weapons," Fin said, raising his eyebrows at Katherine. Theirs was the only vehicle parked in the driveway.

"It doesn't look open to me," Katherine remarked. "What a shame! It looks so intriguing..."

Fin was not so easily dissuaded. He climbed the steps to the veranda and tried the handle of the outer door, stepping into the porch.

"Hello?" he called out. A middle-aged lady wearing a traditional black and white waitresses' outfit appeared from an inner doorway.

"Are you serving refreshments?" Fin asked.

"Yes, do come in," beckoned the perfectly coiffured lady. They walked into a lounge with a few small, polished, wooden tables, each accompanied by a pair of straight-backed chairs arranged around the large leaded fireplace.

"We have no fire today," the waitress explained, "but you're welcome to sit and take in the view of the gardens if you wish." She pointed them in the direction of the sofa and easy chairs facing the large bay window, overlooking the secluded gardens. Katherine noticed the old books behind the glass of a large locked cabinet and decided she would take a closer look later. They took their seats and the waitress asked if they would like to see a menu.

Looking at his watch, Fin remarked on the hour. "It's no wonder I was feeling peckish. If we order some food to eat here, we'd be hard pressed to catch the ferry," he pointed out to Katherine. "We can just order a drink if you'd prefer?"

"Let's eat!" was her response. The waitress took an order of drinks from them and said she would return shortly with the menu.

The room was reminiscent to Katherine of the lounge at the

Welsh retreat where she had first met Fin. She smiled to herself, remembering one of their earlier conversations. "Do you remember our first chat in the library on the island?" she asked. "The one when you asked me if I had ever been here? When you told me that the mountains were too beautiful to miss?" Fin had a vague recollection.

"Well, you were right, Fin Byrne!" Katherine exclaimed.

"It takes a great beauty to appreciate a great beauty," said Fin who, feeling rather bold, had decided to seize the moment. Katherine smiled as an involuntary blush coloured her cheeks. She could not think of a suitable reply and, sensing her embarrassment, Fin decided not to say anything further. The awkward silence was broken with the arrival of the menus and both busied themselves with the offerings of suppers comprised of the local, organic produce. After placing her order, Katherine asked if the gardens were accessible from the lounge. The immaculate waitress advised them that the meals, which would take a little while, would be served in the restaurant, from where guests could walk out into the garden. She said that they were welcome to take their drinks into the garden where one wrought iron table and two chairs stood alone on an old stone patio.

"This place certainly has an air of intrigue about it," commented Katherine, looking at the high, ivy-clad wall surrounding the whole of the garden. For her, its atmosphere was reminiscent of an age of elegant decadence. "I wonder what's through that gate."

"That's to make a quick getaway, to avoid being caught," Fin said, trying to subdue his comment, although there was no one else around to hear.

The quiet waitress was keeping a discreet distance and Katherine began to feel as if there was only her and Fin in the world. "Perhaps this place is now used for clandestine meetings of another kind," she commented with a suggestive smile. "Do they rent rooms?"

Fin laughed and the two relaxed, enjoying their drinks under the evening sun. Just as the light began to fade, the waitress called them into the dining room. Although each of the tables had been laid with sparkling white porcelain crockery and elegant silver cutlery, they had the candle-lit room to themselves. He raised a glass of water and suggested a toast, "To incidental meetings, accidental pregnancies and clandestine locations!"

Katherine laughed, then added, "To mothers, fathers, brothers, husbands and lovers."

Both grazed slowly over their meals, neither of them eager to draw a close to the evening; each being equally attentive to the looks, smiles, and comments of the other. The waitress watched from a distance, smiling to herself as she polished the glassware.

Feeling that he needed to say something to draw the evening to a close, eventually Fin glanced at his watch and joked, "If you still intend to catch that ferry we're going to have to airlift you halfway across the Irish Sea. Alternatively, there's a quaint farm cottage not too far from here, where I'm sure the friendly owner would be pleased to make up a bed for you for the night."

They drove in silence. Both filled with a warm anticipation, the excitement overriding the doubts and fears in their minds. However, as the jeep turned into Lusmore lane, Fin felt a knot form in the pit of his stomach. Approaching the turning into the farm, he caught sight of something moving in the field under the moonlight. As he drove nearer he could see a team of horses.

"Jaysus! The ould man wasn't joking!" Fin exclaimed. "I turn my back on this place for a day and he moves them in."

"I leave you for a few weeks and you develop the vernacular!" Katherine joked. However, she quickly realized that Fin was serious. "Those aren't your horses?" she asked.

"I met this pedlar a couple of weeks ago and he asked if he could keep some horses in the front field for a while. I don't know what made me agree to it. There was something weird about the whole situation. I just hope he'll keep to his word and move them on before too long," Fin explained as he drove slowly alongside the field, counting at least half a dozen cobs and wondering what exactly he had gotten himself into.

Inside the cottage, Fin led Katherine into the kitchen and offered her a cup of tea. Taking a seat at the table, Katherine declined anything to eat or drink. Looking around at her surroundings she commented, "This is a great place. Did you do all the work here yourself?"

Fin explained that he had help from contractors for the plumbing and the electrical work, but that he had carried out most of the woodwork, plastering and painting himself. "The cottage renovation was the easiest part. The restoration of the farmhouse was far trickier," he explained.

Katherine commented that she was looking forward to seeing the farm in daylight.

"Yes, it's getting late. Are you cold? I can light a fire. Or are you tired?" Fin asked. "I'll make up a bed on the sofa and you can sleep in my room." Without waiting for a response, he showed her into the lounge and proceeded to load up the sofa with pillows and blankets he retrieved from the drawers of an old painted chest under the stairs.

"I'll be fine here on the sofa," Katherine protested, arranging the pillows and spreading out the blankets. As if to prove the point, she lay down and pulled up the covers.

"O-k-a-y," Fin said slowly. "If you're sure you'll be comfortable enough…"

"Sure!" Katherine replied. "But first I'll need to use the bathroom."

"That's upstairs," he gestured.

As she stood up from the sofa, she turned to him and kissed his cheek. "Thank you. Thank you for bringing me here and letting me stay."

Wrapping his arms tightly around her, Fin kissed her passionately. The events of the past four weeks faded away and he felt transported back to that moment in the lighthouse keeper's cottage on the island, where the two had melted into each other's bodies, and each other's hearts. Katherine responded whole-heartedly, her body simultaneously comforted and excited by his touch. Once more he began to explore the curves of her body with a gentle touch.

As his grasp became tighter, his caresses more urgent, she hesitated and stepped back.

"Things have changed," she said quietly.

"Yes, circumstances have changed but how we feel about each other hasn't," he urged, taking a step towards her. "Or has it?"

"Fin, I don't know. I just don't know how things are going to work out," she protested.

"Did you ever know?" he asked. "Did you ever know how it was going to work out with Darrel, with Henry? We can never know how things are going to work out, with anyone, or anything," he said gently.

"I just don't know…"

"You don't *have* to know," he reassured her. "We can work things out together."

Gently cradling her head in his hands, he once more he fastened his lips firmly on hers.

Katherine reciprocated the kiss, but did not embrace him.

"I think it's best if I sleep upstairs, alone, tonight," she said, gently, turning to climb the stairs.

Socrates and the Pedlar

Rudely awakened in the early morning by the sound of raised voices in the courtyard, Katherine looked out of the open bedroom window to see three people engaged in an animated conversation. A shrunken figure was waving his arms around, with a taller man leaning over, appearing to be listening. A short, stout woman stood alongside, in something of a no-nonsense stance, her arms crossed firmly across her ample chest. Pulling on a sweater over Fin's pyjamas which she had borrowed for the night, she headed downstairs to see what all the fuss was about. She found Fin in the kitchen, frying bacon and listening to a loud transistor.

"Good morning," he greeted her with his signature smile and then clocked that she was wearing his pyjamas. "How did you sleep? You're looking very fetching this morning."

"I hope you don't mind," Katherine blushed.

"Not in the slightest! Fancy some breakfast? This is just about ready," he said, taking the pan off the heat. Then turning down the volume on the radio he explained, "I found this old thing when I cleared out the farmhouse. It's ancient, but it still works."

"Who are those people outside?" she asked.

"What people?"

Fin went to look through the small window in the lounge.

"That's him, the pedlar with the horses," said Fin. "I wonder what the Briens are doing here."

As he walked out into the courtyard he explained to Katherine that they were his closest neighbours.

Dan Brien waved and called out across the courtyard, "Fin, glad you're here. We spotted this ould fellow and his horses in the field and came over to see what he was about. He says he has your permission to tether his team there and had come around to check on them this morning. We came to knock to check this out with you, but there was no answer at the cottage."

"Ah, Fin!" It was the pedlar's turn to speak. "I'm glad you've arrived, you can put this kind man's mind to rest. I explained that we had an agreement, but he it seems he wanted to hear it from you. He's just looking out for you, I know, and that's grand."

Maire Brien frowned, remaining silent.

"Yes, we did make some sort of agreement, a couple of weeks back now," Fin volunteered. "I seem to recall you wanted to leave the horses here for a couple of months?"

"That's right," confirmed the pedlar whose name Fin had

neglected to ask, "from the Solstice to Samhain."

"I've a feeling you're up to no good," Maire tutted. "We don't have time for the likes of you around these parts. We're just dairy farmers trying to earn an honest living."

"Maire!" Dan scolded his forthright wife. "There's nothing to say he's up to any nonsense."

"Then why has he chosen *that* field?" she spat.

"You've nothing to fear from me," said the pedlar, "but I would think twice about lighting that bonfire you've got piled up high over on your land. It is midsummer and such a bonfire could attract some trouble for you."

"Stuff and nonsense," Maire spluttered. "Keep your superstitious fearmongering to yourself, and best you keep yourself away from our farm."

Katherine appeared at the doorway with ruffled hair and wearing Fin's pyjamas. Maire looked her up and down, taking in every detail.

"This is Katherine," Fin said, to introduce her, but he found himself at a loss for anything else to say.

Dan Brien lifted his hand to welcome her, whilst Maire stood motionless and silent as if awaiting further information. Katherine waved politely but remained in the doorway.

However, the pedlar was determined to make her acquaintance. Walking across to the doorway, he doffed his cap and said, "Pleased to meet ya."

Feeling herself momentarily frozen by his gaze, she was unable to reply. It was as if he could see right into her soul, reading every aspect of her, neatly laid out on the pages of a book.

"I hope you'll be very happy here in the hills," he winked.

"Oh, I'm just visiting!" Katherine protested.

"Of course you are," he smiled, switching his gaze to focus on Fin. "Thank you for your kindness, I will honour our agreement and be gone from your land before the winter sets in. Now, if you please, I will be on my way."

"Don't let him leave his horses here on your land!" Maire Brien said, unable to contain herself. "That front field of yours is best left fallow, Fintan Byrne!"

"Come along now, Maire. Let's leave them to their business. What Fin does with his land is none of our concern," chided Dan.

"It is our business too!" she said adamantly. "We don't want any more of the likes of him and his ways around here."

"Imeacht gan teacht ort!" the pedlar said, addressing Maire from across the courtyard in his native tongue.

"What did you say? Did you hear that, Dan? He cursed me!" Maire's ruddy complexion deepened.

"Well, if you don't believe in all of that stuff, why are you getting so het up about it?" asked Dan.

"I must first know myself to be curious about that which is not my business!" the pedlar said with a wry smile on his weather-beaten face.

"Socrates?" The phrase struck a chord with Katherine.

"Aye, tis the very same," the pedlar confirmed. "So you're familiar with his words?" Katherine nodded in response. "And have you read the works of John Mahaffy?" he asked her.

"Can't say I have…" Katherine replied somewhat vaguely.

"Well, you'd be wise to heed his advice," winked the old fellow. "In Ireland the inevitable never happens and the unexpected constantly occurs!"

Sensing Katherine's embarrassment at the situation, Fin decided it was time to take charge.

"Thanks a millions for your neighbourly concern. I am very grateful," he said to the Briens. "It's grand to know that you're looking out for me and if there's anything I can do to return the favour, please just ask."

Then he turned his attention to the pedlar. "And we have an agreement," he said. "And we shall both honour it."

The old fellow nodded and sought to take his leave. Fin shook his hand. As he turned to go, the pedlar once more spoke to

Katherine saying, "May the saddest day of your future be no worse that the happiest day of your past."

Dan beckoned to his exasperated wife, "Na bac leis! Come on now, Maire, let's go and leave these people in peace. It's all in hand."

The stubborn woman refused to move. "Not until I see the back of this fella," she said, setting her mouth in a straight line.

However, the old man had the last word. As he walked past Maire Brien he commented, "Be it so that you may scratch a beggar man's back, one day."

"Did you hear him? Did ya?" screeched the distraught woman, as her husband wrapped his arm around her shoulders.

"Come on, Maire, let's go home," Dan said.

The 49th Day

"And just what was that all about?" Katherine asked Fin, as they stood alone in the courtyard.

"Just some old folklore nonsense," he replied. "Some people around here still believe in all of that stuff!"

"What stuff?" asked a curious Katherine.

"The myths and legends, the folktales about the faeries, and how it's bad luck to cross them," Fin explained. "Some people take it seriously, some don't."

"Like Maire Brien," Katherine noted. "What was that about curses? I heard the old man say something. Was it in Irish?"

"Yes, I think the old guy muttered a mallacht or two," laughed Fin.

"And what was all that kerfuffle about the front field?" Katherine asked.

"Ah well, there's a history to that. Apparently, the name of the farm, 'Earrach Tobar', meaning 'Spring Well', gets its name from the well in the middle of the front field. I'm not sure of its exact location. It got filled in a few generations back when some children fell in and drowned. I've just overhead snatches of adult conversation about it, when I was a kid." Fin shrugged his shoulders. "I guess some people believe it's an omen of bad luck, and pedlars trade on this type of material. It upsets some people, though not me. In fact, I have a book that the old fella gave me last time he was round here. I'll show it to you."

He walked over to the fire and picked up the brown, smoke-stained pamphlet from the mantelpiece. He handed it to Katherine.

"It's very old," she commented, turning it over and flicking through the pages.

The book contained a series of poems or short stories written in Irish and each headed up by a rough etching. Katherine's focus was drawn to the illustration of a man walking beside a lake and a silhouette of a woman holding up a looking glass.

"Why did he give you this?" she asked.

"It's the rent for the field!" Fin smirked, and Katherine laughed in response.

"Let's hope Mrs Brien doesn't see it! She'll have apoplexy! Do you have to hand it back to him when he leaves? Anyway, about that breakfast…"

Fin remembered the bacon. It wasn't too cold. "Can I make you some eggs?" he offered. "There's juice in the fridge and I'm going to make a pot of coffee." For the first time in nearly two months, Katherine could stomach the aroma of coffee. After a plate of scrambled eggs and bacon and two refills of freshly brewed coffee, Fin asked, "What time's the sailing? Have you got time to take a look around the farm before you head off?"

Katherine opted for a tour of the farmstead and said, "I'll catch the later sailing, if that's okay with you?"

She watched with pleasure as an animated Fin led her around the old barn, explaining how each of the traditional pieces of farm equipment still worked. She learned how he had used old photographs to restore the interior of the farmhouse to render an accurate version of how it would have looked at the time it was built. He showed her the stables which now only awaited occupation, and outlined his plans for the outbuildings, in which he planned to open a shop stocking local farm produce for the benefit of his neighbours.

"Of course, this is only half the story," he added nonchalantly, when he could see by her expression that she was impressed with his accomplishment. "And now you are asked to release your powers of imagination, suspend all judgement and take a leap into my vision for the future," he laughed, leading her down towards the lake.

"Does Cillian appreciate all that you have achieved here?" Katherine asked.

"He didn't hang around long enough to find out," responded Fin. "The only thing he's interested in is a quick return...for *my* seven-year investment!"

As they reached the bottom of the field, the landscape flattened out in front of them, revealing the lake. Katherine caught her breath at the sight of the reflection of the morning sun on its gently rippling surface.

"I have plans to stock fish here," Fin explained, "for recreational fishing purposes. If I get a licence I can offer specialist holidays."

"What's over there?" she asked, pointing to the woodlands.

"That's where Cillian and I used to play as kids," he replied. "Soon to be the site of holiday accommodation in the form of eco-friendly log cabins."

"Ooh! Can we get to it from here?" Katherine asked, looking at the wooden walkway edging the lake. "A bridge over the lake from here would be ideal!"

Fin could see it quite clearly and said, "You're right! That would be a beautiful feature. We could have a main walkway with lower platforms either side, for casting off. But for now, we'll have to walk around the perimeter."

Chatting as they walked, Katherine felt comfortable enough

to raise a few poignant issues with Fin. Apologetically she said, "I didn't mean to cause any confusion last night. I hope you don't think I'm playing games with you."

"No, not at all," Fin said, failing to admit that he had felt slightly confused.

"I don't know why I ever thought that going back to Henry was the answer, you can never go back and there's no way that he was ever going to be happy to venture into new territory. I guess I knew that deep down, but I panicked, feeling alone...and pregnant. Then last night, I was fearful that if we tried to go back to our brief time together on the island things might have ended up the same way," Katherine explained.

Fin thought before replying. "Then I guess the only way to go is forward," he suggested. "As I said last night, there are no guarantees, but we have the choice to try something out, to put our trust in each other, or not. All we have is the choice."

On hearing his words, Katherine felt relieved. All she knew was that her life was about to change in ways she had never dreamed possible, mainly due to the advent of motherhood, and that she loved being in his company. The fact that he did not seem to be looking any further beyond for answers or commitments was comforting to her. For the first time it seemed as if she was in the company of someone who did not have their own personal agenda; or if he did, it was not the dominating factor. Katherine recognized that it was her choice to be here with Fin. With Henry it had been easy; she had fallen into a relationship with an authority figure and had felt safe and protected. With Darrel, she had been swept off her feet and into a whole new world; one in which she had never felt she belonged.

Despite having known Fin for such a brief time and her surroundings and situation all being new to her, inexplicably it also felt curiously comfortable. Life somehow took on a magical dimension when she was in Fin's company. It was as if they both walked on a different plane when spending time together and yet, for the first time, she also felt she was able to walk alongside someone who respected her, someone who was not intent on sucking her into the slipstream of his own life. Feeling that there was nothing else to say on the previous night's events, Fin was happy to explain all of his ideas and plans for the holiday village to Katherine and she was eager to listen and learn. Now feeling more relaxed, she too could picture it quite clearly in her mind's eye and felt excited to be sharing his dream.

"If you come to live here, in Ireland, you'll be able to see the progress of this place at first hand. You can be involved, help out during the high season, if you wanted," Fin said. The possibilities were racing through his mind. "Once you settle in, with the baby, you'll have the long academic holidays during which you could work here, for money of course, and it would be somewhere safe for the baby," he added excitedly. "The two of you would always be welcome…as long as I'm here."

"Well, there's nothing and no one to keep me over the water," Katherine said thinking aloud. "As far as Henry is concerned, we'll only be in touch if I choose to contact him. I'm sure Darrel will show up at some point, if only to finalize the divorce as soon as he's got some other poor victim in his clutches. My future and that of the baby is solely in my hands, so I guess that could work if I'm offered a place on the research programme."

"When are you expecting to hear?" Fin asked.

"At interview the course director said they would let me know before the end of the week, so anytime now," she replied.

"Well, unless you find anything to go back over the water for you're welcome to stay here," Fin offered. "I'm not sure how things are going to work out, whilst I have Cillian's threats to sell this place hanging over me. But they can't last forever."

Katherine smiled in gratitude. "Thank you! It was starting to feel as if I didn't have a friend in the world and that I would be facing motherhood alone. Pregnancy allowing, I'm happy to fight your corner for the farm."

The two continued to walk in a comfortable silence. As they approached the opening to the wood, Katherine caught sight of a wooden structure amidst the trees. "Is that one of the cabins?" she asked.

"No, I haven't started building them yet," Fin answered. "That's the start of a treehouse I built out of leftover timber. I haven't got around to the roof yet."

They made their way through the trees towards a small clearing. On closer inspection of the treehouse Katherine again felt a strange surge of familiarity. "I've seen one just like this, but I can't remember where," she said, searching her mind. "But I'm sure it was made of bamboo, perhaps it's the tree that's so familiar."

"The sessile oak is a popular tree over here," Fin explained.

"Oh, it's really high!" Katherine exclaimed, looking up at the wooden structure from the base of the tree.

"That's because I started to build it on the branch that Cillian and I used to climb up onto when we were kids," Fin laughed. "I guess it's not so easy for adults to climb!"

They both rose to the challenge, Fin scrambling up first then reaching over to offer Katherine a hand. As her foot slipped, he grabbed her arm.

"Should you be doing this?" he asked. "I mean is it safe, what with the baby and everything?"

Reassuring him that she was fine, Katherine clambered up onto the platform. "Perhaps you need to build a ladder?" she suggested, slightly out of breath.

Fin laughed, "Yes, perhaps a rope ladder. As kids we were able to hide from our parents by climbing up here. Now there's no one to escape from." He had managed to complete the platform and two walls of the tree house. The two stood together in silence, admiring the view over the lake and to the mountains beyond.

"This is a dream," Katherine said, feeling light-headed.

"This is reality," Fin responded gently, as his attention was drawn towards the fluttering of wings in the branches of a neighbouring spruce.

"It's a merlin, in that tree," he whispered. "There!" He pointed out the bird to Katherine.

"What's a merlin?" she asked, looking at the black stripes on the bird's blue-grey wings as it ascended into the space between the trees.

"It's a type of falcon: a bird of prey. Look, it has a yellow cere on its beak and yellow feet." Fin watched the movements of the bird. "I think it's breeding season. I bet there's a nest in that tree. That's the male. He has an orange underbelly. I'd say he's off hunting," he said, turning to Katherine.

She was standing with her eyes closed. Whilst knowing this was the first time she had ever stood in this spot, she felt an overwhelming sense of déjà vu: the curve of the lake, the gentle roll of the hills beyond, and the sharp silhouette of the mountain ridge were all etched into her memory. Closing her eyes, she breathed in the fresh mountain air and enjoyed the gentle brush of the summer breeze on her cheek. The only sound being the swish of the bird's wings as it sailed past her through the air. Then there was only stillness. The atmosphere took on a different quality and Katherine found herself standing alone on the platform in the dark. She wanted to call out to Fin, to grasp his hand, to feel his arm around her shoulders. However, she could neither speak nor move. She was frozen. The paralysis felt timeless. She felt a chill in her bones and a relentless emptiness eating away at her, from deep inside.

As her breath turned cold on her lips, she wondered, *Is this how it feels to die*? She could no longer feel the wooden platform beneath her feet. She heard the faint voice of a young woman asking, "Are you warm enough, Ma? We can get some more blankets for you if you're cold."

Then another voice faded in from the background, "Ma's fine.

Let her be, Aislinn."

Katherine was aware of the sound of choked sobs amidst comforting words. She sensed a great sadness. The muted voices were surrounding her, but she could not see or feel anyone. She continued to listen until the voices quietened and a sense of calm descended.

"Katherine!" Fin shrieked as he caught her in his arms. "Katherine! What happened? Are you okay?"

She opened her eyes. "Yes, I'm okay. I don't know what happened," she responded.

"I think you passed out," Fin said, sounding concerned. "Your eyes were closed and you lost your balance."

Katherine replied, "I could hear voices. There were others here."

"No, it's just you and me," he frowned. "Perhaps it was the climb. You really should see a doctor. When we get back to the cottage I'll look up the nearest clinic."

"I feel fine," Katherine protested. "It was just as if I drifted off somewhere else for a while."

Fin was not convinced. "We'll sit here for a time," he instructed her, holding both hands and lowering her to the floor of the platform.

"It was strange," she said, trying to explain the weird feeling she had just experienced. "I felt very cold and alone, although I could hear voices. It was as if they were here and I was passing through."

"Well you were right here with me, and only me, the whole time," Fin replied. "This happened a few times on the island. Perhaps it's just a part of your condition? We really should get you checked out."

"I had tests at the hospital. There was nothing untoward detected at that point," explained Katherine. "I'll register with a doctor as soon as I'm settled," she promised.

Climbing down very carefully from the treehouse, the two

walked back to the farmhouse in silence, each occupied with their own thoughts. Fin was unsure as to what Katherine would decide to do and was trying not to let his thoughts race ahead into future possibilities. She was more concerned with her experience in the treehouse. It may have looked to Fin as if she had passed out, but to her it felt as if she had passed through into a different dimension. She was convinced that she had been at the point of death and had traversed the plane into a deep sense of peace. As they walked, she welcomed an enhanced sense of energy. *Perhaps being pregnant heightens sensitivity in all areas, not just smell and taste,* she reasoned.

Then she recalled Peter Wheeler, the past life regression therapist, explaining to her how some people were able to hypnotize themselves. What if she had unintentionally created her own regression to another past life? However, she was conscious that there had been a very different feel to this experience. Katherine wondered about the voices. She had heard only the words of females. Had they been talking to her when they used the word 'Ma'? And who was Aislinn? Had she been afforded a glimpse into her own future? Was the baby, her baby, a girl?

The thought that she was now carrying a female soul soothed Katherine's fears. Perhaps this was the end of the cycle of cruel and violent men in her lives. All Katherine knew was that she felt enlivened. Happier and more settled than she had been for weeks, she just needed confirmation of a place at the university and she would know, for sure, which way her life was leading her.

Over lunch in the secluded cottage garden, the two chatted incessantly about the farm and the business. Katherine's vibrant repose was proving intoxicating for Fin. They discussed designs for the bridge and the season for stocking the lake with fish. She asked how many cabins could be built in the woods and suggested some lifestyle magazines to target with advertising.

There was a sparkle in her eyes and vitality in her manner which Fin had not previously witnessed. It was as if she had tapped into a new source of energy. She could feel it too.

"I have such a good feeling about this place," she announced. "It's weird. I know I've never been here before but it feels so *right*. Everything feels just as it should do. Does that make any sense to you?"

It made perfect sense to him. Since she had arrived at the farm, he had felt the same. It was as if a missing piece of the puzzle was now firmly in place, but he knew he could be very wrong. Common sense was telling him that he hardly knew this woman and there were already a few challenges lining up for him to face, in the form of an unborn child and an absent ex-husband. However, she invoked in him a sense of purpose and a strengthened resolve. He paradoxically felt supported and challenged at the same time. Her presence injected an air of excitement of the unknown, and yet he felt very safe with her.

As the late afternoon set in and the two could not linger any longer over the late lunch in the walled garden, Fin shifted about uneasily in his seat, not sure how to broach the question of the evening sailing from Rosslare to Pembroke. He needed to ask the question; he just had to know whether or not she intended to stay. He was not so sure he would be happy to hear the answer.

Finally, he managed to ask, "You're not catching the ferry today, are you?" Closing his eyes, he held his breath until he heard her response.

Following a painful pause she replied, "If it's okay with you, I'd like to stay a while..."

On hearing her words, he opened his eyes and sighed with relief. Katherine watched a wide grin spread across his face.

"I think I've stopped looking back," she continued thought-fully, "and finally stepped into the future." For a moment, neither could think of anything more to say; both were content to bathe in the magic of the new moment. However, the silence was short-lived.

"Jaysus! What's that?" Fin yelled. From over the top of the walled garden, he could see smoke rising.

"Is that in the front field? I have to take a look. Stay here." Running out into the courtyard, he jumped into the jeep and started the engine. As he raced towards the field, he could see the distressed horses charging around. *What the fuck is she thinking of?* he asked himself when he could see the flames of the bonfire from next door's field licking the bramble hedgerow bordering his own.

There was no doubt in his mind that Maire had deliberately lit the fire so close to the hedge for maximum effect. Fin thought that he would have to get around there and put it out himself, before the flames caught a hold of the hay in the field and the horses bolted. He hurtled along the lane and turned in through the opening to the next field.

"Why in God's name would you do such a thing?" he hollered, storming across the field.

"It's St John's Eve," Maire Brien shouted back. "It's to keep away the faeries from your well. If we let them have their way they'll poison us all."

Jaysus! The woman has lost her mind. Fin looked around for any sign of Dan. "Where's Dan? Is, he home? Does he know you're doing this?" he shouted in desperation. The fire was spreading and he knew there wasn't much time before it moved along the hedgerow to reach the hay stacked for the horses. "Put out that damned fire before it gets out of control!"

Realizing he had no facilities to tackle a fire of this size, Fin decided he couldn't take any chances. "Mrs Brien, I'm calling the fire brigade," he warned, before realizing he had no idea of the location of the nearest station. "Where's the nearest station?" he demanded, fired up by his own frustration. The stubborn woman refused to answer.

"Mrs Brien! Someone could get hurt! A fire this size could

cause so much damage!"

Panic was now setting in. He was torn between staying to keep an eye on the bonfire and getting back in the jeep to find whatever materials he could use to douse the flames. He was slightly relieved to see someone else approaching from across the Briens' field.

"Dan!"

As he ran towards the corner of the field, Dan raised his hand to Fin and called out, "It's all in hand, Fin. I've called the fire brigade. They'll have an engine around in no time."

Fin's heart was still racing.

"I'll keep a watch here," Dan continued breathlessly. "You get back to those horses and keep them away from this hedge."

Scrambling over the shrubbery, Fin ran to the stack of hay which stood in the path of the rapidly spreading flames. As the horses stamped restlessly at the gate to the field, he started to pick up the bales and carry them into the centre of the field, as far away from the hedge as the strength in his arms would allow. As he threw the last bale, sticky with sweat, he looked up to see the pedlar at the gate.

Jaysus! This is the last thing we need! he thought to himself, fearing another altercation with the Briens. However, the old man appeared to be concerned only with the horses. Removing his bramble-torn T-shirt, Fin wiped his brow and the front of his chest. He watched as the red and yellow engine drove along the lane, slowing to a halt outside the Brien's field. Not wanting to brave the brambles again with a bare chest, Fin headed for the gate to his field. He would walk around and thank them for putting out the fire. And he would talk to the old fellow on the way, and advise him to stay away from the Briens. When he reached the gate he could see that the horses were calmer.

"Are the horses okay?" he asked the pedlar.

"They are now," the old fellow replied. "Though I'm afraid I can't say so much for that woman. People like her cause more problems than they solve. She needs to stop meddling with things she doesn't understand."

"Leave it to me," Fin instructed the old man. "I'll deal with her."

"Don't waste your time!" the old man exclaimed. "Some folk will only ever choose to see what they want to see. She's no threat to you, Fin. You need to be keeping an eye on things closer to home."

"What do you mean?" Fin asked, intrigued.

"There are people who want to take things away from you," the pedlar told him. An image of Cillian's face flashed into Fin's mind. "But this land belongs to you now. You don't need to be worrying about that. Just remember to keep *her* close," said the old man with a wink. "It's not the midsummer faeries who will want to whisk her away from under your nose."

Fin wondered what the old man was getting at. Did he know something? What or who was he talking about? But this wasn't the time for riddles and games. He had more urgent matters to deal with. Approaching the fire tender, Fin could see that the fire crew had the blaze under control and there was no sign of Maire Brien.

"Are you going to report this matter to the police?" he asked the nearest officer.

Fin was told that bonfires were permitted on midsummer and that the incident was being treated as an unfortunate accident.

"You know that she lit it too close to the hedge on purpose, right?" Fin said, checking the information that the brigade had been given. The officer looked at Dan Brien who shook his head and turned away.

"The situation is under control here," the officer replied firmly, "and we have advised the landowners not to be lighting any more fires in this field."

"What on earth...?" Katherine exclaimed when she saw the bloody scratches on Fin's back, arms and chest.

"You wouldn't believe it!" he responded, brushing the stray bits of hay from his hair. "That mad old Maire Brien had set a fire in the next field to frighten off the faeries! The fire brigade turned up to extinguish it but they said there's nothing else we can do as the Briens said it was just a bonfire that got out of control!"

"Why would she do that?" Katherine asked, clearly puzzled. "What about the horses? Were they hurt?"

"And then the old fella turned up," Fin continued. "Thankfully, all he was interested in was the welfare of the horses."

Katherine was more concerned with the state of his body. "These nasty cuts need some attention," she stated. "Let me clean them up for you. Do you have any antiseptic cream?"

"I'll take a shower first, and then you can treat them for me," answered Fin.

Ten minutes later they both stood in the bathroom, with Katherine tracing a gentle line over the deepest scratch on his chest with a fingertip of cream. Fin shivered.

"Is it sore?" she asked.

"No, just cold," Fin replied, feeling the goose bumps rising on his arms and the hairs standing up on the back of his neck. He loved the feel of her touch.

"I don't think I've ever seen quite so many scratches on one body," commented Katherine as she traced the marks spread over his torso, his neck, and his arms, massaging the remains of the cream over his chest.

"There must be at least 40…"

Her comment was interrupted as he leaned forward and kissed her on the cheek. In response she turned to face him and he reached out to draw her mouth to his. After a long, lingering kiss he pulled away gently. Looking directly into her eyes, he said, "I'm glad you're here. I wanted you to stay."

Katherine's heart rate rapidly increased. "I'm so happy to be here, it feels like somewhere I belong." Smiling, she took a step closer to facilitate another kiss.

However, Fin had other plans. He reached for a clean shirt and ran towards the stairs. "Come on! Give me a hand," he beckoned to her. "Grab a cushion or two and come with me."

"What are you up to?" she asked.

"You'll find out, trust me!" he laughed.

Following him downstairs, Katherine heard the clink of glasses from the kitchen. Fin was placing them, a bottle of wine, and some strawberries into a bag.

"Where are we going?" she asked.

"I've got something special to show you, but we don't have much time," he replied, looking at his watch. "I'll take the blankets; they're heavy. Can you manage the cushions?"

Fin strode out of the cottage and into the courtyard. Katherine could see that he was headed in the direction of the field and the lake beyond.

"What's the hurry?" she called after him, trying to keep up.

"A midsummer sunset waits for no man, or pregnant woman," Fin joked, and waited for her to catch him up. The two enthusiastically trekked across the fields.

"If we climb the tree you're not going to pass out on me again, are you?" he asked as they arrived at the base of the great sessile oak. She assured him that she felt fine and had no plans to scare him again.

From the half-built house in the tree, the couple sat amongst cushions wrapped in warm blankets chatting, laughing, and exchanging warm smiles as they watched the magical rays of the midsummer sun setting through the hollow in the mountain ridge. As the spectrum deepened to a crimson hue, Fin raised his glass to propose a toast.

"Today is my birthday," Katherine smiled, "my 30th birthday."

"Well you are full of surprises!" exclaimed Fin in response. "To your birthday!"

"To my birthday in the hills!" Katherine gently clipped his glass with hers.

"To life, here in the hills!" he reciprocated.

"To a new life," Katherine said with a knowing smile as she gently rubbed her abdomen. "To a new soul, to a daughter, and to a new way of life for us all in these hills."

"Subject to interference from greedy brothers and ex-lovers," Fin added, before realizing that Katherine had mentioned the word daughter. "Did you say it's a girl?" he asked.

"It's just a figure of speech," Katherine replied. "I have a feeling, but I'm not sure. We can't be sure of anything, but we can trust that we will always have the choice to change the things that need to be changed and the power to shape the future."

"*Our* future," emphasized Fin.

"Yes, *our* future," she said with a smile, and just the slightest unease rising in the pit of her stomach.

Soul Rocks is a fresh list that takes the search for soul and spirit mainstream. Chick-lit, young adult, cult, fashionable fiction & non-fiction with a fierce twist